PRAISE FOR DIANA PALMER:

"Nobody tops Diana Palmer when it comes to delivering pure, undiluted romance. I love her stories."
—*New York Times* bestselling author Jayne Ann Krentz

"Diana Palmer makes a reader want to find a Texan of her own to love!"
—*Affaire de Coeur*

PRAISE FOR ANN MAJOR:

"No one provides hotter emotional fireworks than the fiery Ann Major."
—Melinda Helfer, *Romantic Times* magazine

"Ann Major is a top-notch writer who conjures up well-paced plots that consistently deliver to her readers."
—Bestselling author Pamela Morsi

PRAISE FOR SUSAN MALLERY:

"Susan [Mallery] writes a powerfully emotional Western...."
—*Affaire de Coeur*

"Susan Mallery dazzles. Her stories are unforgettable. If you haven't read her yet, you must!"
—Bestselling author Suzanne Forster

DIANA PALMER

With over ten million copies of her books in print, bestselling, award-winning author Diana Palmer is one of North America's most beloved authors. She got her start in writing as a newspaper reporter and published her first romance novel for Silhouette Books in 1982. In 1993 she celebrated the publication of her fiftieth novel for Silhouette Books. *Affaire de Coeur* lists her as one of the top ten romance authors in the country. Diana Palmer is the winner of numerous national Waldenbooks Romance Bestseller awards and national B. Dalton Books Bestseller awards. Her fans the world over treasure her sensual and charming stories.

ANN MAJOR

Ann Major, the author of more than thirty-four novels, is one of Silhouette's bestselling and most beloved authors. Her larger-than-life characters, compelling plotlines and sensual prose have touched the hearts and emotions of millions of readers all over the world. Whether she writes a simple love story or a more intricately plotted tale of romantic suspense, she always delivers. Her books have repeatedly placed at the top of national and international bestseller lists.

SUSAN MALLERY

Susan Mallery lives in sunny southern California where the eccentricities of a writer are considered fairly normal. Her books are both reader favorites and bestsellers, with recent titles appearing on the Waldenbooks bestseller list and the *USA Today* bestseller list. Her 1995 Special Edition novel, *Marriage on Demand,* was awarded Best Special Edition by *Romantic Times* magazine.

DIANA PALMER
ANN MAJOR
SUSAN MALLERY

MONTANA MAVERICKS
Weddings

Silhouette Books

Published by Silhouette Books
America's Publisher of Contemporary Romance

Special thanks and acknowledgment to Diana Palmer, Ann Major and Susan Mallery for their contribution to the Montana Mavericks: Return to Whitehorn series.

 SILHOUETTE BOOKS

MONTANA MAVERICKS WEDDINGS

Copyright © 1998 by Harlequin Books S.A.

ISBN 0-373-48357-0

The publisher acknowledges the copyright holders of the individual works as follows:

THE BRIDE WHO WAS STOLEN IN THE NIGHT
Copyright © 1998 by Harlequin Books S.A.

BRIDE, BABY AND ALL
Copyright © 1998 by Harlequin Books S.A.

COWGIRL BRIDE
Copyright © 1998 by Harlequin Books S.A.

CONTENTS

Mavericks:
Return to Whitehorn—

*Welcome to Whitehorn, Montana—
the home of bold men and daring women.
A place where rich tales of passion
and adventure are unfolding under the Big Sky.
Seems this charming little town has some mighty
big secrets. And everybody's talking about...*

Abby Turner: Returned to Whitehorn to plan her wedding.
Since she can't have Chayce Derringer, she figures she
might as well marry a nice guy and make the most of it....

Chayce Derringer: Kept his distance from Abby to protect
her virtue. But can he bear to stand back and watch her walk
down the aisle with another man?

Felicity Evans: Prim, proper and pregnant, she's learned
never to be impulsive in love again. And love-'em-and-
leave-'em Kirk Conroy is the *last* man she'd get involved
with—even after he comes to her rescue....

Kirk Conroy: He's never been turned down by a lady before,
and sultry yet shy Felicity has become his only challenge.
But is this Don Juan of sorts ready for instant fatherhood?

Sierra Conroy: Gave up on love ten years ago—after
wealthy Dylan McLaine broke her heart. Now Dylan's back.
But how long can she hold out against his irresistible,
powerful appeal?

Dylan McLaine: He still secretly carries a torch for Sierra.
And though it won't be easy convincing Sierra, this Montana
Maverick intends to make her his Montana bride....

THE BRIDE WHO WAS STOLEN IN THE NIGHT

Diana Palmer

For Amanda Belle

Chapter 1

Abby Turner of Whitehorn, Montana, was getting married. There never was a more reluctant bride. She stared at the small diamond solitaire on her left hand with sad gray eyes in a pretty face framed by wavy dark hair and wished with all her heart that she'd said no instead of yes when Troy Jackson had proposed. He was a kind and sweet man, but she knew for certain that within a month of the wedding, she'd be walking all over him. She was a fiery, impulsive woman with an outrageous sense of humor, and she embarrassed him. She'd tried to deny that part of her nature, but it kept slipping out. Inevitably people noticed.

Whitehorn was a small town where people lived as they had for generations. A ranching community sprawled outside the city limits and Troy, along with his father, ran several hundred head of Hereford cattle on their third-generation ranch. It wasn't as large as Chayce Derringer's spread, but then, Chayce had more money than most local people. He was involved in mining as well as ranching. He'd been Abby's guardian since the death of her father, his foreman. Abby had been ten at the time. Her mother, Sarah Turner, had been crippled in the same wreck. Chayce had taken mother and daughter right into the big house with his housekeeper, Becky, and assumed total responsibility for them.

Whit Turner, a former rodeo cowboy, had been not only his foreman, but his idol and surrogate father as well. Chayce had loved him. He was fond of Abby, too, and he'd spoiled her rotten. At least, until she was sixteen. That had been when the arguments began, each one hotter than the one before.

Abby had given Chayce fits, not because she was rebellious, but because she was feeling the first stirrings of love for him. He was fifteen years her senior and completely impervious to her, and it hurt. Consequently, Abby's temper grew steadily worse until she was eighteen. She'd pushed him too hard only once, and something had happened that had kept him completely out of her life ever since. It had been almost four years since Abby had seen him at all. He made sure of it.

He'd arranged for her to go away to college as soon as she graduated from high school, just two weeks after their disastrous encounter. It had been traumatic. Her mother had died that same year, and

Chayce had been determined that she needed the change of scene—and to get away from him. What had happened, he told her grimly, couldn't be allowed to happen again.

So Abby had gone to college at California State University, taking her degree in business, and Troy Jackson had come to her campus to do some work on his teacher certification. They'd started dating and very soon Troy had proposed. They lived in the same town, he pointed out, and he'd inherit his father's ranch one day. What could be more natural than to marry Abby and have kids to inherit it when he himself passed on?

It had seemed logical. Abby's encounter with Chayce had put a wall between them that hadn't ever come down. He was a fiery and independent man who'd had a devastating love affair when he was little older than Abby was now at twenty-one. He'd never gotten over the loss of his fiancée, and he'd never let another woman close enough to wound him. He'd made it crystal clear that Abby didn't have a chance, despite his headlong ardor that night so long ago.

Abby had just graduated the first week of June, with only Troy and her college roommate, Felicity Evans, to watch her accept her diploma. Chayce hadn't come near the campus, although he'd sent a telegram of congratulations.

He wasn't home, now, either, of course. He found reasons to go on long business trips the minute Abby announced any plans to stay at the ranch. She'd writ-

ten him about her engagement to Troy and asked him
to give her away at their August wedding in Whitehorn. He hadn't replied. She wondered if he would.

She tried not to talk about Chayce, but he was so
much a part of her life that it was inevitable that she
did. Troy made his distaste for her guardian quite
clear, although he promised to tolerate Chayce once
he and Abby were married. He only hoped, he told
her firmly, that Chayce would be a little more discreet in future about his love affairs. Chayce was
handsome and rich and eligible and he was dating a
well-known Hollywood starlet. Therefore, it was inevitable that he was photographed with her and the
pictures ended up in the tabloids. The publicity nauseated Troy, who was even more old-fashioned than
Becky, Chayce's housekeeper.

Because Troy made so many tart comments about
Chayce, Abby made sure that she didn't let her own
feelings for him show.

She stared at the ring on her finger, wondering
what on earth had possessed her to agree. Despite his
glacial treatment of her, she loved Chayce. She was
never going to be able to give her heart or her body
to anyone else. After four long years, that was painfully apparent. But Troy was kind and sweet and after one ardent kiss that Abby hadn't been able to
respond to, he'd confined his affection to hand-
holding and lazy smiles. Perhaps he hoped that his
reticence would succeed where his ardor hadn't.

What he didn't realize was that Abby was inca-
pable of feeling physical desire for him. It was a

problem that she hoped they could work out after they were married, but she didn't dwell on it. She couldn't go around forever mooning over a man who didn't want her and who had made it perfectly clear.

Becky was working in the kitchen when Abby joined her there, smiling as she took down a glass and poured iced tea into it.

"Thirsty, are you?" The gray-haired woman smiled affectionately at the younger woman in tight jeans and a pretty pink tank top. "And so you ought to be after all that cleaning. You've been in the attic almost since daybreak."

"I've been in hiding," Abby confided with a grin. Her gray eyes sparkled and around her face, wavy but untidy dark hair curled. She had a lovely figure and she wore clothes these days that emphasized it. Troy didn't like that, either. In fact, Troy didn't like a lot about her, she realized worriedly.

"What are you hiding from?" Becky wanted to know, interrupting her thoughts.

Abby sighed, sipping her tea. "I'm hiding from Troy. He's miffed with me again."

"What did you do this time?"

"Not much," Abby defended herself. "I just decorated his new vet's car for him."

Becky put her face in her hands. "Oh, no."

"It wasn't bad! Listen, I didn't even write a dirty word on it! I just drew pictures of cows and calves and silos and things with cans of that pretty colored children's bath foam...come back here, I'm not through!"

"Troy's father is a deacon in the Baptist church!" Becky choked. "Troy teaches school, for heaven's sake! And the new veterinarian is his best friend from grammar school!"

Abby put her hands on her full hips. "I know that," she said. "The vet has a wonderful sense of humor. *He* thought it was hilarious! But Troy didn't. He was so angry that he wouldn't even speak to me when I left." She threw up her hands. "He's so somber, Becky! Like a judge. He needs to lighten up. I was just giving him a nudge in the right direction."

"What sort of nudge?"

Abby shrugged. "Well, I sort of hinted that he did the writing on Dan Harbin's truck."

Becky stared at her. "Hinted, how?"

"I sort of signed his name to it," Abby said pertly. She held up a hand when Becky turned red. "It was very discreet. I signed his name in a dignified black script."

Becky put her face in her hands again. "He'll shoot you. His father will shoot you, too."

"His father approves of me," she said pointedly. "Why, he said that Troy takes himself much too seriously and that anyone should be able to take a little joke."

"Yes, and I remember when he said it. He only did it to keep Sheriff Hensley from arresting you when you pulled that last crazy stunt!"

"It wasn't crazy," Abby defended herself stoically. "And Judd wouldn't have arrested me."

"You could have gone to jail!"

"Nobody got hurt."

"By the grace of God!" Becky was all but waving her arms now. "You turned one of Sid Jackson's best young bulls loose on the streets of Whitehorn! It chased the pharmacist at BobCo right into the Hip-Hop Café!"

"It didn't get inside," Abby stated. "It stopped at the door and trotted right back to the 4-H corral for its dinner! Anyway, it was a tame little bull that followed people around like a dog. It only wanted the pharmacist to pet it." She looked indignant. "What sort of pharmacist runs from an itty-bitty bull, anyway?"

"Of all the crazy stunts…!"

"Now, Becky, Troy had just been talking about how exciting it would have been to be at the running of the bulls in Spain, like Hemingway wrote about. I was only helping him to experience it firsthand."

"The bull ripped off Miss Ellison's skirt," Becky snorted. "And *her* a maiden lady of sixty-five!"

"It was only because she'd petted it, and it was trying to get her to do it again. She laughed," Abby reminded her.

"Chayce wouldn't have."

Abby bit her lip and turned away. "Chayce never laughs…not at me, anyway," she said tersely. "I irritated him from the age of ten. I haven't stopped yet. I wrote him that I was getting married in August and I wanted him to give me away at my wedding and he hasn't even bothered to answer the letter."

"It may not have caught up with him," Becky

said. "He was going to take Delina back to California after her filming in the Bahamas finished. He didn't say exactly when that would be. The letter may still be on its way."

"I suppose." She glanced at Becky. "What's Delina Meriwether like?"

"She's dark-haired and dark-eyed and very sweet," came the reply. "And she adores Chayce."

"Maybe he'll marry her," she said without any real enthusiasm.

"Chayce won't marry," Becky said as if she knew. "He had a hard time of it when Beverly Wayne let him down so badly. You were ten," she recalled, "so I don't imagine you'd even remember how hurt he was. He loved her. And all she wanted was pretty things and a lot of male attention. Chayce wasn't enough for her. She loved men, plural. He caught her with one the day after they became engaged, and she laughed. It amused her that he hadn't known she had other lovers." She shook her head, searching out ingredients for a pie. "He was twenty-four and in love for the first time in his life. He took it real hard. I don't think he's really trusted another woman since. Not even Delina, although she's crazy about him."

Abby was more depressed than ever. Women had come and gone in Chayce's life until now. Delina had lasted over a year. She'd worried Abby more than all the others put together, but she couldn't let herself get overly concerned. She had to look ahead, not behind. Asking Chayce to give her away was a sort of test. If he agreed, it would start them on a new relationship, and hopefully cauterize the wounds of the past. They could start over. He'd never love her, but they might find some sort of common ground.

"Have you bought your wedding gown yet?" Becky asked.

She shook her head. "I wanted to wait until we settled on a definite date in August."

"What's holding you up?"

"I want Chayce to be here," she said simply.

Becky hesitated, not quite looking at her as she began to make pastry for a pie. "I wouldn't count too much on him agreeing to do it, Abby," she said gently.

"But why not?" she replied. "He's looked after me since I was ten."

Becky still hesitated. She busied herself with the dough. "He has...other interests."

"He could bring Delina with him. She might like to be a bridesmaid. I wouldn't mind." That was a vicious lie, but she told it with a calm expression.

"He wouldn't do that, I'm sure." She added the shortening to the flour. "He's possessive about you. I've wondered ever since you mentioned the engagement if he was going to come back at all while you were still here. He doesn't, usually." She glanced at Abby worriedly. "You must know that he doesn't like Troy."

Abby looked astounded. "No, I didn't know. When has he even seen Troy to dislike him?"

"Troy went to talk to him while you were both in school last summer in California," Becky said reluctantly. "To get his blessing to court you. You know how old-fashioned Troy is."

Abby's heart turned over. "Troy never said a word about it!"

"I don't guess so, after what happened." She grimaced. "Chayce told him that you needed to grow up before you thought about getting married. He wasn't pleased at the news. Not at all. I expect when he gets this letter of yours about the wedding, he'll go right through the ceiling, Abby."

Her breath seemed strained. "That's surprising. I thought it would delight him to know that I'd finally be out of his hair."

"He's taken care of you for a long time, Abby," Becky said. "Despite the fact that he's kept his distance all these years, he's kept a careful eye on you. It isn't going to be easy for him to hand you over to another man."

"He doesn't want me around," Abby said with helpless bitterness.

"That isn't true!"

"Yes, it is." Her gray eyes met Becky's blue ones. "He couldn't even be bothered to come to my college graduation. But Troy did. And so did my friend Felicity."

"That isn't why you're marrying him, is it?"

Abby stiffened. "Of course not. I'm marrying him because we have a lot in common and we get along well together."

"Do you love him?"

Abby wouldn't look at her. "I'm very fond of him."

Becky started to speak and then thought better of it. She grimaced as she poured milk into her dough mixture and began to form it into a ball.

Abby drank the last of her iced tea. "I'm going to finish clearing out the attic," she announced. "If Troy comes looking for me, I went to town."

"He'll see the car in the garage."

"I was arrested and they took me in a police car," Abby improvised.

Becky tried to suppress a grin and failed. "You're incorrigible, dear."

"Not yet. But I'm working on it."

Up in the attic, she unearthed the photo album that she hadn't wanted to share with Becky. It was one that Chayce's mother had kept, and it was full of pictures of Chayce when he was in school. Even then, she thought, tracing the beloved face in adolescence, he was incredibly handsome. Chayce had olive skin and beautiful black eyes under thick eyelashes and elegant eyebrows. His nose was straight and he had a perfect, chiseled mouth over a square chin. His hands were beautiful, too, long and graceful and dark. She ached just remembering how those hands felt on her bare skin, there in the exciting, secretive darkness of his study, late that long-ago night...

She closed the photo album with a snap, raising

dust. It wouldn't do to dwell on that night, especially with her upcoming marriage. She was going to marry Troy and have his children and forget this nonsense. If only she could learn how to forget Chayce and the aching hunger that just the thought of him engendered.

Her eyes closed and she shivered a little as she tried to imagine doing the things with Troy that she'd done with Chayce. Love was such a necessary part of lovemaking, she thought miserably. She'd responded to Chayce so passionately only because her heart belonged to him. Troy had her respect, even her admiration, and she was fond of him. But something inside her curled up and died when he touched her.

There was a saying, a myth, that she remembered from high school, about a man being taken to paradise for punishment and then going mad when he was sent back to earth. She felt a little like that. The most exquisite joy she'd ever known was in Chayce's hard arms. Now, for the rest of her life, the memory of it was going to destroy any hope of feeling it with someone else.

She wondered if it was fair to marry Troy, when she still loved Chayce. If there had been a chance, even a slim one, that Chayce might one day return her feelings for him, she would never have agreed to marry Troy. But there was no chance. There was no hope. The alternative was to live her life alone, without children or companionship. By comparison, even life with Troy had a certain appeal.

She smoothed her hand over the cover of the old photo album and wished that she could have known Chayce's mother, who had died when he was only nine years old. She had a pretty face and Becky said that Chayce's father had loved her beyond bearing, that her death had turned him into a bitter alcoholic who took out his grief on his only child. Poor Chayce. His life had been no bed of roses, either. In his way, he was afraid of love. It had been cruel to him.

"Abby!" Becky called from the top of the staircase. "Troy's here!"

"I'll be right down!" she called back, not wanting Troy up here, where memories of Chayce were almost alive for her.

She scrambled to her feet, rushing to put the albums away and close the box that concealed them from view. In a sense she was putting her own memories away with them. She'd have to make sure that she didn't take them out again. She was getting married. And not to Chayce.

She and Troy ate a leisurely lunch and then went riding in his new red pickup truck.

He patted the dash as he drove. "Isn't she a beaut?" he asked with a grin that made his dark brown eyes light up. He was redheaded and had freckles, and when he smiled, they seemed to stand out like measles.

"Why isn't a truck a 'he'?" she asked.

He just shook his head. "You can't call something this pretty a boy truck," he explained.

She didn't share his enthusiasm for pickup trucks, but at least he wasn't still irritated at her, so she settled back and adjusted her seat belt without a protest.

"Heard from Chayce?" he asked abruptly.

Her heart jumped, but she didn't let him know how the sound of Chayce's name excited her.

"Not yet," she replied in what she hoped was a careless tone. "Becky said that he might not have received my letter. He was in the Bahamas with Delina when I sent it, but Becky said he'd gone on to Hollywood with her when she finished shooting her film."

Troy glanced at her suspiciously. "You don't like her."

"I don't even know her!" she said with a hollow laugh. "She's Chayce's business, not mine."

"Suppose he marries her?" he persisted.

She clenched her hands together over her blue jeans. "He's got to marry someone eventually," she said stiffly.

"Why? He has women coming out the doors and windows."

"Not for the past year," she returned. "There's just been Delina."

He was still giving her a narrow look. "How would you know that? I thought you hadn't seen him in almost four years. Hard to believe that. You live in the same house."

"Chayce hasn't been at home when I've been there," she said through her teeth.

"Why?"

She let out an irritated breath and turned to glare at him. "What is your problem, Troy?"

"Chayce doesn't want you to marry me, that's my problem!"

She took a steadying breath. "Chayce can't tell me who to marry. I'm surprised that he said anything to you. I haven't even had a postcard from him."

"I'm not surprised," he murmured, watching the road ahead of them. "He still thinks he owns you, but I'm going to prove to him that he doesn't. I think we should set the marriage date forward. To next month."

She felt her stomach clench. It was too soon, too soon, too soon...!

"If you love me," he persisted angrily, "you'll agree."

She closed her eyes. He was making so many demands, all at once. She needed time to think, to plan, to argue her case.

"You don't want to move it forward, do you, Abby?" he asked bluntly. "You don't want to marry me at all."

"I do!" she protested, turning in her seat to look at him with wild eyes.

He sighed softly. "Okay. That's all I needed to know. I thought you were going to try to back out of it. In fact, Dad said you might."

"Your father? Sid? But why?" she asked, stunned.

He changed gears as they went onto a dirt road that led to the holding pens of his father's ranch. "He said that you were in love with Chayce Derringer."

She stared at his hands on the steering wheel. They were clenched so hard that the knuckles were white. That was when she knew that she couldn't lie to him any longer. But she couldn't tell the whole truth, either. She decided on a compromise.

"All right," she said after a minute, not looking at him. "I had a frantic crush on Chayce when I was about sixteen. He found out and we had a long talk." She turned her hands over and looked at them. "He's fifteen years older than I am and he never wants to get married. I knew then that it would never matter how I felt about him, because he didn't want me." She looked out the window. "I can't stop caring about him, Troy. I don't know how. But he doesn't feel that way about me, and he never will. So you're not going to be competing with Chayce."

"If that's true, why did he try to warn me off you last summer?"

"I'm sure he didn't," she said resignedly. "He only wants to make sure that we'll have a good marriage. He's taken care of me for a long time. Maybe it's hard for him to let go, even if he doesn't see much of me."

"And you're not the divine Delina, after all," he said without meaning to wound her further. "She's such a knockout." He shrugged. "I guess I overreacted. I didn't think past what he said. But when you come to think of it, not many women could compete with a Hollywood goddess. And she is. Heaven knows, my blood pressure shoots up every time I see her picture in a magazine."

"Apparently so does Chayce's," she replied, "because he spends most of his free time with her."

"And if he ever does marry, she'll be in the front running," he agreed.

"Yes."

He glanced at her. "I didn't mean to sound as if I don't think you're pretty," he said. "You're sweet and cute and I love being around you. When you aren't acting like one of the cutups in my history classes," he added darkly.

"I'm not cut out to be staid and retiring, Troy," she said firmly. "I won't change. If you want to marry me, you have to accept me the way I am."

"You're fine, with a few minor adjustments," he commented imperturbably. "You need to tone down that sense of humor and learn how to act with a little dignity in public. And you need to let your hair grow out, while we're on the subject," he added with a glance in her direction. "I don't like short hair on a woman. In fact, I don't like those tight jeans, either. You'll have to wear something more staid when we're married. After all, I have a reputation to maintain, in my profession."

She tried to convince herself that it was a big joke, that he was kidding. But he wasn't. His somber expression was proof of that. She could see herself in long dresses and no makeup with her hair in a bun, trying to live down to Troy's image of the perfect woman.

"You should have proposed to Eve Payne," she remarked, referring to a fellow teacher of his who was the very image of a conservative woman.

"Oh, Eve doesn't like me," he said easily.

"Why not?"

"She thinks I'm damaging my reputation by being seen with you!"

Chapter 2

"I beg your pardon!" Abby flared.

He laughed, but not with any real humor. "You're not exactly the soul of discretion, Abby. And after that stunt with the bull, a lot of people around here think you're totally out of control. In fact, my mother did wonder if you needed therapy."

Her chest puffed up. She wrapped her arms around herself and tried to remember that this was the sweet, kind, biddable young man who'd been her good friend for over a year and had pleaded with her to marry him only three months before.

She glared straight ahead through the dirty windshield. So she needed therapy, did she? And a bun and long dresses and to tone down her personality…!

"Don't smolder. You know I'm right," he commented. "You've run wild too long already. You needed a strong hand and you never got one."

She had, when Chayce had been part of her life. But after he retired from the field, there was no one else to hold her back. She had run wild. Perhaps she did it to try to make him notice her. But it had never worked.

"Which reminds me, there's one more thing we have to talk about," he continued.

"What other fault of mine needs correcting, pray tell?" she asked through her teeth.

He changed gears again after they reached the top of the hill. "I want you to give up that environmental rights group you belong to. Putting wolves back on the range around here is the government's way of wiping out private ownership of land. It's subversive. We don't need wolves taking down cattle."

"I've explained this to you a dozen times," she began. "In the old days before wolves were almost hunted to extinction, the rodent numbers were kept down by them. Predators do much more to support the balance of nature than they do to harm it."

"That's right. Nature." He looked at her coldly. "Cattle-raising isn't part of nature. It's a business, like any other. If wolves multiply, cattle herds diminish. We've already got enough trouble trying to fight the government for water rights and public grazing. Other cattlemen are having fits because the buffalo in the national park are roaming free and infecting our cattle with brucellosis. Do you know what it is? It's a disease that causes cows to abort calves before term. Have you any idea how much money we lose every time a calf isn't born alive?"

"Yes, I know," she said. "Chayce owns a ranch," she added sarcastically, "and I do read cattle journals. But I'm not backing down on this. We have to preserve the..."

A huge black pickup truck with a double cab was bearing down on them on the narrow road. It was one of several that belonged to the Derringer ranch. She recognized the small white pistol emblem on a black field in a white circle that denoted the Derringer brand. It could have been handsome Kirk Conroy, a confirmed bachelor who ran the ranch in Chayce's absence. But it wasn't. Because Kirk drove like a preacher on Sunday visits compared to the way Chayce did it. And whoever was behind the wheel of that powerful machine was driving like a bat out of hell.

"Well, I'll be," Troy murmured. He pulled off onto the side of the road as the big truck came alongside them. "I thought you said he wasn't coming home."

"I didn't know he was," she said through her teeth.

A window powered down, and there was Chayce framed in it, his black eyes snapping in a face so handsome that it drew women everywhere he went. His hair was black, like his eyes, and he looked formidable.

"How are you, Chayce?" Troy asked with an effusive grin, trying to placate him. "Good to see you!"

Chayce didn't answer. He sat there as if he were

carved out of stone, with a powerful chambray-clad arm resting on the steering wheel as he glared past Troy, whose complaints about Chayce seemed to have become a thing of the past.

Chayce glared at Abby and she glared back. Four years, almost, and he couldn't even smile at her. She was bitter, and she looked it. But along with the bitterness was a painful maturity, and that showed, too.

"I thought you were in the Bahamas," Abby said curtly.

"I was. I got your letter this morning. They forwarded it to California, but it was held up." He glared at both of them. "What's this nonsense about the two of you getting married in August?"

"N...nonsense?" Troy blurted out. "We...we just want to get married, Chayce. Now you don't have to do a thing, except give Abby away. I'll even buy her wedding gown..."

"I'll buy the gown," Chayce said icily. "*When* she marries."

Troy went as red as his hair and began to look nervous.

Abby's chin came up as she faced Chayce. "You heard him," she told her guardian. "We're getting married. And we'll probably be moving the ceremony up." *And you can do what you please,* her eyes added coldly.

"Why the rush to the altar?" Chayce replied curtly. He glanced at Abby with eyes so intimidating that she actually moved back an inch. Seconds later, his gaze fell on Troy. "Is she pregnant?" he asked in a tone so soft and cutting that Troy swallowed visibly and put an arm around Abby for comfort and support.

Abby didn't even feel the arm, she was so outraged. "How dare you, Chayce!"

"She's...she's no...no such thing!" Troy blurted out. "For the love of heaven, I have a responsible job and I'm an upstanding member of the community! Decent men don't seduce women before the wedding!"

Chayce's eyebrows arched up at the statement.

"This isn't going to get us anywhere," Abby said.

Chayce's eyes narrowed. They didn't blink. They glittered. In this mood, he was dangerous. Abby felt chills run down her spine. Troy's arm around her wasn't quite as steady as he made it seem, either.

"We'll discuss this at home, Abby," Chayce said after a minute. He gave Troy a curt nod, powered the window back up and sped away, leaving a trail of dust as high as the truck behind him.

"Whew!" Troy exclaimed, removing his arm. "What brought that on, do you suppose? He was against it last year, sure, but you're of legal age now!"

"I haven't the slightest idea. Not that it matters," she said furiously. "He isn't telling me when I can get married!"

Troy glanced at her warily. "Now, honey, try not to get into a fight with him. We can't afford to make him too mad. He's a powerful man."

She searched his eyes. "You aren't afraid of him?"

He laughed, but it fell short of humor. "Of course not. Now let's get on down to the holding pens. I want to show you our new bulls." He glanced at her. "You won't do anything impulsive around my father, like opening gates...?"

"No," she said with resignation. "I'll be the perfect girl. You can count on me."

"Can I?" he murmured. "I hope so!"

She thought about that comment later, when Troy had left her at the front door without going inside. It was already dark and he was quite obviously reluctant to face Chayce again while the man was in such a black mood. Desertion in the face of battle, Abby thought irritably, watching him speed away. Some protector he was going to be!

On the other hand, why did she need a protector? It was only Chayce, whom she'd known since her tenth birthday. He might frighten the whole world, but he wasn't going to intimidate Abby!

She squared her slender shoulders and marched right in the front door, geared for battle.

It was anticlimactic that Chayce was nowhere in sight.

She stood in the hall, breathing uneasily, almost trembling with fury. All afternoon she'd thought of having to face Chayce when she got home, and he'd taken off again. Well, what more could she expect?

He'd spent years avoiding her. Nothing ever seemed to change...

"Is that you, Abby?"

The deep, smooth drawl came from the study. She went only to the doorway and looked in. Chayce was sprawled across a burgundy leather armchair with his long legs crossed and a brandy snifter in his lean hand. The room was dark except for a lamp burning beside the armchair.

"Yes, it's me," she said. She didn't take a step into the room. This particular place held memories that she couldn't bear.

"Come in," he said quietly. "We have a lot to talk about."

"We have nothing to talk about, Chayce," she said with quiet dignity. "I'm twenty-one."

He just stared at her, his black eyes going slowly over every inch of her in the tight jeans and clinging tank top. "You've filled out more," he murmured. "And you've cut your hair."

"Little girls do grow up," she replied with a mocking smile.

"So they do." He took a sip of brandy and a deep breath afterward. "Come in here and close the door, Abby," he said.

"I'd rather stay where I am," she replied tersely. "You can say what you have to say from there."

"I said, come in here and close the door!"

His voice, soft and deep, could cut like a whip when he wanted it to. Added to that even, threatening black glitter in his eyes, it was enough to back down a tiger, much less Abby.

She moved hesitantly into the room and closed the door behind her. But she didn't move away from it. The cold wood was somehow comforting at her back.

He hadn't moved. His eyes were still riveted to her body, seeking all the changes, hunting weaknesses. They narrowed.

"Your heart is beating you to death," he remarked coolly. "I can see the fabric of your top shaking over your breasts every time your heart beats."

The remark only made it worse. She swallowed hard and wrapped her arms across her breasts, uncaring that it only confirmed what he'd said.

"What do you want to say to me?" she asked stiffly.

He made an amused sound deep in his throat. "I don't really know," he admitted with a sigh. "Four years," he murmured as he studied her. "You're older. Your hair is short. You've gained a little weight. You speak your mind, but then, you've never been afraid of me. Troy is. Did you notice?" he added with soft laughter.

"It isn't something to laugh about," she returned.

"I need something to laugh about," he said curtly. "All this rushing around when you and Troy have known each other all your lives. You don't have to set new speed records for getting to the altar!"

"My marriage is none of your business."

"Like hell it isn't," he said flatly.

"I know how much I owe you," she returned.

"But you don't own me because of it. Why did you come back?" she asked miserably. "Why didn't you just stay away? You don't care if I marry Troy, you're just angry that I asked you to give me away!"

He put the snifter to his lips and drank the rest of the brandy, still glaring at her. "I'm angry, all right. I'm not old enough to be your father," he said in a deadly soft tone.

"That isn't what you said four years ago." She choked. "You said—" She stopped, midsentence.

He dangled the glass in his lean hand, having apparently forgotten it altogether as he looked at Abby. "You laid in my arms, in this room, on that sofa over there," he said roughly, nodding toward the burgundy leather-covered couch. "With your blouse on the floor and my shirt unbuttoned. I held you like that, kissed you until we both shook like leaves in a strong wind. I put my mouth on your bare breasts and you caught my head in your hands and clung, pulling me to you as if it would kill you if I stopped."

Her eyes closed. "Please. Don't."

The leather creaked as he slammed to his feet, putting the snifter on a table as he went toward her.

She lifted a hand, helplessly, as if to ward him off.

He didn't even see it. His hands went to the door on either side of her head and he looked into her frightened eyes at point-blank range.

"I had you down on your back, with my legs between yours," he said, his voice husky, almost choked with feeling. "You were sobbing. I unfastened your jeans...and the phone rang. Do you re-member what you said? You begged me not to an-swer it. You wanted me, you whispered, so badly that you felt sick all over with it." His eyes blazed as they stared into hers. "I touched you..."

She couldn't bear the memory. She sobbed and buried her face in his chest. "Don't!" she moaned.

His face nuzzled hers. He lowered his body so that his hips ground into hers, arousing him instantly, ob-viously. He shivered for a few seconds before his mouth dragged across her wet cheek and found her searching lips.

There was no time between then and now. She belonged to him the instant he touched her. She yielded completely, opening her mouth to his as he'd taught her that night. Her hands flattened against his shirt and she began searching helplessly for buttons.

He stiffened, but he didn't lift his mouth. "Unfas-ten it," he whispered against her lips. "Touch me!"

It was wrong. She was engaged. Troy's ring was on her finger. She was promised to him. But this was the only man she wanted, had ever wanted, could ever want. She fumbled the buttons apart from their holes and her hands caressed him hungrily, feeling the familiarity of the warm, hard muscles with their thick covering of curling black hair. She drew her mouth away from his and pressed it against his chest, drinking in the clean scent of him, the feel of his muscles against her lips.

"It never stops," he murmured, shaken. His hands

slid under her tank top, up to the fastenings in back. "I tried to stay away. Dear God, I tried so hard...!"

She lifted her tormented face to his, watching him, enraptured, as he loosened her bra and his big, lean hands found her soft breasts and tenderly explored them.

His breath caught at the feel of her skin. His thumbs and forefingers met, teasing the nipples until they went hard and sensitive. He searched her eyes as he touched her, feeling her pleasure as he felt his own.

"You know what I want," he whispered.

She did. It was some primitive rite of passage that neither could ever forget. Without a single thought for her chastity or the promise she'd made to Troy, her hands caught the hem of the tank top and whipped it off. She let the garment fall onto the floor and she arched her back and let him look at her full, firm breasts while she shivered with the most obsessive desire she'd ever known.

"And you know...what I want," she murmured.

"Yes." He touched her breasts, with a reverence that made her shiver, and his dark head bent. He lifted her and slowly, tenderly, took her inside his mouth to suckle her in the hot, tense silence of the room.

His free hand went behind her, pulling gently until she was lifted and riveted to his hips. His arousal was so blatant that she gasped when she felt him against her.

"When I get like this," he whispered at her breast,

"I can go all night long. I could love you until you were too exhausted to hold me. And I'd still want you."

Her hands were on his flat stomach, barely touching, shy even in the throes of desire.

He lifted his head and looked into her eyes, seeing fear and anguish and need. All that. And love.

He winced.

She hung there in his grasp, without wiles, without protest, without coyness. Even without shame.

He looked down at her body, arched in a bow, pleading. He touched her, traced her, ached for her.

She was trembling all over, sobbing with her frustrated longing.

He bent and lifted her close in his arms and stood there rocking her against him, his powerful legs shuddering as he fought the need to throw her down on the floor and ravish her.

"Oh, dear Lord," she whispered brokenly, pressing her mouth against his throat. "Why? *Why?*"

"I don't know why," he whispered back, holding her even closer. His eyes closed as he savored the feel of her against him. "I've never lost my head the way I lose it with you." He buried his face against her breasts. "I can't even look at you and stay sane."

She touched his cheek as he caressed her with his mouth, watching him at her breast, shivering with the realization that he was as hungry as she was.

"Can't we...lie down?" she choked.

"Baby, if we lie down, I'll have you in two

minutes flat." He ground out the words. "I won't even take time to strip you."

She put her mouth against his warm shoulder and trembled. "Yes," she sobbed.

He groaned. He couldn't help it. He had to. He had to...!

He turned, sudden resolution in his hard face, his eyes. He started back toward the sofa and as she looked up at him, he knew that he couldn't stop. He could already feel her under his body, feel her accepting him, feel his possession of her, feel it become urgent.

He made a sound deep in his throat and she clung to him, ready, aching to belong to him. Finally, she thought feverishly as she pressed closer, finally!

He started to put her down on the leather sofa when the doorbell rang, so loudly that it burst like a bomb on the heated silence of the room.

They stared at each other as if they were just coming out of a daze. His brows drew together as he registered the sight of her bare breasts pressed hard into the hair and muscle of him, her arms tight around his strong neck.

She stared, too, at his swollen mouth that had possessed hers so feverishly, at his eyes that told her how desperately he desired her.

And reality snapped them both back to painful comprehension.

He put her on her feet, holding her while she found her balance. He looked at her breasts as if he wasn't able to stop. He touched them gently, feeling her body tauten, hearing her helpless gasp of pleasure as he stroked her.

"Someone's here," she whispered.

"I know." He bent and put his mouth gently against her soft breast. "I want you."

"I want you...too."

His cheek turned against her breasts and he held her hard, rocked her there. "Oh, God, Abby!"

"I know." She smoothed his damp hair. Her eyes closed. "I know, Chayce. I know."

He was shivering, and she understood why. She soothed him as best she could and wondered absently if the door was locked. If it wasn't, and someone opened it...

There was a sharp knock.

Chayce lifted his head, still shivering. *"What?"* he demanded in a tone that didn't invite company.

There was a thick pause. "Uh, Chayce?" his foreman and good friend, Kirk Conroy called hesitantly. "Could you come down to the barn for a minute? We had to call the vet out about those heifers that miscarried and he needs to talk to you."

Chayce had to take a deep breath before he could answer. "I'll be there in a few minutes," he called back tersely.

"Okay, boss man!"

There were retreating footsteps. Chayce had Abby by the arms. He looked at her as if he couldn't bear the thought of letting her go. He drew her with him to the door, reached behind her and locked it. His eyes were black, alive, demanding.

"We...can't," she whispered brokenly.

"Why not?" he asked harshly. "He won't come back."

"Chayce...I'm...engaged..." she sputtered.

His eyes were on her breasts. He drew her to him, dragging her against his chest, shivering with pleasure. "Is this how you feel with him?" he asked unsteadily.

"I don't...I can't...do this...with him," she moaned.

He seemed to freeze against her. He lifted his head and studied her flushed face. "Never?" he whispered.

"Never. How could I?" she sobbed, her eyes anguished as they met his. "I love you. Damn you, Chayce, I love you...!"

His mouth settled on hers, tasting tears and the warm wonder of her soft lips as he kissed her with exquisite tenderness, framing her face in his warm, strong hands.

He let her go long minutes later, gently easing her away from his body. He brushed the tears from under her wet eyes, frowning as he watched her.

She felt cold without the comfort of his body. Unnerved, she searched the floor for her blouse and bra.

He followed her gaze, retrieving them. As if it was routine, he eased her back into her clothing between soft, tender kisses and kissed her hungrily when she was dressed once more.

"Your...shirt," she whispered.

He bent and retrieved it, too, shouldering into it.

He invited her hands back to the buttons that she'd unfastened and watched them reverse the process.

When she finished, he tucked it back into his expensive jeans, still watching her.

Her eyes were eloquent as they searched his face.

"It's all right," he said quietly. "Nothing happened."

"Nothing." Her voice broke on the word.

He drew in a long, harsh breath. "It's just as well that you want to move the wedding up," he said with cold self-contempt. "It may be the only thing that will save you from me."

"I don't understand."

"Don't you?" He laughed coldly. "I didn't have an idea in my mind that I was going to come near you tonight. I meant to keep you halfway across the room and offer to give you away at the wedding." His jaw tautened. "And you see what happened. I can't even be in the same room with you without getting aroused, even after four years of keeping my damned distance!"

Chapter 3

Abby was supposed to go and pick out her wedding gown on Saturday. She'd asked Becky to go with her, but at the last minute, Becky had an emergency of her own. Her sister fell and although she wasn't seriously injured, she had to be taken to the hospital and Becky had to go with her.

It was like an omen, Abby thought miserably. Chayce had been back three days and her heart was breaking already, especially after what had happened the first night he was home again. He'd acted as if nothing had happened, and she'd tried to, but the memory haunted her. She'd seen Troy only the day before and he was as morose as she was. It was as if he knew how she felt about Chayce. But they were both trying to get past it. Maybe buying the wedding dress would help.

She started out to her little foreign car and found Chayce leaning against the banister on the front porch, dressed in boots and jeans with a blue-patterned shirt and a white Stetson. His arms were folded over his broad chest and he studied Abby in the concealing ankle-length black-and-white patterned dress she was wearing, with her hair brushed firmly away from her face with its waves tamed by hair spray.

"Trying out for the lead in 'Arsenic and Old Lace?'" he drawled as he studied her unappreciatively.

"Troy likes me to dress this way," she said.

"Then perhaps he should marry someone's maiden aunt instead of you," he said pointedly.

She shifted her purse to her shoulder. "Are you going somewhere?"

"With you," he said, indicating the pickup truck. "We're buying a wedding gown, I hear."

"You'll look interesting in one," she returned.

He chuckled. "Not a chance. I'm allergic to lace and flowers. Come on. Becky said one of us should go with you. Now," he added with a dark glance at her clothing, "I understand why she thought so."

"I like old-fashioned dresses!"

He opened the truck door for her and moved abruptly before she could get in, so that she cannoned right into him and found herself riveted to him.

"You don't," he said quietly, staring at her. "He's trying to make you into Eve Payne."

She actually gasped.

"And don't pretend that you don't know it," he added curtly.

"How would you know? You haven't been around me for four years!"

"Becky has," he replied, his jaw taut, his eyes glittering as he looked at her. "She seems to feel he's found fault with everything about you."

She lowered her eyes to his broad chest, feeling all too comfortable this close to him. Cocooned between his long, powerful legs and the truck, with his arm propped against the body of the cab, he felt warm and reassuring despite the excitement his nearness fostered.

"He thinks I'm flighty," she confessed. "And his mother thinks I should have therapy."

He sighed heavily. His fingers touched her hair, tugging it forward, out of the stark style she'd sprayed it into. "Even your hair," he remarked. "It curls, and he doesn't like that, either, does he?"

"He thought I could have it straightened. Chayce!" She tugged at his fingers as they suddenly contracted on her hair.

"Sorry." He loosened his hold and smoothed over the curls he'd pulled. His eyes were worried as they searched over her wan face. "You don't like him to touch you, do you?"

The question brought her eyes shyly up to meet his. "I never said that."

He didn't smile. His face was somber. "Your body said it for you. You were starving to death for a man's kisses."

She laughed without humor. "Only for yours," she said dully. "It never changes. It never stops." She closed her eyes. "You shouldn't have come back."

His hand moved to her cheek. He drew it to his chest and stood just holding her in the soft, warm summer breeze, staring blankly over her head toward the deserted yard. "I had to. That letter knocked the breath out of me."

"I only asked you to give me away," she stated.

"I never expected you to want to get married right away. You're still so young, baby."

"You're the only person I know who thinks that."

"I'm older than most people you know. Thirty-six. Almost thirty-seven." His lips touched her hair tenderly. "The years are wrong."

"Dear old man," she whispered, nuzzling her face against his chest.

Even through the fabric, he could feel her touching his skin. He shivered.

She heard his heartbeat race, his breathing change. The hand holding her face to him moved to her shoulders and paused there.

Her fingers went to his shirt and slowly unbuttoned it. His hand covered hers, but only for a minute. With obvious reluctance, he removed it.

"This," he whispered, "is a very bad idea."

He didn't sound as if it were. She smiled as she pushed the fabric away and put her mouth against thick hair and warm muscle. He smelled of spicy cologne and soap, and her hands buried themselves in the hair that covered his chest while she kissed him with aching delight.

His hands caught her head, but they didn't pull it away. They simply rested there.

After a minute, his breathing became even more strained. He shifted and his hands dropped to her hips, bringing her against the powerful muscles of his thighs.

He was very aroused, but she wasn't frightened. Her hands slid around him, savoring the hard muscles of his back as she moved her mouth against a hard masculine nipple and began to suckle it.

He jerked back, holding her away from him. "No!" he said hotly, barely able to breathe at all now.

She looked at his rigid face and then back at his bare chest, at the faint marks where her mouth had touched him. "That was how I felt," she said softly, "when you kissed me there."

"We're on public display," he remarked.

"In a deserted yard," she replied. She lifted her eyes to his face and searched it hungrily. "And you let me."

"Yes," he had to admit, struggling for breath. "I let you."

He moved her hands away from his skin and slowly rebuttoned his shirt. He looked more unsettled than ever when he moved away and helped her into the truck.

He took longer than necessary to climb in beside her. He stowed his hat on the rack above the visor and pushed his hair back, glancing at her with un-usual intensity.

"Who taught you how to do that?" he asked.

"I watched a movie on a late-night cable chan-nel."

He started the truck. "You shouldn't be watching programs like that."

"Why not?"

He searched for a reason and couldn't find one.

She crossed her legs under the long skirt and pushed her hair away from her face. "Troy says they should make the cable company take it off the air, anyway."

"I'll bet he watches it."

"Not Troy," she said with a sigh.

He glanced at her as he backed the truck around and started through the open gate. "He's pretty staid, I guess."

"Yes," she agreed. "He has to be. He's a teacher, you know."

"Does he like kids?" he asked.

She shrugged. "Not much. But he does say we have to have a son to inherit the ranch when we're gone."

He made a rough sound in his throat.

"Something you should be thinking about, too," she chided. "An heir."

His breath caught in his throat. He hadn't let him-self think about children. He stared at the road ahead, trying not to react to the words.

"Does Delina like children?" she persisted.

"I haven't the faintest idea."

"Don't you talk to her?"

His hand clenched on the steering wheel.

"Sorry," she said quickly, thinking that she'd put her foot in her mouth. He probably slept with the woman... She closed her eyes on the painful thought.

He saw that, and knew why she'd done it. He let out a long, weary sigh. He couldn't bear to hurt her, not in any way at all. "I don't sleep with her, Abby," he said after a minute. He stared at his hands on the steering wheel instead of at her shocked face. He glanced at her after a minute and his eyes slid all over her as if they were hands. He looked back at the road. "I haven't slept with anyone. Not for four years."

He was telling her something utterly profound. She caught her breath. "Oh, Chayce!"

It was more a groan than a whisper. Her face was tormented.

He wasn't feeling much better himself. The whole damned situation was giving him fits. Abby was going to marry a man she didn't love, a man who wanted to change every unique thing about her. She didn't seem to mind that Troy found fault with her, but he did. It wounded him. He kept telling himself that she needed a younger man, but why did it have to be Troy?

He drew in a worried breath. "Where are you going to look for a gown?" he asked.

"In Whitehorn, of course."

"There's only one good shop there."

"I know."

He didn't say another word. He turned on the radio and gave every indication of listening to the news. Abby stared out the window and thought of how empty her life had become.

The dress shop was small, but it was the place local brides went to choose their gowns. The owner, a delicate little lady in her sixties, had been a famous couture designer in her youth and had retired to Whitehorn years before. Her name was Madame Lili.

"Yes, I have heard that you were to marry this summer," the tiny little woman said, with a moue of distaste as she looked at Abby's current manner of dressing herself. "Would you like to see some samples of the gowns I've made recently?"

"Yes, thank you," Abby said, surprised that Chayce had come into the shop with her. He settled in a chair near the window and just stared, his face hard and impassive.

Abby looked as the smaller woman pulled out gown after gown, but there was no enthusiasm in her. At least, not until the owner produced a sample that she'd been working on. Abby's gasp brought Chayce out of his chair. He moved close to her, his lean hand going out to touch the delicate lace of the Victorian wedding gown.

It was made of satin, with exquisite lace trim. It had embroidered flowers on the skirt and bodice, overlaid with more lace. Its sleeves were puffed at the shoulder, mutton-leg sleeves that narrowed and came to a point over the back of the hand. The cuff was embroidered, too.

"It is frightfully expensive," Madame Lili said. "But worth the price, don't you think?"

"Well worth it," Chayce said. He looked down at Abby with eyes dark with pain. "It will...suit her."

She looked back at him with her heart in her face.

Madame glanced from one to the other. "A handsome couple you make," she murmured with a smile. "You will want a veil, yes?"

Abby started to speak. Chayce caught her hand in his and pressed her fingers.

"Yes," he said quietly. "She'll want a veil. Something long and delicate," he added, searching Abby's face covetously.

"I have just the thing! One moment...!"

The little woman went into the back of the shop.

"She thinks...we're marrying each other," Abby murmured.

He tilted her sad face up to his and searched her eyes. With a long, hungry sigh, he bent his head and touched his lips tenderly to hers. This, she thought, is the way a man would kiss a new bride, with breathless tenderness.

A sob broke from her lips.

He lifted his head and looked at her tormentedly. "God, Abby!" he breathed roughly.

She touched his hard mouth, trying to fight back tears.

Before she could speak, Madame was back, pretending not to notice the tension in the air.

"Here," she said, proferring a long lace-trimmed veil with the same embroidery that graced the gown, all of it supported by a tiny cap lavishly sewn with seed pearls. "It matches the gown perfectly, yes?"

"Yes," Abby said. She touched it, her face drawn. "But I don't think..."

"She'll have it," Chayce said curtly. "The dress, too."

"But, Chayce," Abby argued.

"She'll need your measurements," he told Abby. He turned to Madame Lili. "Will you bill me, or shall I give you my credit card?"

"You are Mr. Derringer, yes?" she asked with a smile at his faint surprise. "I shall bill you. And may I offer my congratulations?"

"I'm not marrying Mr. Derringer," Abby said without looking at Chayce. "He's my guardian."

Madame was visibly taken aback. "Forgive me! I thought..." She laughed nervously. "Of course, there is an affection between you. I was mistaken. Come, my dear, let us take your measurements."

Chayce went out to the truck with his hands deep in his pockets, morose and anguished. Of course Madame had been mistaken. Abby was fond of him, just as he was fond of her. She'd marry Troy and learn to love him. He was close to her own age, a hard worker and a fine man.

Sure, he thought irritably as he climbed impatiently into the cab of the truck. He was going to remake Abby into Eve Payne, too, and she was going to let him. He hit the steering wheel hard with his hand, furious at the misery his life had become. Four years he'd stayed away, kept his distance, protected Abby from his headlong ardor. And it hadn't made a difference at all. He looked at her and wanted her. He touched her and she was his, yielded and hungry and full of secret fires.

His eyes closed. He had to stop this. He was too old for her. She'd loved him all her life and she was just confused. It had to be gratitude and affection, along with a natural curiosity about sex. He was kidding himself that it could be anything more, at her age. He excited her, but Troy could probably do that, too, if he approached her in the right way. He couldn't risk his future and her happiness on some crazy juvenile impulse. Besides, he'd had a taste of love eternal, hadn't he? Beverly had taken him for a hell of a ride when he was only a few years older than Abby was now, and he'd never recovered.

He tried to picture Abby going from his arms to another man's and failed miserably. She couldn't even let her fiancé touch her. His eyes closed. Dear God, when he thought of her in that wedding gown, he felt sick. Troy would probably complain about the expense of the dress and the fact that Chayce had bought it for her. He wouldn't care how glorious she looked in it, because he didn't really think much of the way she dressed. He'd keep her in garments suited to elderly ladies and lose his temper if she tried to wear anything that showed her exquisite figure.

She was coming out of the boutique, walking

slowly back toward the truck, her face hardly that of a woman expecting to be a bride within a month. She looked more like a condemned prisoner going to the gallows.

Without even thinking, he got out and went around to open the door for her. It was an act of old-world courtesy that was as much a part of him as his black hair with the silver sprinkled around his temples.

She smiled with pleasant surprise, because Troy didn't open doors for her, ever, despite his old-fashioned ideas in other ways. But to Abby, it was another indication of Chayce's affection for her that he did, the protectiveness that denoted his personality. She looked at him and thought how he'd be with a child, gentle and nurturing, and ferocious if it were threatened.

The thought brought tears to her eyes. She lowered them quickly as she went to climb into the truck. He caught her waist, gently holding her back, bending from his great height to look into her misty eyes.

"What's wrong?" he asked softly, wiping the tears away with his forefinger.

She bit her lip, hard. "Nothing..."

His hand lingered on her soft cheek. "Tell me, sweetheart."

She looked up, anguished. "I was thinking how you'd be with a child..." She averted her eyes from his shocked face and took a steadying breath. "Don't mind me. I'm crazy from the sun, I guess. We'd better go."

She sidestepped him and climbed up into the cab.

She didn't look at him as he closed the door or when he got in beside her and started the truck.

He couldn't talk to her. His mind was spinning, too, and not from the sun. He'd refused to think about having a child. But when Abby had mentioned it, his whole body had gone rigid. It was all too easy to see her with a baby in her arms, and toddlers clinging to her skirts. He could picture her in the kitchen with Becky, making cookies and cakes, or outside in the yard catching baseballs or flying kites. Abby had that sort of personality, and she loved children so much.

He pressed down on the accelerator, only anxious to get home and get away from her. Perhaps he could find something to do out of town. God knew, he'd managed that very well over the long four years since she went away to school and only came home for brief visits.

She watched the fields go past the window and never really saw them. Her future seemed so uncertain, so frightening. She clasped her hands tight in her lap and tried to imagine driving around with Troy and a child or two. He was a teacher—but his pupils were of high school age. She'd only seen him with one of his cousin's young sons. He hadn't liked the boy and it showed. He didn't get along with young children. Chaycc, on the other hand, seemed to forever have the cowhands' children on his heels when he was around the ranch. He attracted them the way honey brings flies.

"You're very quiet," he remarked when they were almost home.

She stared at her hands. "There's not much to say, is there?" she replied. "Except...thank you for the wedding gown."

He didn't answer her. He slowed for the turnoff that led to the ranch, easily controlling the big truck, and left a dust trail behind him.

When he pulled up in the yard, it was still deserted. He came around to open the door. Abby stepped out, right into the path of a bumblebee. It hit her cheek and she yelped.

"What is it?" Chayce asked, turning on his heel when he heard her cry out.

"A bee!"

He moved close, tilting her face up to his. "Did it sting you? Where?"

"I...I don't know!" She had a terror of flying insects, a holdover from childhood. She pushed at her hair, afraid that it might be caught there.

Chayce drew her hands down. "Let me look, sweetheart," he coaxed, tilting her face up. He studied it, looking for any sign of a sting, but she seemed to be all right, beyond having had a fright. Tears were in her eyes. Her face was flushed. He winced at the lingering traces of fear. "Here, now," he said softly, brushing away the tears that spilled over her eyelids. "It's all right. I'm not going to let anything hurt you, not anything at all." As if he couldn't help himself, he bent and put his mouth against her wet eyelids, absorbing the tears.

Abby was so stunned, so overwhelmed, by the tenderness, that she almost stopped breathing. Her face lifted to his mouth like a flower to the sun. She could barely get her breath at all.

He drew her into his arms and held her against him while his mouth gently touched her eyes, her wet cheeks, and finally, finally, her parted lips.

She stood in his embrace without a hint of struggle, loving his mouth against hers, loving the breathless sweetness of his touch.

"Couldn't you pretend to struggle?" he whispered against her warm, eager mouth.

"I don't know how," she whispered back. Her eyes were closed. She stood on tiptoe to tempt him into lowering his head again.

His big, lean hands slid into her hair and tilted her head at just the right angle. She didn't look, but she could feel his eyes on her before he bent again. This time the kiss wasn't tender. It was hard and rough and deep.

She gasped as his arms tightened, riveting her to his lean body there in the deserted yard. She lifted her arms around him and held on for dear life, so enthralled that she couldn't think past the moment. He tasted of coffee and his mouth was every dream she'd ever had.

He bit her lower lip and lifted his head, violence in his black eyes as they stared, unblinking, into her yielded gray ones. "Why did you have to start talking about children?" he asked half angrily.

Her gaze fell to his hard mouth. "Is that...why?"

"Does he like children?" he asked.

Her gaze fell once more to his broad chest. "Not much."

"And you do," he said huskily. "You love them."

She leaned her forehead against him with a miserable sigh. "Don't make it worse than it already is," she pleaded quietly. "You've already said that you don't want me in any conventional way."

His hands tightened on her waist. "He won't like the wedding gown, Abby," he said grittily. "He won't like the idea that I bought it for you, either."

"I don't care. It's the most beautiful dress I've ever seen."

"Only because you'll be wearing it," he said quietly.

She lifted her eyes. His were sad and quiet and intent. "Will you marry Delina?" she asked softly.

His face was like stone. He searched her face slowly, with a kind of deep-buried anguish. "I don't love her."

"Is love really necessary?" she asked on a hollow laugh. "Most people make do with what they can get. That's what I'm going to do."

"Don't talk like that!" he muttered. "He's a good man, Abby. He's young and steady."

"He could be perfection on a white horse and it wouldn't matter," she replied. Her eyes met his accusingly. "And you know why, Chayce."

He let her go, inch by inch, as if it hurt him to let her go. He stood back. "This is all my fault," he said. "I should never have come home." He drew in a long breath. "I've got some things to see about. I might as well do them before the wedding. But I'll be back in time to give you away," he added firmly.

He was closing doors. He couldn't have made it plainer. He was going away, to remove temptation from their paths. She'd lose him all over again. But did it matter? She was hurting so badly inside that she thought she might bleed to death in front of him. And she couldn't say so, or show it. Because he didn't want her love, or even her. Not for keeps.

She turned away. "As you wish," she said in a subdued, careless tone.

He watched her walk toward the house with impotent fury in his black eyes. She didn't want to marry Troy. She was going to do it only because she knew she couldn't have Chayce, and they both knew it.

For the first time in four years, he wondered if he was doing the right thing by turning his back on the love Abby wanted to give him. If only there were some way that he could be sure of her feelings for him!

But all he could do was step back and let her decide for herself what she wanted to do with her life. His part in all this was something he didn't dare think about. He should never have touched her in the first place. He'd had no right! If he'd left her alone, none of this would have happened.

With a rough sigh, he followed her toward the

house. He was going to pack a suitcase and do what was best for everyone. He wouldn't permit himself to think of the consequences.

Chapter 4

It didn't surprise Abby one bit to find Chayce gone when she came back downstairs an hour later. It only surprised her that he'd waited three days to go. He wasn't going to give her a chance to change his mind about things. He wanted her to marry Troy and he'd gone away to make sure she didn't back out.

But after the way he'd been in the boutique that morning, she could no longer bear the thought of spending her life with Troy. It might be the best thing, but she hadn't the nerve for it. To cold-bloodedly marry a man she didn't love seemed the worst sort of betrayal of everything those vows meant.

Becky glanced up from the magazine she was reading out in the kitchen when Abby came in.

"I'm baking some cookies," she said with a smile. "Want some iced tea?"

Abby shook her head. "How's your sister?" she asked.

"She sprained her ankle. She's at home propped up in bed with five new romance novels and a box of chocolates," she said with a chuckle. "I'm thinking about spraining my own ankle..."

"You wicked thing!" Abby teased. She went to the coffeepot and poured herself a cup.

"You don't like coffee," Becky said.

"I wish it was arsenic," Abby replied miserably, sitting down at the kitchen table with the older woman.

"Don't tell me Chayce is gone again."

"How did you know?"

"Saw the Mercedes backing out of the garage about an hour ago," she replied. "He left a fire trail behind him. You two have a fight?"

"No, we didn't. That's why he left."

"I don't understand."

"He got funny after he saw the wedding gown," she replied sadly. "He said I had to have it, despite how expensive it was, and then he started talking about how good Troy was going to be for me. That was just after he'd said that Troy was trying to make me into Eve Payne and I shouldn't let him change me."

"Whew," Becky whistled. "Sounds like a midlife crisis for sure."

Abby glowered at her. "He isn't middle-aged!"

Becky's eyebrows lifted. She grinned.

Abby sighed and sipped her coffee. "I want to run away, too. You can come with me."

"You could turn another bull loose."

Abby glowered at her. "That's not a lot of help."

Becky crossed her arms on the table and stared at Abby with affection and worry. "Do you love Troy?"

"No."

"Do you really want to marry him?"

"No."

"Then why do it?"

Abby ran a hand through her short hair. "Because Chayce says he's too old for me and I have to marry somebody younger. Troy's the only person who wants to marry me."

"That's a shameful reason to put on an engagement ring."

Abby actually blushed. "It didn't seem like a bad reason at the time. I hadn't seen Chayce for four years and he'd already made it clear that he...that he..." She hesitated.

Becky smiled. "I may be old, but I'm not blind," she murmured dryly. "I know how you feel about Chayce, Abby. I've always known."

Abby shrugged. "It doesn't matter how I feel, though," she said miserably. "He says he's too old for mc and he's determined that he isn't going to get married at all."

"You know why he's that way."

"She was a fool, and she never loved him," Abby

said shortly. "I do. I'd never play around with other men."

"He knows."

She lowered her eyes and picked at a fingernail. "Anyway, he said I should marry Troy." She looked up belligerently. "He said he'd give me away. He can't wait, in fact. That is, if he can force himself to stay here long enough for the ceremony!"

She burst into tears unexpectedly as the reality of her situation crashed down on her. Becky got up and comforted her, smoothing her hair while she cried.

"Oh, Becky, I can't marry Troy! I can't! Not when I feel this way about Chayce. It would cheat Troy and me both!"

"I know that, baby," she said gently. "I know."

"What am I going to do?"

"Give Troy back the ring."

She sniffed. "Chayce will go through the roof when he finds out."

Becky had a faraway, amused look in her eyes that Abby didn't see. "Think so? I wonder."

"He didn't say where he was going, did he?"

"No."

"He's probably on his way to see Delina," she muttered, wiping her eyes with the tissue Becky brought her. "She doesn't want to get married."

"I'll bet she does," came the dry reply. "No woman in her right mind could look at Chayce Derringer without seeing him at the end of a wedding aisle."

Abby leaned forward, red-eyed and fatigued. "She

may be hoping for a wedding, at that," Abby said. "She doesn't sleep with him."

The older woman's eyes widened. "And how do you know that?"

"He told me," Abby said absently. "He said he hadn't slept with anyone in four years."

There was a shocked silence from the other side of the table. When she looked up, Becky was still all eyes.

"Maybe he was lying," Abby said, hoping to erase the shock.

Becky shook her head. "We both know he doesn't lie." She let out a breath. "Well, well," she said, and even sounded amused. "And he's gone away, has he?"

"So I'll marry Troy and leave his house. Then he can come home again, and he won't have to leave every time I cross the property line," Abby grumbled. She pushed up from the chair. "Maybe I'll go away myself. I've got a degree and it's a big state. I can arrange that he'll never have to see me again, ever, and I won't have to marry Troy to do it!"

"Don't do anything rash," Becky cautioned.

"It won't be rash," she promised. "But I'm going to go see Troy right now."

Becky didn't say a word. But she'd have loved to be a fly on the wall.

"You what?" Troy exploded when Abby told him what she'd run him to ground at the corral to say.

She caught his hand and put the engagement ring

into it firmly. "I said I don't want to be made over into Eve Payne," she repeated quietly.

Troy's expression was indescribable. "Abby, I swear, I never...!"

"Listen," she interrupted wearily, "you don't like the way I am. That's basic, and I'm not going to change. You can't turn me into someone I'm not."

"But I'm not trying to change you," he protested weakly.

"What would you call it? Troy, you don't like the way I dress, the way I behave, or the way I look."

He drew in an angry breath. His freckles stood out even more. "I can get used to it."

"You can't," she said.

"What brought this on?" he asked suspiciously. "Are you still mooning over Chayce?"

Her heart skipped, but she only smiled. "Chayce has Delina," she said with forced indifference. "He'll marry her one day, and I'll be very happy for him. But one thing he said was right on the money. I'm not ready to get married and settle down just yet."

"You want us to be engaged for a few months longer?"

"I don't want us to be engaged at all," she said flatly. "I'm sorry. I don't love you. Without love, marriage is a piece of paper."

He clenched the ring in his hand. "You need to think about this, Abby. Give it a little time. You've had a lot of turmoil lately—graduation, our engagement and Chayce coming back after four years of avoiding you. It's too much for you, that's all. You take a week or two and just think about it. We've got a lot in common. You may not love me right now, but you like me. Love will come later."

It wouldn't, but she could see that she might as well talk to the fence as to Troy in that mood.

"I won't change my mind. I'm sorry."

He made a rough sound. "Well, what am I going to tell my folks?" he exclaimed, voicing his real objection to canceling the wedding. "What am I going to tell all the people who know we're engaged? For God's sake...!"

"Tell them I ran away to join the circus," she replied. "Or that I got kidnapped by aliens and brainwashed. Tell them whatever you please, I don't care."

"You can't jilt me at the altar!"

She didn't dare laugh. It wasn't funny. "We're nowhere near an altar. And I'm not jilting you, Troy. You're jilting me."

"I am?" He waited, brightening. "Okay, I am." He frowned. "But why am I?"

She thought for a minute and then smiled. "Because Chayce bought me a very expensive wedding gown and you realized that you'd be taking on Chayce as well as me if we got married and he'd run both our lives." She nodded. "How's that?"

He pursed his lips. "Not bad," he murmured lightly.

"Fine. You have my permission to use it."

"Did he?"

"Did he what?"

"Buy you an expensive wedding gown?"

"Yes," she replied. "But I won't need it now, you understand."

He stared at her quietly. "Are you really sure you want it this way?"

She nodded. "I'm sorry. I can't marry you." She turned toward her little foreign car and paused to glance over her shoulder. "Why don't you tell Eve we're not engaged anymore?" she asked, and went to her car before he could reply.

The broken engagement was a gossip-fest for two weeks in and around Whitehorn, but it didn't really raise eyebrows all that much. Most people who knew Troy and Abby had wondered from the beginning why two such different souls would want to get married. Especially when Troy went all red-faced around Eve Payne.

That wasn't all, either. Ever since Chayce had taken Abby to Madame Lili's and he'd bought that glorious wedding gown for her, gossip had run rampant about the two of them. Madame Lili had told people that it seemed very odd for Mr. Derringer to be buying a gown for Abby to wear for some other man, when he looked at her as if he would die to have her wear it for him.

Whitehorn held its breath and waited for new developments. Meanwhile, Abby discarded her Troy-inspired image and went back to body-hugging clothes that flattered her lovely figure. She let her

hair grow, too, and allowed it to wave and curl out-
rageously, as it naturally did. Last of all, she canceled
the beautiful wedding gown. It broke her heart, but
she had no need for it. She told Madame Lili that
she hoped some other lucky girl would get to wear
it, when she heard the sadness in the little old
woman's voice even over the telephone.

The Fourth of July came and went without a word
from Chayce. Becky and Abby went to the town celebration and watched the fireworks. Troy was there,
and so was Eve Payne. They hadn't come together,
but they sat together. He was friendly to Abby and
she was friendly to him, and the gossips just
shrugged and walked off without remarking on the
broken engagement.

A week later, Abby gave up hope that Chayce
might come back, and she started checking through
the want ads of the Butte and Billings daily news-
papers to look for work. She found several promising
jobs for someone with her business education and
started sending off résumés. It was the only thing to
do, she decided, since Chayce quite obviously wasn't
coming home until she left one way or another.

"You aren't really serious about this, are you?"
Becky asked worriedly a few weeks later. "I mean,
you won't know anybody in these places."

"It isn't as if I'll be going to L.A. or New York
City," Abby murmured. "Butte and Billings aren't
that big, really."

"You'll be alone," came the morose reply.

"I'll be alone here," Abby said heavily.

"He phoned last night."

Abby's heart leapt. "You didn't say anything."

"Not much to say. He asked were you all right, I said yes, he asked if you had everything set for the wedding."

"And?" Abby prompted, all eyes.

Becky shrugged. "I didn't know what to tell him," she said worriedly. "I said you hadn't picked a date. Well, that was true enough. He said it was already July, and why hadn't you? I said I didn't know. Before I could say anything else, he hung up."

"He didn't say where he was?"

Becky hesitated. "Yes."

"Where?"

Becky grimaced. "He was at Delina's house."

Abby turned away, her gray eyes full of dead dreams. "I'll carry that cake you made for the boys out to the bunkhouse for you, if it's ready," she said in a deceptively cheerful tone.

"It's ready. I'm sorry, baby."

Abby smiled lifelessly. "I'm going to be all right," she said. "I'm just about to find my own two feet. Don't you worry. I'll be fine."

"I know that."

Abby picked up the cake in its neat carrier and wandered down to the bunkhouse to give it to Billy Cates, who did the cooking for Chayce's outfit.

Billy grinned toothlessly from ear to ear. "Bless me, that was sweet of our Becky! The boys love her apple cake. So do I."

"You've all worked extra hard lately," she said.

"We both thought you deserved a treat." She glanced around at the empty living room, where the boys usually sprawled in front of the satellite-fed television when they weren't working. "Where is everybody?"

"Out rounding up stray calves," Billy told her. "Mr. Conroy was afraid we might lose some in this drought if we didn't get them all in. Weather's been frightful. Sure wish we had some rain."

"We're not likely to get much this time of year, but we can hope."

"Plenty of thunder and lightning," Billy remarked. "But no rain to go with it."

"Par for the course."

He relayed his thanks to Becky again and Abby wandered back toward the house, her mind far away.

She wasn't watching for a car, which was why she didn't see the black Mercedes coming pell-mell up the driveway until she was at the back door.

Chayce swung the car right up to the steps, snapped the key out of the ignition, and reached her in two long strides.

He was wearing a vested gray suit with a white shirt and patterned tie and highly polished gray boots. But his face didn't match the elegance of his clothing. He looked as if he hadn't slept in days and he needed a shave.

Abby stared at him from dead eyes. "Why are you back?" she asked.

"What do you mean, you aren't marrying Troy?" he demanded without preamble.

Her eyebrows arched. "I haven't told you anything about it."

"You're the only one who hasn't! Troy's father phoned me in Hollywood and asked why you'd broken off the engagement. He said it was the talk of the community, along with that damned wedding dress I bought you!"

"You didn't buy me a wedding dress," she said solemnly. "I phoned Madame Lili the very next day and canceled it. Someone else will wear it to the altar," she added coldly. "Someone who's loved and wanted and appreciated." She laughed harshly. "That description certainly doesn't fit me!"

"Troy loves you!"

"The devil he does!" she flashed back, furious at her situation and his sudden interest in it after a month's absence. "He's crazy for Eve Payne. Once he realizes that he loves her, they'll get married and live happily ever after. She's been eating her heart out for him for years!" Which was the truth, even if Abby had only just found it out from a mutual acquaintance, anxious to know if that was why Abby and Troy had canceled their wedding.

"And what about you?" he asked curtly.

"I have job interviews in Helena next Monday," she said, turning to go into the house.

"Helena?"

She paused with her hand on the screen door handle. "Yes, Helena! I'm going to work there. Aren't you glad?" she asked with flashing gray eyes. "You'll be able to come back and live in your own house. You won't even have to go to such great lengths to avoid me anymore!''

She went into the house, ignoring the hot, furious curses that followed her.

She didn't stop. She went straight up the stairs to her room, ignoring Becky's quick call as well. Once inside the door, she locked it, and went to her chair by the window. She was shaking all over. Chayce had come home at last, but only to demand to know why she'd canceled her wedding. She really wondered why she'd expected anything more from him. If he'd wanted her at all, he'd never have left four years ago.

A few minutes later, there was a sharp knock at her door. She got up from the chair to answer it, expecting Becky to be standing there, concerned.

It wasn't Becky. It was Chayce. He'd changed into jeans and a patterned brown shirt, and he was wearing boots and his beige working Stetson and worn leather chaps.

''Well?'' she asked belligerently.

His eyes went over her exquisite figure in tight jeans and tank top. ''Put on your boots and grab a hat.''

''Am I going somewhere?'' she asked.

''Put a long-sleeved shirt over that,'' he added, nodding toward the tank top that hinted of the sweet curves underneath. ''So you don't get sunburned.''

''I have to...''

He put his thumb squarely over her mouth. ''You have to change clothes.''

She didn't know how to take this sudden change of attitude. She almost refused. But even a few stolen minutes in Chayce's company was such a tempting thought that she didn't have the will to refuse him.

She nodded and turned back into the room. Surprisingly he followed her, closing it behind him.

She pulled out a long-sleeved shirt from her closet, glanced at him and started to put it over the tank top.

"You'll burn up. It's hot out there."

She hesitated and then turned toward the bathroom, since it was evident that he didn't plan to leave.

But even as she took a step in that direction, he moved in front of her. He tossed the shirt onto the bed and with a deft motion, he whipped the tank top over her head and tossed it aside. She was wearing the briefest kind of lacy bra. She stood there in it, her mouth half-open, her eyes like saucers.

"The first time I touched you, I did that," he recalled, his black eyes narrowing on the generous view of her breasts that the lacy garment afforded him. "Neither of us was expecting it. You were soaked to the skin and we'd argued about something. You refused to change into anything dry, despite the fact that you were shivering from the cold. I herded you into the study and closed the door. We argued. You refused to take off your wet clothes. And that's exactly what I did. Except," he added in a husky, deep tone, "that you weren't wearing anything under that top. And I didn't realize it until it was too late."

She felt his eyes like brands on her soft skin as he looked at her.

"Do you remember what I did next, Abby?" he asked, still staring at her bare shoulders and throat. "I put my mouth on your breasts and you cried out. I thought I'd frightened you until I lifted my head and looked at your face." His chest rose and fell heavily. "Dear God, I'd never dreamed of passion like that. I pushed you onto the couch and followed you down," he continued quietly, holding her spellbound. "I never even realized what I was doing to you. Every soft little cry, every bite of your nails into my back only made it more urgent. It took every bit of willpower I had to draw back in time." He touched her breasts where they rose above the lacy cups, and she trembled with memories and sensation. His eyes met hers, seeing the embarrassment she couldn't hide even after four years. "I managed it, just. But I damned near satisfied you right through your clothing," he whispered. "You, and myself. And that's why I couldn't come home again. It was such a near miss that I was afraid it might happen twice. Except that I knew I'd never be able to pull back a second time. I wanted you too much."

She averted her eyes, red-faced.

"We burned together like twin flames," he whispered. "I've had women all my adult life, but I never lost my self-control so completely with anyone until you came along. I was embarrassed and ashamed by what I almost let happen between us."

Her shocked eyes met his. "You were?"

He scowled. "Didn't you know?"

She shook her head. "Oh, heavens, no. I thought..." She swallowed and let her gaze fall to his chest. "I thought men did that all the time with women. You were older than I was, and I'd never even let a man touch me before. It didn't occur to me that it was anything unusual for you." Her hands fumbled nervously with the fabric of his shirt. "I thought I'd done something wrong and you blamed me."

"Something wrong." He laughed mirthlessly. "I came within a breath of stripping you and going the whole damned way, right there," he added roughly. "It's still my first inclination every time I look at you."

That was a little shocking. She glanced up at him uncomfortably and saw the fires burning in his dark eyes. "Inclinations don't mean much, though, do they, when you leave skid marks getting away from me?" she asked sadly.

"Don't look like that!" he said sharply. "You know why I left. You know why I stayed away."

"So it wouldn't happen again," she agreed with a tiny sigh. Her eyes searched his face slowly, with a longing that she couldn't begin to hide. "But it doesn't seem to matter, does it, Chayce? I can't have anybody else. I don't want anybody else."

He drew in a heavy breath. "Neither do I," he said shockingly.

She didn't believe she'd heard him say that at first. Her eyes were riveted to his lean, handsome face.

"Didn't you understand what I was telling you, when we went to look at the wedding gown?" he asked gently. "I was telling you that I'm not capable with other women. I haven't been since that night with you."

"Was it...something I did?" she asked.

He shook his head. His arm reached around her waist and brought her to him. "It was this." And he kissed her.

Chapter 5

It wasn't a demanding kiss. It wasn't invasive. It was tender and full of respect and breathless longing. Abby slid her arms around Chayce's neck and her body went soft against the hard length of his.

His lean hands met and passed around her back. His mouth grew slowly more insistent, pushing her head against his broad shoulder while he kissed her as if he needed her mouth to survive.

When he finally lifted his head, his eyes were turbulent, and one hand was hesitating at the fastening between her shoulder blades.

His jaw tautened and his eyes narrowed. He took a sharp breath and his hand moved back down to her waist. "No," he said shortly, jerking back from her. "Oh, no, not this time!"

She felt shaky all the way to her toes. Her helpless eyes sought reassurance, hope, in his face.

He was still trying to get his breath. He backed away a step and then another. His hands went into his pockets and he swallowed, hard.

"I came to take you riding," he said heavily. "And that's what we're going to do." He reached for her shirt, which was still lying on the bed. He held it while she slid into it, and then he fastened the buttons right up to her collarbone.

She wasn't thinking at all. Her eyes couldn't leave his face, no matter how hard she tried to make them. He was her whole world.

He hesitated at the last button and saw that look. It seemed to take the breath out of him, because he stopped breathing for a moment.

"Fires burn themselves out eventually," he said roughly. "But not before they consume everything in their path. We have to build a firebreak, while there's still time."

"You mean, you don't want me," she said.

He shook his head. "That's not what I mean at all." He finished buttoning the last button and his hands went to her shoulders. "We're going to live one day at a time. Starting right now. We're taking a tour of the ranch. I've been away a long time. I want to see what's happened while I've been gone. I want to get reacquainted with my men. You can come along."

It was something. He seemed willing to let her into his life, even on a limited basis. She wasn't strong enough to refuse. "Okay," she replied.

He touched her flushed cheek with the back of his

lean fingers. He smiled in a way he'd never smiled at her before.

"What about...Delina?" she asked worriedly.

His fingers brushed across her lips. "What about that job in Helena?"

She shrugged.

A corner of his mouth pulled up.

"I hope you haven't forgotten how to ride," he remarked and, taking her hand, he led her down the staircase. The feel of his strong fingers linking with hers sent a thrill all the way through her. She couldn't remember ever being so happy.

It had been years since they'd been riding together. Chayce sat a horse as if he'd been born to it, which he had. His own father had tried his hand at rodeos, although he'd never been very successful. It was Abby's father who'd won event after event and had become Chayce's hero. Whit Turner had tried to turn Abby into a champion rider, but she didn't have the seat for it. She could ride, but there was nothing special about her abilities. She could stay on the horse's back and not much more, although she did enjoy it.

Chayce glanced at her, approving the picture she made in the Atlanta Braves cap he'd loaned her. She didn't like Western hats, because she could never find one that fit her properly. She liked bibbed caps, like this one.

"All you need is a hound dog and a shotgun," he murmured. "And a truck."

She made a face at him. "I look fine, thanks."

Her eyes slid over his lean, fit body in the saddle with admiration and pure pleasure. "You always did look at home on a horse."

"It's where I'd rather be, most of the time, not stuck in some boardroom with spreadsheets between my hands."

"You have your finger in a lot of pies," she recalled.

He nodded, absently watching the lazy circling flight of a hawk overhead. "The ranch would be enough for most men. I sit on the board of three corporations, head a committee for the national cattlemen's lobby and chair my own companies. It keeps me running." He glanced back at her. "Lately I think it keeps me running too much."

She averted her gaze to the wide pommel of her Western saddle. "I thought you were running from me."

He chuckled. "Maybe I was."

"Not anymore?" she asked and tried not to sound hopeful.

He drew the reins more securely through his gloved fingers. He averted his face so that she couldn't see it. "I haven't decided yet."

"I won't marry Troy, in case you thought you could change my mind," she said firmly.

"You don't suit him the way you are," he said quietly. "But I feel responsible for the way you broke up. Maybe I shouldn't have come back until the wedding."

Her hand caught the pommel and held it, hard.

He saw her fingers clench, saw her stiff stance, and reined in his own mount. "Talk to me!"

She reined in, but she didn't look at him. She stared off in the distance at the buttes that seemed to run along forever against the blue sky. "If I'd married Troy, it would have been the biggest mistake either of us ever made. You don't marry one man to work another one out of your system. I may not be mature, but at least I know that. I would have cheated Troy every day I lived with him. Eventually he might have hated me for it."

"Love can be learned."

She turned and looked straight at him. "No, it can't. Not where there's no spark of interest to begin with and nothing in common except being born in the same town. He liked football games and I liked fishing. That's pretty basic."

He leaned forward in the saddle and pulled his Stetson farther over his eyes. "I like fishing myself. I haven't been in years, of course."

"We used to go, when Dad was alive." She smiled, because the memory wasn't so painful now. "I'd sit on the bank with a cane pole and try my best to catch something."

"You were patient enough," he agreed. "But you wouldn't use the right kind of bait."

She glared at him. "I am not torturing worms and spring lizards...!"

"Dough balls for crappie," he indicated. "And artificial flies for trout fishing. You needed a good rod and reel, not a cane pole, but Whit was always afraid you'd hook yourself in the hand or the eye. I knew better, but I wouldn't argue with him."

"He loved you," she said, glancing back toward the distant river.

"He loved you, too. If he'd had ten kids, I think you'd still have come first. You were unique, Abby, even at the age of ten."

"You liked me then."

"I like you now," he said, and his voice was deeper, softer.

She wouldn't look at him. What she felt was too near the surface. "Billy said the boys were chasing strays. Know where to look?"

"I think so. Come on."

He led the way down a long wooded trail that passed across the shallow river and into a small canyon. The sound of bawling calves was loud in the face of the soft wind.

"There they are," Chayce said, nodding toward two hands who were driving a few calves out of the brush toward a corral set up in the grassland beyond. He scowled. "I thought I told Kirk to buy polled cattle to replace the culls. Even these damned cows have horns. That's an open invitation to a bad accident."

Abby hadn't been home enough to get a look at the cattle this far from the house. She was puzzled, too, because Kirk Conroy was very good at his job.

"Speaking of Conroy," Chayce murmured, his keen eyes scanning the valley, "where is he?"

He wasn't one of the riders; that was immediately

apparent. Chayce urged his mount into a canter and reined up beside one of the cowhands.

"Where's Kirk?" he asked curtly.

The man, surprised, gaped at him. "Mr. Derringer?" he asked, leaning forward as if he couldn't believe his eyes. "We thought you were in the Bahamas, sir!"

"I said, where's my foreman?"

The cowboy sighed. "He's at the doc's."

"Why?"

"He really ought to tell you himself, Mr. Derringer," he said nervously.

"Is he hurt?"

There was a pause. "He got stepped on by a bull," the man confessed finally. "Bruised his foot real bad and he's going to limp for a week or so." The cowboy shrugged. "He didn't want you to know. Said you'd take a strip off him for being careless."

"Oh, hell," Chayce muttered. "Anybody can get stepped on by a bull. I've been stepped on by a surly horse. That's nothing to be embarrassed about!"

The cowboy smiled, relieved. "He'd sure like to hear that, I expect."

"And I'll tell him, just as soon as he gets back," he added. "I'm going to be home for good now. I can handle things if he needs to rest that foot for a few days."

He gave the man brief orders about the roundup and moved ahead with Abby. He stopped to talk to another rider and Abby rode ahead a few hundred yards, where she spotted a red hide in some thick underbrush.

"Poor little guy, are you stuck?" she murmured, smiling. She struggled down off her horse and went toward it, vaguely aware of an angry shout behind her as she tugged at the bawling calf. She was totally oblivious to the horned cow that heard the bawling of her calf and came thundering down a hill with her head lowered, right at Abby.

Chayce saw the charge and knew he'd never be quick enough to ride the cow down. "Brady!" Chayce yelled, holding out his hand. "Throw me your Winchester!"

The rider complied in a heartbeat. Chayce stood up in the stirrups, whipped the rifle to his shoulder, sighted and started firing, right in front of the cow.

She bawled and, frightened, turned. He held the Winchester steady, ready to bring her down if he had to.

"Abby! Get out of there!" he yelled.

She'd turned at the shock of the shots being fired and only then realized her danger. She went back to her horse on shaky legs, mounted and rode quickly up to Chayce.

He only lowered the rifle when she was reining in beside him. "You little fool!" he raged. *"Don't you look?"*

She felt shaky. It had been a long time since he'd been so angry with her. "No, I didn't. I'm sorry," she said in a choked tone.

Chayce put the safety on the rifle and gave it back

to the man he'd borrowed it from. His face was pale under its olive tan, and he looked wild-eyed as he swung down out of the saddle.

Her hands trembled on the reins as she began to realize how close a call she'd had. "I just wanted to free the calf."

He didn't say a word. He reached up and lifted her down from the horse with deft, sure motions. His face was as rigid as stone, and the black eyes that met hers were frightening. Around them, the men could sense trouble brewing and the man Chayce had been talking to yelled for the men to come on and take their morning break. It was almost comical how quickly they scattered.

With the horses grazing just behind them, they were alone in the deserted pasture, a good distance from the calf and its mother, with whom it was now reunited.

"You could have been gored," Chayce said through his teeth. "You could have been killed, damn it!"

She bit her lower lip hard. She felt like a fool already and here he was, rubbing it in. She didn't know why she'd done something so stupid in the first place. She'd never thought of any danger with Chayce nearby.

"Come here, you little idiot!"

He jerked her into his arms and wrapped her up bruisingly tight. She could feel the wild racing of his heart, hear his quick, sharp breathing.

Only then did she realize that she'd frightened

him. Imagine that, she thought dazedly, frightening Chayce, who never felt fear at all.

"I wasn't in any danger," she mumbled against his damp shirt. "You were here."

"I knew I couldn't get to you before the cow did," he growled out at her temple. "The only hope I had was to spook the cow or bring her down, and my hands were shaking."

Her heart turned over. She drew back a breath, just enough to let her see his hard face. It was amazing, the look on it. He was afraid for her.

His eyes narrowed as he realized what she was seeing. His jaw tautened and he put her away from him abruptly. He could barely get a complete breath.

"Don't do that again," he said curtly.

She shook her head, still fascinated by his concern for her. He'd always stood between Abby and danger, but it had never affected him quite like this. Not so that his hands shook.

"And don't get any ideas," he added impatiently.

She shook her head again.

His nostrils flared. He looked around them, took off his hat, wiped his sweating brow on his sleeve and slammed the hat back onto his head.

"Let's go," he said shortly. "We've got a lot of ground to cover."

He helped her to remount with careless efficiency and swung back into his own saddle. He didn't say a word as they rode from place to place, watching small groups of cowboys work cattle from one range to another. It was a huge operation, and Abby had never realized just how big it was until now. It was a responsibility that would make mincemeat of the nerves of a lesser man. She remembered all the things Troy had said about the obstacles that beset ranchers in the modern world.

"Do you agree that wolves shouldn't run on cattle range?" she asked abruptly.

He glanced at her. "I get along all right with wolves," he said. "If I have any problems, I call the wildlife people and have the threat removed."

Her eyebrows lifted. "What about park buffalo infecting the herds with brucellosis?"

"If you inoculate your herd, they can't catch it," he said simply.

"How do you feel about conservation?"

"Is this a quiz?" he asked. "And if it is, what's the prize?"

"Sorry." She withdrew again.

He reined in and pulled her horse around as well. "I think that conservation is essential," he told her. "We're experimenting with hardy forage that doesn't require tons of fertilizer to grow. In fact, we're processing animal waste to meet that requirement. We're experimenting with grass strains that thrive in the conditions here, and we've cut back even in our graze plantings to natural ways of controlling insect pests." He frowned. "Didn't you know that I sit on the board of the local resource conservation and development authority as well as the local cattlemen's association?"

She stared at him with quiet curiosity. "You never talked about it."

He laughed shortly. "You were a child, Abby," he said simply. "You've grown up."

"Yes." She turned her attention to the wide pasture, noting the lack of moisture. "The drought is biting hard."

"In spite of the snow melt, too, and we had record drifts this year. Amazing how we still have to fight nature to make a living."

"Drought doesn't affect mining," she reminded him.

He chuckled. "Diversity has distinct advantages." His eyes narrowed. "What are you going to do with that degree?" he asked out of the blue.

She started. "Get a job," she faltered.

"What sort of job?"

"I don't know," she said. "Something in management maybe, or a junior executive position working for a company."

"What company?"

She pursed her lips. "Is this a quiz? And if so, do I get a prize?"

He chuckled, hearing his own questions thrown back at him. He turned his horse and rode on, waiting for her to catch up.

They stayed out for several hours, stopping to eat steak and beans at the chuck wagon with the men at lunchtime. It was midafternoon before Chayce had seen what he wanted to see and was willing to go back to the house.

"Are you sore?" he asked, noting how she stood in the stirrups occasionally.

She nodded. "I haven't done much riding lately."

"Have a hot bath. It will help."

"I'll do that."

They rode on in silence, watching a hawk fly over and, closer, a rabbit jump and run for cover. It was so beautiful here, around Whitehorn, she thought wistfully. She was going to miss it terribly. But she'd have to go somewhere away from Chayce. Just being with him was a sort of torment. She couldn't bear living in the same house with him and knowing that he was never going to be able to return the feeling she had for him.

Her brush with the horned mother cow had shaken him, but so had seeing her with the wedding gown in Madame Lili's shop. He'd still left the ranch, regardless of the tenderness he'd shown her.

"What did you tell Madame Lili about the gown?" he asked suddenly, and she jerked, because it was as if he'd read her thoughts.

"That I hoped she'd find someone who would love it as much as I did," she said stiffly. "I'm sure she will. It was...exquisite."

He glanced at her quietly, seeing the pain and resignation and love in her soft eyes that she tried to hide. He sighed with a kind of resignation and smiled to himself as he urged his horse forward at a faster clip. Four years hadn't worn down her feeling for him. It was a fair bet that what she felt wasn't infatuation, and he'd never been more sure of what he felt himself. It was time to stop running.

Abby languished in a whirlpool bath when they got home, having left Chayce heading for his study without a backward glance. He could forget her so easily. All he had to do was walk away. Abby had never been able to do that, not in any way at all. She closed her eyes and let the jets soothe away the soreness that stabbed at her tired muscles. The warm water felt so good, and so did the bubble bath she'd added to it. The fragrance was of violets and it wafted around her nostrils in a delicious haze.

The sound of the jets had canceled out any other sounds. She didn't realize that she was no longer alone until the jets suddenly stopped and she looked up in time to see Chayce move his thumb from the button that controlled them.

Her breath caught in her throat. The bubbles covered her, just, but the most shocking thing was that Chayce had just come from a bath himself. He was wearing a long silk navy blue bathrobe; and apparently nothing under it.

"Go ahead," he invited as he drew the towel from the warming rack. "Ask me what I'm doing in here."

She had to clear her throat before she could speak. Her face was flushed, and not from the heat of the water. "What are you doing in here?" she asked.

He held the towel in one hand and searched her face. "Make a guess."

"You ran out of water?"

He smiled and held the towel. "Come out."

She flushed even more. "I can't."

"Why?"

"Chayce, I don't have any clothes on," she said in an abnormally high-pitched tone.

He shrugged. "Neither do I."

"You're wearing a robe!"

He glanced at it. "So I am. Does it make you feel at a disadvantage?" His black eyes twinkled. "That's a problem that's very easily solved."

He took one lean hand from the towel, twitched open the tie that held the robe and shrugged it off.

She didn't mean to look. She didn't want to look. And then she couldn't stop looking. He was beautiful all over. Her eyes searched him like caressing hands, helplessly.

He held the towel up. "Now we're even," he said.

With a sigh of resignation, and feeling as if she were taking a step off the edge of a cliff, she got to her feet and stepped out of the tub.

He looked at her for a long time before he wrapped her in the towel, his eyes possessive and quiet and full of tenderness.

"Is it hard to breathe?" he asked gently as he toweled her dry. "You're all but gasping for air."

"I'm afraid," she whispered, avoiding his piercing gaze.

He leaned to speak into her ear. "It won't hurt."

She flushed. "Chayce!"

He chuckled. "It's wicked to tease you. I'm sorry. Maybe you don't realize that it's as difficult for me as it is for you."

"What...is?"

He searched her eyes. "This first time."

Her lips parted. Her heart was running wild. "First time...for what?"

He didn't answer what must have sounded like an inane question.

"Becky's right downstairs!" she said in a squeak.

"She's gone to spend the rest of the day with her sister. She may not even be back tonight."

He finished drying her and tossed the towel into the laundry hamper. He met her eyes levelly. "Do you want me to protect you?"

"From...what, you?" she asked on a high-pitched laugh.

"From becoming pregnant," he said solemnly. "Children should be planned and wanted."

She swallowed. This was getting entirely out of hand. She couldn't believe that they were standing together stark naked talking about babies.

"Yes, and you don't want to get married," she said in a rush.

He took her face in his warm hands and searched her frightened eyes. "I love you," he said quietly. "I want to get married. I want children. What I'm asking is if you want them this soon with me."

She blinked in sweeping confusion. Her heart felt

as if it might explode from the sheer joy of what he was telling her. "I don't understand."

"I called Madame Lili," he whispered. "She still has the wedding gown and the veil. I said that we'd be in to get them tomorrow."

"In the…but, I told you, I called off the wedding!"

"You called off one wedding," he said, correcting her. He bent and touched his mouth softly to hers. "You didn't call off ours. We're getting married by a Methodist minister right here on the ranch. We'll hold the ceremony in a marquee with arches of roses and as many guests as we can fit in the yard. We'll have a catered reception afterward. The minister said that he could perform the ceremony the second week of August. By then we'll have the rings, the blood tests, the license and invitations sent out."

She stared up into his black eyes. "Married? Us? You and me?"

"Married. Us." He drew her against him, flinching a little at the intimate contact. He inhaled sharply and shivered. "Oh, God, Abby…"

She reached up to him. Her hands, cool and nervous, slid into his thick hair and tugged his face down to hers. She kissed him with all the love she'd hidden for so many years and felt his immediate, explosive response.

He swept her up into his arms and carried her to the bed, following her down without lifting his mouth away. With all the barriers down, it was like a brushfire burning. His mouth was all over her, warm and thrilling and insistent, his hands touching her intimately, rousing her with expert deliberation.

She was weeping when he finally gave in to her pleas and, holding her eyes starkly, slid down to become part of her shivering body.

She gasped at the feel of him, so intimate, so invasive.

"Too quick?" he whispered tenderly, pausing to let her get used to him like this. He smiled even through his raging hunger. "I've waited a long time. I can give you all the time you need."

She swallowed. "It...stings a little," she whispered, dazed by being with him like this.

"Yes." He brushed back her damp hair. "It won't be uncomfortable for very long. Look at me, Abby," he whispered, bending to nibble her lips. "Watch me."

It was so erotic. She thought she'd never experienced anything in her life that was so vividly intimate. He talked to her. He whispered things that made her blush, moved against her, laughed with pure pleasure as she responded suddenly and starkly to the teasing, caressing motions of his body.

"I'm...sorry!" she gasped when she realized that her nails had scored his shoulders.

"For what, Abby?" he asked huskily. His eyes seemed to blaze, his face was alive with passion, his body expert in the skill of kindling it. She sobbed, shocked by the sudden transformation of pain into throbbing, hot pleasure. She surged under him, shivered, gasped with the sensation of it, with his piercing stare as he watched her face.

"It's so intimate," she gasped.

"The most intimate thing a man and a woman can do together," he agreed. "And the most beautiful, where love exists." His body became insistent, demanding. Above her, his face hardened as the pace increased.

She held on for dear life, certain that what she was feeling now was going to kill her. She looked into his eyes and he vanished in a red haze of pure surging ecstasy that left her arched stiffly and convulsing. And still he watched and watched, until finally she felt his body join hers in the exultant surrender to fulfillment.

They lay together, not speaking, not moving. His skin was damp against hers and their hearts throbbed in a disjointed unity.

She felt him in every pore of her body, with every beat of her heart, as if he were part of her very breathing. Her hands touched his back experimentally, to make sure that he was real and it was no dream.

"You never answered me," he whispered after a minute.

"About what?" she whispered back.

He smiled tenderly and his lips teased at her throat. "About whether or not you wanted me to make you pregnant."

Chapter 6

She felt his heartbeat quicken and his arms tighten around her, as if he were poised, waiting for her answer.

She smiled against his warm, damp throat. "I want lots of babies," she whispered, nuzzling him.

He caught his breath and then let it out. "Thank God," he breathed at her ear. "Thank God, thank God...!"

He found her mouth and kissed her until they had to come up for air. His eyes were blazing with his feeling for her, with love so sweeping that a blind woman could have seen it.

"I couldn't stop," he whispered, tracing her mouth. "I'm sorry, I meant to give you a choice."

"I made a choice," she replied softly. Her eyes searched his. "I love you with all my heart. I never stopped loving you. I want it all, marriage, children, living with you, working with you. I never dreamed it would happen."

"You seem very sure that it has."

She nodded and touched his hard mouth. "You'd never have done this unless you loved me," she said simply.

He nodded. "I love you too much. I'll never know if I did the right thing by coming home. Perhaps you'll be sorry one day that you didn't marry Troy."

"Never," she said with certainty. She sighed. "I wish we were already married."

He pursed his lips. "Do you?" He chuckled, looking down the length of their bodies, pressed so closely together. "I don't think even marriage would get us closer than this, Abby. But I take your point." He drew away from her, laughing at her expression. "You'll get used to it."

"Of course I will." She sat up, her eyes full of wonder as she looked at him. "What are you doing?"

"Getting dressed. Put on something. Anything. It doesn't matter." He shrugged into his shirt and picked up the telephone.

Two hours later, they were in Las Vegas, standing together in the same clothes they'd worn that afternoon in a wedding chapel where a justice of the peace was performing a brief ceremony.

When Chayce kissed her, she cried. It was unbelievable. "But what about my beautiful wedding gown, and the ceremony," she blurted out.

"A lot of people have both a civil and a religious service," he said pointedly. He grinned. "You'll feel even more married then," he added, holding her hand tight in his. "And for years, people will talk about the prospective bride who was carried off in the middle of the night by her ardent husband-to-be," he added wickedly.

"Nobody knows about it," she scoffed.

His eyebrows rose over indulgently amused eyes. "Think so? Wait and see," he retorted.

They slept very late the next morning in Chayce's big bed after the return flight from Las Vegas, tired and relaxed and both wearing wedding bands. These they were obliged to show to a shocked and gasping Becky who opened the door to Chayce's room at ten o'clock in the morning and found him in bed with Abby.

"But...what...where...how?" Becky cried from the doorway.

"Las Vegas," Chayce said. He put a finger to his lips. "The local service is the second week of August, right here at the ranch, and it will be performed by a minister, not a justice of the peace," he added. "So you don't know that we're already married. Understand?"

Becky was quick. She put a finger to her lips, gave them both a rakish, gleeful grin and closed the door.

Chayce rolled over, ripping the sheet away from

Abby's relaxed body in the process. "I want to test a theory," he whispered with a grin as he bent his mouth to her soft body.

"What sort of theory?" she gasped, moving restlessly under the sweet contact of his lips.

"I want to see if it feels different with a wedding band. Game?"

She lifted her arms around his neck and raised her face to his. "Oh, yes," she whispered. She drew him down to her. "I'm game. I love you, Chayce."

"I love you, too, Mrs. Derringer," he whispered. And after that, he didn't say anything intelligible for a long, long time.

"Well?" she asked on gasping breaths, much later.

"It's definitely better with the ring," he murmured against her mouth.

She smiled under his demanding mouth. "I thought so, too." She sighed. "And the nice thing is that nobody will know we're already married."

After twenty people had congratulated them in Whitehorn the next morning, Abby made a face and looked sheepishly at her new husband.

"I told you so," he said comfortably with an arm around her as they walked down the street.

"But how?" she asked.

"That will probably be one of the remaining mysteries of life," he replied. He looked down at her with pure pride. "But we're having all the prewedding parties and a big society wedding just the same.''

"I'm glad," she replied. "I wanted so badly to wear that wedding gown for you."

"As you will," he said, searching her eyes. "Just seeing you with it was enough to tear the heart out of me. I came back early because I knew I couldn't let Troy marry you."

"You said you came back to talk me into marrying him!" she gasped.

"I lied," he said with a faint smile. "I wanted to make sure you didn't change your mind. I gave in while I was away. I'm fifteen years your senior, but I don't guess it really matters if you love me and I love you."

"I tried to tell you that," she murmured dryly.

"Next time you try to tell me something, I'll listen." He drew her closer. "I've been an idiot, Abby. But I woke up in time, thank God."

She closed her eyes and pressed her cheek to his shoulder. "I was so afraid that you were going to let me go."

"I don't think I could have, when it came down to it. It was best that you broke the engagement when you did. I had visions of stealing you away in the middle of the night and flying you off to Las Vegas to marry me while you were still engaged to Troy. That would really have started tongues wagging around here!"

She glanced around them at hastily closed curtains.

"I think they're already wagging," she said pointedly.

He turned her to him on the deserted sidewalk. "They might as well have a reason," he whispered. And he kissed her right there, with enough passion and tenderness to prompt a whole new wave of gossip.

The wedding was a local occasion. There were showers and parties and all the celebration Abby could ever have hoped for. The wedding itself was the culmination of weeks of festivities. Even though most people knew that Chayce and Abby had already been married, this exquisite service was just for Whitehorn. Not only were almost all the local citizens packed onto the Derringer ranch for the ceremony and a huge catered reception with tents to follow. Even the news media had been allowed in. Cameras flashed as Abby walked down the red-carpeted makeshift aisle to Chayce in the wedding gown that he'd bought for her. She caught a glimpse of a tearful Madame Lili crying and nodding her head as she saw the radiant face of her client.

Chayce smiled at the picture Abby made in the gown, with the gossamer veil pulled over her eyes as she spoke her vows in a floral arch to the minister with his vestments and open Bible. When Chayce lifted her veil at the end of the service, and looked at her, she thought her legs might give way. On his face was an expression that she'd never seen in a man's eyes before, not even in Chayce's. It was beyond love.

"Forever, Abby," he whispered raggedly, and bent to kiss her with such breathless tenderness that sobs were heard in the audience.

"Forever," she whispered back, her soft eyes full of tears and overflowing love.

Eventually they remembered where they were and stopped looking at each other long enough to smile sheepishly and accept the minister's congratulations before they walked back down the aisle.

Abby paused and looked out at the people in the crowd, neighbors and friends alike. Troy was standing with his arm around a radiant Eve Payne, and Abby grinned at him as she realized that he'd found his own heart's desire, and vice versa.

She gathered up her gorgeous bouquet of white roses and lily of the valley and baby's breath and fern and with a sharp breath, tossed it into the crowd.

She'd hoped that Eve Payne would catch it. But with the irony that sometimes accompanies best wishes, the bouquet seemed to suddenly develop a mind of its own. It flew, as if guided by some unseen hand, right into the hands of Chayce Derringer's bachelor foreman, Kirk Conroy, who'd also served as best man for the service.

Poor Kirk, with streaks of ruddy color down both cheeks, had to endure a storm of ribbing from his buddies. He muttered something and handed the bouquet to the nearest woman, who turned out to be

Felicity Evans, Abby's college roommate who had acted as a bridesmaid.

Felicity glanced down at the bouquet and back up at handsome Kirk with her heart shrinking in her chest. She was going to stay on the ranch while Abby and Chayce went on their honeymoon. Chayce had asked her to go through some old Derringer family papers and put them into order. Chayce's kind job offer came at a time Felicity was in dire need...

The dismayed look on Felicity's sad face drew Abby's attention, but Chayce caught her hand and brought it to his lips warmly just before Becky, in her Sunday best and in tears, hugged them both affectionately.

"I told you it would all work out," Becky reminded Abby.

"Yes." Abby looked up at Chayce with her whole heart in her eyes. "And it did."

Chayce smiled with pure pleasure as she met his downward gaze. His fingers contracted around hers. "My stolen bride," he murmured in a voice that only she could hear.

She chuckled and nuzzled her cheek against the jacket of his elegant suit, the faint scent of the white carnation he was wearing tickling her nose. She thought of her parents and the long, painful years that had led to this moment. Then she glanced at the wedding band on her finger and lifted her eyes to her husband's handsome, beloved face.

"Deep thoughts?" Chayce murmured at her head.

"Sweet ones," she countered.

"No regrets?"

She shook her head. Stars were shimmering in her gray eyes and she looked gloriously happy. "Dreams come true," she whispered.

He sighed gently. "Indeed they do, my darling," he said softly, smiling at her soft color when he used the endearment.

A firm cough interrupted them. They turned to look at Becky, who was holding a big knife.

"The cake," she prompted. "The wedding cake? The one you both have to cut together." She jerked her head toward the waiting crowd at the table. She leaned forward. "Just between us, if they don't get some cake pretty soon, this nice wedding may turn into an ugly riot. Remember that cake started the French Revolution."

"Cakes don't start revolutions!" Abby exclaimed.

"That's what Marie Antoinette thought." Becky handed her the knife.

Abby glanced at Chayce and grinned back at him. Together, they walked to the table that held the elegant wedding cake, hands clasped tightly together, looking like two halves of a whole.

Chayce put his hand over hers as they cut the cake, and when he looked into her eyes, the love that blazed forth from them was as exhilarating as the champagne Becky was pouring into crystal flutes. The photographer they'd hired to document the wedding snapped a picture of them at that exact instant.

He would tell his assistant later that it was the closest he'd ever come to capturing the very essence of mutual love on film.

BRIDE, BABY AND ALL

Ann Major

To Ted

Prologue

Kirk Conroy wearily tossed his mail onto the kitchen table. There was an interesting-looking prospectus from his broker, a bond brochure, a stack of junk mail and three bank statements. Damn, so much stuff came to him, he sometimes thought he could do with a secretary.

Ruthlessly he singled out the one letter that wasn't addressed to him. With a guilty frown he studied the long, expensive-looking envelope from the Whitehorn law firm. Then he went over to the counter and flung it into a drawer.

Some people didn't know when to give up.

Since he was right by the fridge, there was no way he could miss the calendar page that a certain, rather willful bride-to-be by the name of Miss Abby Turner had taped ever-so-firmly at his eye level.

If Abby has me going to another damn wedding party tonight, so help me I just might be tempted to head for the hills, even if she is my good friend and boss's fiancée.

A slow grin broke across Kirk's handsome, dark face when he saw that tonight's date was blank.

He was off. Which meant maybe he could do something fun…like sorting through the foot-high pile of mail that had been gathering dust on his desk.

As ranch foreman, the Derringer wedding festivities and roundup had Kirk working overtime. Just as he was about to open the fridge, he heard the roar of a big engine and the squeal of rubber outside on his driveway.

What did Chayce want now? There'd better not be some problem.

Curiosity rather than enthusiasm propelled Kirk out to his front porch. He'd just gotten home. He was hot and gritty from a long day in the saddle. The last thing he needed was company…unless *she* was pretty and blond and female.

And *willing.*

She'd better be real willing 'cause she'd pushed him to the limits of his patience last night.

He wasn't used to women teasing him the way Mary Lou kept doing. Any more than he was used to women rejecting him, the way Abby's bridesmaid, that snooty librarian, did every time he tried to be friendly. Like last night at the wedding social when he'd noticed how pale she looked when she'd set her plate of food down and rushed to the window. Hell, all he'd done was smile charmingly, put a hand on her waist, and ask if she was okay. She'd jumped away as if his hand had been a branding iron. When he'd offered to get her a glass of punch, she'd almost bitten his head off.

After that his mood had been pretty low and his ego in need of consolation. Not that he'd gotten more than a few chaste kisses from Mary Lou. Oh, she'd snuggled up close enough in his pickup, pressing her trim little body against his, letting her heat seep into him as she kissed him so sweetly and ardently. But then after only a few nibbles, she'd put her slender hands on his chest and levered herself free, acting as virginal as that ice queen Miss Evans when she'd jumped away from the window, spitting like a scalded wildcat, "I'm feeling just fine! Don't waste your practiced charm on me! I can get my own punch, thank you very much, Mr. Conroy!"

"But *no* thank you!" he'd murmured, his gaze glued to Miss Evans's swaying, curvaceous backside as she'd swished away from him toward the punch bowl.

"You got her goat! You losing your touch or what, old fella?" Chayce had taunted.

"I'm dating Mary Lou," Kirk had growled, annoyed that the ice queen's barb had stung him so sharply.

"Have you heard the rumor that our Mary Lou has a powerful yearning to get herself married, and that she's set her sights on the handsome Kirk Conroy?"

"Handsome?" Kirk braced his hands on his hips and gave his friend a wicked smile. "Thanks for the compliment—old fella."

"It wasn't mine, I assure you."

"Well, you can tell your gossipmongers that no way is the extremely charming Mary Lou hauling this boy to the altar."

"You'll marry fast enough—soon as the right girl sets her hooks in you and yanks back on the line."

Kirk frowned at the tattered photograph on his fridge of himself wrapped tightly in Mary Lou's possessive arms.

Not this boy.

He'd been married.

Once.

A long time ago.

Big mistake. Huge.

Not that he ever talked about it.

He could get what Mary Lou and Miss Felicity Evans guarded as their most precious gem—anywhere, anytime—without getting himself married. But Mary Lou *was* fun. And prettier than most. Prettier than that stuffy Miss Evans by a long shot. Which was why he'd been dating Mary Lou for nearly a month and behaving himself, too. Settling for kisses at her door, making her want it, too. Still, it was about time she thawed. He was growing bored with Mary Lou…probably because of the lack of sex.

The sun was low over the mountains when Kirk stepped outside, and the air held a distinct chill. Not that Fred, his lazy, black hound dog, who lay sprawled across his top step seemed to feel it.

Chayce Derringer, his friend and his boss slammed his truck door and strode grimly up the walk straight toward him.

"You look like you've got wedding jitters, old fella. And got 'em bad." Kirk smiled, even though he knew Chayce and Abby had already been married in a civil ceremony earlier. This big ceremony was the icing on the cake.

Chayce had to leap three stairs to avoid the big dog. His black boot missed the dog's nose by less than an inch, but Fred didn't blink so much as an eyelash.

"That no-account hound of yours looks dead."

"He's just tired."

"You got an extra beer?" Chayce demanded shortly, ripping off his dark glasses as if he intended to stay.

"Sure I do. Relax. Come on in." Kirk grabbed the door Chayce had flung open, and bowed low, in mock homage, as if he'd let a king pass.

Chayce didn't relax. To Kirk's surprise, Chayce glanced warily around his tiny cabin and even pushed the door of his bedroom ajar and stared into the room suspiciously.

"What the hell are you doing that for?"

"Just making sure we're alone."

"You clearing me for some top secret mission." Kirk couldn't find his beer opener in the kitchen mess, so he used his dinette table to pop the caps off two beers. Then he turned a chair backward and plopped down onto it, straddling it with his long legs. He leaned his broad chest against the chair back and stared up at his friend. "You're in a strange mood. What is it with you tonight?"

Slowly Chayce pulled the bedroom door closed, but not before they'd both gotten an eyeful of the rumpled bed upon which blankets and sheets and pillows had been thrown in a sloppy tumble. Not before they'd both glimpsed the pair of lace panties dangling from a knob on a dusty chest of drawers.

What were they doing there...anyway?

"You're one messy housekeeper, Kirk Conroy."

Kirk beamed at his friend affectionately. "We all have our failings. The ladies don't seem to mind."

Chayce strode past him to the kitchen and lifted a pot from the sink. There was a thick black residue of burned leavings from the frozen chicken casserole Mary Lou had given him, which he'd ruined two days ago.

Kirk got up and took the pot and slammed it back down into the sink. "Is it a crime if I'm fresh outta steel wool? I'll wash up tonight."

"You're one lousy cook, too. You ought to get married. Like me."

"No girl ever asked."

"Hell...you could have anybody."

"Which is a big part of why I'm not married. I'm having too much fun with all of them to settle on any one girl."

"Which explains your messy bed...and those panties..."

"I won those off a lady in a poker game...a long time ago." He'd won more than the panties.

"Gossip has it you've been putting that bed to better uses than stretching sheets real tight across it."

"I'm surprised you've got such a keen interest in my sex life."

"How come you don't marry your Mary Lou?"

"That's none of your damned business." Kirk took a long pull from his bottle. "You getting jealous all of a sudden...of my carefree bachelor existence...'cause you're about to tie the knot in front of the minister...."

Chayce's expression turned serious. "No, Abby sent me over here. She, er, has a favor she wants me to ask of you." Chayce didn't look too happy or too comfortable to have been sent on this particular errand, either.

Here we go again. "You know I owe you. Ask me anything."

"You know Felicity..."

Here it comes. Kirk's mouth tightened as he remembered the revulsion in her big brown eyes last night when he'd felt worried about how pale she was.

"I'm sorry I teased you about losing your touch—"

"I don't give a damn about her...or your dumb remark—"

"Admit it. You're not used to rejection."

"The way she took off, you'd think I was a snake or something. Not that I care..."

"Maybe her reasons aren't about you." Chayce grew silent as if he could say more on that subject, but chose not to.

"Well...at least she won't be here much longer."

Chayce frowned. "Now that's what I wanted to discuss—"

Something in his friend's voice gave Kirk a mighty bad feeling. He shrugged, waiting for Chayce to continue. But Chayce didn't seem overly comfortable about continuing, so Kirk's bad feeling didn't go away.

"Well," Chayce began after a peculiar, awkward spell. "After we go on our honeymoon, Felicity's gonna stay right here...for a while."

"What?"

"Abby talked me into hiring her."

"To do what, I'd like to know?" Kirk couldn't think of one damned thing somebody as puny as Felicity Evans could do around here. "I thought she was from back east...and rich and too high-and-mighty for the likes of us."

"Well, you're wrong about... She likes it here. She can't go home right now. She likes the mountains and finds the deep valleys...and the people warm and refreshing." Chayce avoided his eyes. "At least...some of the people..."

"Did she say something mean about me?"

"Well..." Chayce hedged. "Well...I don't think

she exactly takes to you. That's why I wanted to clear this with you.''

"Maybe I don't want her here, either."

"Okay. Hear me out. You remember me finding all those old papers and books up in the attic a few years back? You remember how I was always intending to go through them—"

"We were talking about Felicity Evans. I was about to tell you why it's a damned fool notion for her to stick around."

"Hold your horses."

"Chayce, wc can't stand the sight of each other."

"Let me get back to those old papers. They're a mess."

"So?"

"Felicity's a college librarian...."

"Damn it! I'll help you with—"

"There are...reasons...why she can't...go back to the university for a spell...and she's, er, most kindly agreed to stay and help out by putting them in order...while we're away on our honeymoon...."

"But—"

"I've already accepted her offer."

"What!"

"So, if you'll just give me your word that you'll take care of her—"

"Take care of her?"

"Since she'll be living out here with you and the hands...all alone...I want you to promise me you'll see after her and protect her. She's big city...and not used—"

Kirk felt as frustrated as a coyote caught in a trap.

Chayce had been Abby's guardian in the beginning. The only girl Kirk had ever felt the least bit protective toward was his sister, Sierra, and he felt damned uncomfortable about what he was doing in that department.

"Felicity hates me," he persisted.

"Hate is carrying things too far. She just needs her own space. You just keep the boys away from her. Abby says she's been through a rough time and has some serious thinking to do."

"About what?"

"I can't go into it, but if you knew you'd understand, and sympathize."

"This is a working ranch, not a prayer retreat."

Chayce's voice was grim. "Usually you're the first to help anybody with a problem."

Kirk frowned. His own tough times had made him sensitive to hard-luck stories. Still, he didn't like the way Chayce and everybody else were always pointing out his gullible nature and teasing him about being a soft touch for anybody with a sob story, especially a story that involved a kid.

"She's Abby's best friend. She's like a sister."

"Abby sure as hell chewed me out when Miss Felicity ran off last night and wouldn't come back to the party. Abby said I was rude."

"Which goes to show you that Abby thinks the world of her. So, you just look after her and make sure she's okay. She's pretty fragile right now. Don't take her behavior so personally. Look, I wouldn't ask you to do this if I thought you had any ideas about her yourself.''

"She's hardly my type."

"Sometimes those things are hard to figure." Chayce shot him a knowing look. Maybe he was remembering how it had been with Abby and himself in the beginning when Chayce had been Abby's protector.

"You mind telling me what's so all-fired mysterious about this fragile iceberg? What's her damned secret anyway?"

Chayce lifted his beer bottle and took a final swig. "It's not mine to tell. Just keep an eye on her, and your hands off her. Don't let her know about our little conversation, either."

"You've made me mighty, mighty curious, Chayce."

"You know what they say—curiosity killed the cat. Put her out of your mind. She's not your type, remember?"

"Where's she from anyway? How'd she grow up? You can at least—"

"Her parents died when she was a little girl. An aunt and uncle raised her. A very rich, very well-connected aunt and uncle. In Washington, D.C. The president's kids came to play…that is, when the man in office had kids."

"So, she was a rich orphan?"

Chayce pitched his bottle into the trash. "Gotta go."

Kirk stared at that trash can a long time. "How rich?"

"Way richer than your Tina, if that's what you're asking."

After what Kirk had gone through, marrying a rich girl his first go-round, big money was no recommendation. It came between people. Made in-laws think they were way better than plain folks.

Put her out of your mind, Conroy!

After Chayce left, Kirk sat in his kitchen musing for a long time about a woman he wasn't the slightest bit interested in. In fact, truth be known, he'd been thinking about Felicity ever since she'd whitened and then flounced off to the punch bowl all by herself. But that was just because he wasn't used to rejection. Especially not from somebody as plain as her.

She didn't know how to dress. Any woman should known how unflattering such a dull-colored, prim, schoolteacher look was. And those wire-rimmed glasses she usually wore—

If she's so boring, then quit thinking about her, Conroy!

Maybe he could have, but his curiosity was working overtime. How come a rich, college-educated, city girl wanted to shut herself away on a Montana ranch?

Another of Kirk's prime failings was that he couldn't think about a woman long—without his brain turning to sex. Suddenly he found himself wondering just exactly how long her chocolate-dark hair really was. Wondering, too, how she'd look with it curling around her slender face instead of pulled back, wondering how silky it would be, coiled around his roughened hand.

Her big, brown eyes were nice, too, even if they were so sad. He liked her generous mouth and her peaches and cream complexion. She was slim and easy to watch when she moved. He began to wonder what she'd look like with less on.

No, it wasn't her looks that turned him off.

It was *her attitude*.

How come she hated men so much?

Or was it just him?

Why did he care?

No telling how long he might have gone on thinking about her, if a loud snort from his bedroom hadn't damn near made him jump out of his skin. He bolted out of his chair as if lightning had struck him. His chair went flying into the wall, and he yowled when he banged his kneecap into the sharp edge of his dinette table. In two furious strides he hobbled across the tiny kitchen and kicked his bedroom door open.

Pillows rained onto his bed. Blankets and sheets erupted from the floor behind his bed.

Heart racing, Kirk took a wary step forward. His ticker didn't slow till Blackie Piel's woolly gray head popped guiltily over the far side of the bed like a jack-in-the-box.

By George, he should've guessed!

"What the hell are you doing behind my bed, you

pop-eyed runt?" Kirk thundered, ripping the rest of his blankets off the bed.

Blackie rubbed his bleary eyes as innocently as Goldilocks might have done upon being discovered by the three bears.

"Glad to see you, too," snapped Blackie's familiar, tart drawl. "Your floor put a kink in my back."

"You snake! You sneak! You deliberately hid... from me and Chayce so you could snoop—"

Blackie grinned, flashing a mouthful of stinky, yellow teeth. "Yep."

"We thought we were having ourselves a confidential conversation."

"Yep." Blackie's brown eyes gleamed. He smiled unrepentantly. "Your boss is a fool. Asking the likes of *you* to protect a single female all alone out here. And a rich girl, at that. I'd sooner set a fox to guard a henhouse."

"If you'd ever seen her— Why, I wouldn't touch that skinny ice queen with a ten-foot pole."

"You wish...you had a ten-foot one. Not that you don't do okay with your God-given equipment, puny as it is—"

"Puny—"

"Settle down. I ain't seen it in a spell. You may've grown some. Why, I'll lay long odds you'll have the lady on her back in this bed in a week. And soon as you offer me a job here, I'm gonna make a few bets on it with the hands."

"You do that—and I'll fire your skinny ass!"

Blackie's bold brown eyes sparkled. "So, I got

myself a job, and it didn't cost me near as much begging and groveling as last time. I'll have to memorize my technique."

"How come you need a job so bad?" Kirk demanded suspiciously. "Did Sheila boot you out again?"

"No..." But Blackie flushed tellingly.

"Vegas. You got drunk and shot craps and lost everything again."

"Damn Sheila. Did she call you—"

"She didn't have to. This isn't the first time you turned up on my doorstep without your truck or a dime to your name."

"How'd you know about the truck?"

Kirk lifted a window shade. The sun was just going down behind the high silvery peaks.

"I don't see it parked anywhere." A pause. "How come you always land on my doorstep?"

"'Cause under that rough, tough exterior of yours, you've got the softest heart in Montana."

Nothing riled Kirk more than everybody throwing that particular failing up to him. "Don't you go spouting such an impertinent, cock-and-bull lie about me being such a sissy to just anybody around here...or I will fire you—damn your sneaky, cowardly, rascally hide!"

Kirk grabbed his Stetson from a peg by his front door. "I need some air."

"You just got here."

"You'd better be gone when I get back, Piel! I've had my fill of conversation for the day."

Kirk cracked his screen door, and Fred stood up lazily, thumping his tail.

It didn't help Kirk's black mood to catch sight of the icy Miss Felicity Evans taking her habitual evening stroll along the road. No, the mere sight of her moving along as lightly and gracefully as a ballerina in that pale, frothy dress made his blood boil and his heart hammer. Nor did he like the fact that Fred left him the second he saw her and loped toward her, tail waving in a jaunty salute.

With a dark frown, Kirk watched her kneel and pet that scruffy, no-account, disloyal excuse for a dog right behind the ears, in that exact spot that always put the useless mutt into such a state of ecstasy.

Fred gave a low whine of pure canine pleasure.

Man's best friend! Hell!

With a disgusted frown Kirk set off toward the darkening mountains. So caught up was he in his own fury that he didn't see the slender young woman look up from Fred and watch after him till long after he'd disappeared. He had no way of knowing that her heart was racing with an indignant mixture of unwanted emotions even faster than his. Just as he had no way of knowing that she was telling herself that he was the last man on earth any sensible woman should ever take the slightest notice of, especially not a woman facing the heavy responsibilities she now faced.

She just knelt there ruffling the fur behind Fred's ears, watching Kirk's tall, retreating figure with dark hopeless eyes till Blackie Piel stepped outside and shouted a jubilant greeting her way. When Blackie waved, she stood up and sprinted off toward the ranch house as scared as a startled doe with Fred trotting lazily behind her.

Chapter 1

Felicity stared at the other wedding guests in dawning horror. How could Chayce have asked Kirk Conroy to protect her when Abby had warned her he was a womanizer?

Chayce should have known how such a man would take such a suggestion. With his reputation, the conceited Mr. Conroy probably thought she was staying in Montana after the wedding...to get something going with him.

Dear God.

As if she didn't have enough problems.

Felicity raced up the festooned stairs so swiftly that even before she reached the landing, she felt faint. She seized the railing, her heart near bursting from fury, exertion and shame.

Two minutes before, the sight of Abby in her filmy

wedding veil with Chayce leaning over her had had Felicity sniffling into her hanky. They looked so in love. So openly trusting and affectionate with each other. So unafraid of love…and their feelings. Then she'd heard that skinny runt of a cowboy's odious, low drawl, and rage had washed away her sentimentality.

"Whaddaya say, Ryan, I'll lay you ten to one that instead of protecting our shy maid of honor the way Derringer asked him to, Conroy'll have Miss Evans stripped and flat on her skinny butt in his bed in no time. And she won't be wantin' her beauty rest. She'll have a smile on that pretty face of hers for a change, too. If you get my drift…"

The normally cool and cerebral Felicity hated the way the slightest little thing had her on the verge of tears these days. She never used to cry. Not since she was a little girl and she'd watched them lower her mother's casket into the snowy Pennsylvania ground. Her uncle had taken her hand and told her she could live with him as long as she wasn't a crybaby. The clods of earth had begun to fall. Snowflakes had swirled. She had stood there till the last rose on the coffin was buried. Then she'd felt a door close inside her as she'd walked away with her uncle. She had hurt so badly she had not wanted to ever feel anything again. But now, because of Kirk Conroy who meant absolutely nothing to her, hot teardrops leaked from her eyes and spilled down her cheeks.

Every time she remembered Blackie Piel's cynical

assertion, his cruel words cut her to the quick all over again.

Was Kirk Conroy laying wagers, too? Was everybody laughing at her?

If only she were the bride. She and Abby had joked about it so many times. Older and wiser and settled, cool and collected, Felicity had felt ready for marriage. She had even felt she'd found the perfect man.

The perfect man... A man who read, who shared all her intellectual interests, even her fascination for medieval manuscripts, a man of her own class, a man whom her aunt and uncle would approve.

What a laugh.

How could she laugh when her heart was broken?

Who...who would ever marry her now? This question made her eyes fill with more tears.

Felicity had nowhere to turn.

Even here, where nobody but Abby knew, she was already the butt of cruel, male jokes.

Of one thing she was sure: It would be a cold day in hell before she gave that shallow, egotistical, womanizing Kirk Conroy the slightest encouragement—even if God had blessed him with a gorgeous face and body. Even if God had cursed her with a weak feminine nature that was highly susceptible to his rogue, cowboy charm. And to think, she had thought that being an academic herself, she would always go for brains in her men.

Rather than brawn and sparkling blue eyes.

Why, this caveman in jeans and boots had only to

smile at her and flash his devilish blue eyes and her stomach turned to water. If he combined one of his quick grins with a twinkling glance or a gentle word, her toes almost curled. Whenever he got too near her, she felt comatose. The chemistry was there whether she wanted to feel anything for the devil or not. Logically she *knew* what he was under his charming exterior. Why couldn't she be the stony-faced young woman her aunt had taught her to be in difficult social situations?

The orchestra began to play, and gentlemen took ladies into their arms and began to dance. Felicity blushed shyly, but her right foot boldly tapped out the beat as she stared down at the giddy throng of wedding guests whirling to the music. She brushed away her tears.

Had it been such a short time ago that she had been in love and danced...with Patrick? In love? Easy, charming, professorial Patrick. Patrick, who had been so perfect for her. No. He had only seemed perfect.

She had been his research assistant. He had won her in the library with his shy manners and gentle smiles. Her stomach knotted as a series of once cherished memories bombarded her. He had enlisted her to help him with his Shakespearean research. Funny, how just thinking of meeting him on those wide stone steps outside the library after work every day where he had taken her books and walked her to her car, speaking to her of Elizabethan London, was now enough to make her feel slightly nauseated.

She paled and clutched the railing tighter. Patrick was out of her life forever. And how could she ever tell her aunt and uncle what had happened?

Feeling very alone and isolated, her sad gaze fell upon a tall dark figure lounging a little distance apart from the others. For some reason the man's solitary stance struck a chord. She felt unaccountably drawn, as she would have been drawn to anyone else in the world who felt as alone as she did in this happy crowd.

When she smiled automatically, he looked up and grinned. Suddenly, even before she recognized him, a fierce, magnetic force connected him to her.

Time stopped.

Then the man leapt toward her eagerly, mistaking her casual smile as an invitation.

In the next instant she was thunderstruck as she watched his long-legged strides. She was wearing her contacts instead of her glasses, so the scene was a bit blurrier than usual. Still, with mushrooming fear, slowly, feature by feature, his gorgeous, dark face and tall, athletic physique came into sharper focus.

First she saw that shiny lock of ebony hair that fell across his tanned forehead. Then she recognized his thick, slashing, black brows, chiseled jaw and incredible blue eyes that sometimes seemed hot enough to melt even the thick layer of ice around her heart. Next her gaze trailed to the carved shape of his mouth and remained there, for Kirk Conroy had the sexiest mouth in the universe.

Kirk Conroy! Chayce's best man! Whitehorn's

leading womanizer! The dangerous rogue who had his men laying bets as to how fast he'd bed her! He'd probably never opened a book in his life. He wouldn't fit into the high society life she had been born and bred to live.

It'll be a cold day in hell, Mr. Conroy!

Still, her face went crimson and her wayward heart thumped excitedly inside its protective crypt of ice. She forced herself to remember that flat, cruel drawl laying odds as to how long it would to take this Lothario in sharkskin boots to bed her.

She would have run from Kirk, but she didn't want to do anything that might reveal he had the slightest power over her. Besides, he was already halfway up the stairs. He was in fantastic shape, while she was, admittedly, feeling clumsier and slower than usual.

Two more long strides had the broad-shouldered cad so close every atom in her being had begun to vibrate.

"Nice wedding." His deep, dark drawl caused her to shiver.

She compressed her lips and said tartly, "Yes. Very nice."

"Are those tears of happiness or sadness?"

How could he sound so genuinely concerned? Why couldn't he pretend not to notice the way her aunt and uncle always had?

"Take your pick." She struck a cool, flippant note, determined to shut him out.

"You look pale," he continued. There was an endearing note of sympathy in his husky voice.

"Don't pretend you care."

"Sorry. I thought you smiled at me a while ago."

"So, you came running?" She forced a brittle laugh. "I suppose if I were any other girl, I'd be flattered."

He blushed.

"I'm sorry if my casual smile...gave you the wrong impression." Her voice was chillier than ever.

"Have I done something to offend you—"

"As if you really care."

"I assure you, I do."

"Your reputation precedes you."

"People around here usually say good things about me."

"You might consider what they told me complimentary."

"But you don't?"

"Mr. Conroy, is it true you have only to set eyes on a lady...to get her to your bed?"

"Oh, so that's what they've been telling you." He laughed with what she imagined to be an overabundance of male conceit. "Ladies are safe enough. It's the other kind...who find me...irresistible."

His smile died a quick death when she didn't laugh. "I have never forced myself on any woman."

"You probably see it that way. But then women are a game to you, aren't they?"

"I like women. Is that a crime?"

She looked away.

"I don't understand you," he said.

No. The last thing a man like him could understand was how painful it was for a woman who fell in love with a man who saw her only as a conquest.

"Nor do you need to. Just stop flirting with me. Stop smiling or offering to get me glasses of punch. I'm not looking for a man, Mr. Conroy. Especially not a man like you."

"A man like me? Am I too poor and common, so far beneath you that you can't even deign to be civil...."

"Why, no."

"Then you must have had man trouble. And recently, too, I bet. Do you want to talk about it?"

"Certainly not with you, Mr. Conroy."

"Kirk." His smile remained sympathetic. "I was watching you a while ago. You were crying...before you smiled. You've been doing that a lot lately...looking close to tears and then either smiling or acting cold like you're afraid of what you really feel."

His kind eyes saw more than she wanted him to. He was too easy in his skin, as the French say. Way too easy for her devastated emotional equilibrium. Way too easy for a woman who'd been taught to conceal her pain and imperfections, even from herself.

"Weddings do that to me."

"I've never understood why."

"You either feel certain emotions or you don't."

"Is that so? You don't strike me as the emotional type."

"I—I'm not...generally speaking. It's difficult to explain them."

"Look, Miss Evans—Felicity—why don't you take my arm? Maybe we'd get along better dancing than we do talking."

Before Felicity could protest, a beautiful blonde in a short red skirt dashed up the stairs and seized his hand.

"So, here you are, Kirk, darling. Up here all by yourself." The woman stared straight through Felicity as if she were invisible. "I've been looking and looking for you."

Darling. The endearment grated, as did the blonde's possessiveness toward Kirk. Why? Felicity wondered.

"Hey there, Mary Lou," he said gently in that easy, friendly way that seemed second nature to him.

"Do you want to dance?" Mary Lou asked him.

"But I—I just asked...Miss Evans here." He eyed Felicity quizzically.

The blonde's rude gaze held fire.

Tensions sizzled but silently, not like grease on a fire.

"You can have him," Felicity said coolly to the other woman.

Only then did he let the blonde take his hand and lead him away.

Felicity should have felt relief, but the moment he was gone, she felt even emptier and lonelier than before. She couldn't seem to stop watching him. Her heart filled with sadness as he gracefully whirled the beautiful Mary Lou in his arms. Soon another woman cut in on them, and laughingly, he folded his new partner into his arms. Every so often he grinned up at Felicity as if he had to know whether or not she cared.

Between those grins, she grew anxious, wondering if he'd do it again, and before she thought, she answered one with a smile.

His handsome face broke into a really wide grin, and she felt herself glowing in the laser heat of his searing blue gaze. Then the black lashes of his right eye fanned shut in a flirtatious wink as if to say, "Gotcha!"

He was so sure of his charm. But in that moment it was almost impossible to hate him. He brought her feelings to the surface more easily than anyone ever had. He looked young and lighthearted, as if he had not a care in the world. While she...

Put him out of your mind!

Soon every single woman at the reception was buzzing all around him. He was dancing with all of them...and loving every moment of it.

Felicity was both thrilled and dismayed when he stopped dancing, looked up at her and then led his partner, the tall blonde, to a chair and headed up the stairs to join her again.

She should run, but her feet felt rooted. Only her heart raced away. She felt herself blanch. In the next moment she was light-headed again because he was beside her.

"You were staring down at me again...smiling...

and, this time, you can't say you didn't know it was me."

It was I, she mentally corrected. "I—I'm surprised you noticed...with all the other girls around."

"Jealous?" he teased, grinning at her.

"What if I were? Would that make you happy? Would you take pity on me and leave me alone then?"

"No. I'd tell you that last girl was my sister, Sierra." His easy smile vanished. His voice deepened. "It would mean a lot to me if you'd dance with me. I asked you a while ago, didn't I? You don't know anybody around here.... It was rude of me not to dance with you first. Rude of me to get carried away dancing and forget how it'd feel not to know anybody."

Why did he insist on pretending he cared? For all the money and fancy lessons and high-priced schooling, nobody had ever treated her so solicitously.

He took her hand, and she let him fold it into his long brown fingers that were as warm as fire as she considered her answer. But before she could thank him politely, and insist he not worry, Chayce had the microphone and was announcing to everybody that Abby was going to throw her bouquet.

All the single girls began clumping together at the bottom of the stairs as Kirk gently tried to nudge Felicity downward.

"No." Felicity whispered frantically.

"It's only in fun," Kirk murmured against her ear. His warm breath tickled her earlobe. Her toes curled up like frightened pill bugs. Felicity turned to run, but Kirk had her hand too firmly.

Then the bride and groom were laughing together as if at a private joke. Suddenly Abby thrust her hand forward, and the beribboned blossoms were flying free as a dove above the outstretched hands of the feminine throng.

Exquisite white roses and satin streamers bounced off Kirk's wide chest. He caught the bouquet before it fell. A smile edged the corners of his mouth and brought a glint of warm humor to his eyes as he stared from the flowers to Felicity. "Honey, I think she was aiming for you."

Hesitantly he handed her the roses.

Like characters in an opera they stood grandly poised, his hand held out to hers, the satin bridal streamers flowing over his brown wrist. Before their fascinated audience, their gazes fixed, held. In those dozen or so seconds, they were aware of nothing except each other.

Every gossip in the well-dressed, well-scrubbed bunch registered the electricity in their look.

Nobody, not even the nosiest old busybody in Whitehorn, was more thrilled than Blackie Piel who said in a voice loud enough for Felicity to hear, "Why, she's drawn to him like an iron filing to a powerful magnet. No way can she pull loose. Won't be no time till—"

Till she was flat on her skinny butt.

Did the disreputable old man actually repeat himself? Or was her own mind replaying a recording of his earlier words?

Either way, after his triumphant smirk and prediction, Felicity went hollow inside. Her expression changed from tenderness to fury.

Suddenly it was all too much. The long wedding ceremony, her too-tight gown and this man, this darling, impossible man who made her feel so passionately alive—everything joined forces with the cloying sweetness of the bridal bouquet only inches from her nose.

She was suffocating, fainting.

Even as she struggled for breath and tried to wave away the sweet fumes, the tiny white roses and that unsettling smile of Kirk's blurred. The room spun. She got ill so quickly that the flowers and Kirk's dark face were suddenly lost in a swirl of black stars.

She felt herself falling.

Down. Down.

"Easy, honey," Kirk's deep voice said. Then his strong arms hauled her against a long, lean, masculine body. "There. I've got you, darling."

He said that last so lovingly that for an instant or two, right before she fainted, she felt like some enchanted creature caught in a wondrous spell.

Seconds later she awoke and found herself being cradled in Kirk's lap as if she were a child. His blue eyes were as clear and bright and beautiful as the Montana sky. Barely was she conscious, before a needle-sharp edge of sharp, sexual awareness made her go hot all over again. Her heart raced, and some deep, eternal feeling that she was determined to deny to her last breath was born.

"Let me go!" she snapped weakly, terrified.

"You all right?" he asked.

"Don't you dare pretend you care!"

"Maybe I should get Doc..."

"I'm fine!"

"People don't just faint for no reason."

"I know why I fainted. I'm fine."

"Okay. Okay."

She raised herself up and off him, but as she did, those eyes that seemed to draw her very soul to his flashed with mischief. "Honey, before you skedaddle...aren't you forgetting something?" He held up the bridal bouquet. "Doesn't this mean you'll be the next gal to catch a husband?"

She stood perfectly still, her face paper-white, her mind too befuddled to think of a rejoinder or to reject the bridal bouquet he so swiftly handed her.

Everybody clapped when her trembling fingers crushed the fragile blossoms.

Nobody clapped harder or longer than Blackie Piel.

He was, no doubt, gleefully imagining she'd soon be flat on her skinny unmentionable again.

Chapter 2

Beyond the sea of golden grasses, serrated, snow-capped peaks gleamed. The sky was brilliant cobalt blue. Not that Kirk or his baby sister, Sierra, had time to enjoy the scenery. Not that they could have seen the mountains anyway. The dust was thick and the thunder of hooves loud as they slapped coiled ropes against their thighs to herd the hundred head of cattle they were working into the nearest pen.

Suddenly Kirk noticed the tall slim woman with chocolate-dark hair shyly holding the gate open for them. A big black dog lay sprawled at her feet.

His dog.

Her hair was down.

What was *she* doing here? She was wearing a sheer, summery blouse that hugged her breasts and a skimpy skirt that didn't cover nearly enough of her incredible legs. Blackie was supposed to be holding the gate.

Blackie... Where was that skunk anyway?

Why wasn't *she* in her attic doing her research?

Why wasn't she avoiding him the same as she had ever since she'd fainted and then found herself in his arms holding that wedding bouquet. Funny, how he'd almost forgotten the revulsion that had flamed in her eyes then. Funny, how all he could remember now was how she'd felt—the lightness of her and the softness of her, too. Then she'd started shaking and gotten all breathless and flustered just as she always did if he came within two feet of her.

Suddenly the cattle surged toward him. Distracted by Felicity, he'd loosened his grip on the reins. Suddenly his hard-mouthed roan spurted forward and was stumbling, and it was all he could do not to slide out of his saddle like a greenhorn and get himself trampled right in front of *her.*

His favorite hat did go sailing off his head, and he caught a glimpse of Felicity hiding a cute smile behind her long, slim fingers while a big steer stomped a hole in his hat. All the hands started laughing, too.

Furious, Kirk dug his spurs into the roan's belly and galloped to the far side of the pen where it took him a minute to recover his male dignity. The memory of her smile, even if it had been at his expense soon had him wondering if maybe he shouldn't try being nice to her...just one last time. But when he whipped his mount back to the gate, it was shut and she was gone. He felt disgusted at himself for letting his male pride cost him a chance with her.

Sierra had dismounted and was pouring herself an iced drink. "You looking for somebody or something in particular, big brother? Or are you just looking lost and dumb to amuse us hands?"

The other hands were sure as hell watching him.

His sassy, tomboy sister wore a man's shirt and a pair of faded jeans. Her dark blond hair hung down her back in a thick braid. She could have been beautiful—if she ever half tried.

"How come she hates me?" he demanded sulkily, knowing Sierra would know who he meant. "How come *she* likes you…when you two aren't anything alike? She reads all the time while you—"

"Who says friends are supposed to be clones? She's nice."

"Maybe to you. So, what's eating her?" Kirk grabbed a lukewarm cola from the cooler.

"Nothing that I know of. She just works all the time on those old papers. She's gotten mighty interested in all those folks that have been dead so long. She says she feels at home in a house that four generations of Derringers have lived in. I think her childhood was pretty lonely. Her aunt and uncle don't have friends who can't trace their ancestors back to the Pilgrims or royalty or who don't, at least, make headlines two inches high. I don't think Felicity ever thought she counted much in their eyes. She said they never talked to her, that they only got lively when a celebrity came to visit."

"Does she ever mention me?"

"Not that I can remember. Hey? Why don't you concentrate on Mary Lou? Felicity's the independent, scholarly sort. She likes books and history. She doesn't want—"

"She's not independent! And I do read."

"When?"

"When I have the time. And we are, too, involved!" Kirk declared heatedly, knowing he sounded absolutely ridiculous.

"How?"

"I'm not sure yet."

He wasn't making much sense, and he didn't like Sierra's know-it-all female smirk as she drew her own erroneous conclusion. So, he wisely changed the subject. "How come you don't date anybody, Sierra?"

"'Cause I'm not like you." A shadow passed over her dust-covered face. "I can't just date anybody."

Not such a wise subject change after all. Kirk felt an uneasy twinge of conscience. Why in tarnation did all those unopened letters crammed inside his kitchen drawer keep coming to mind? Damn Dylan McLaine, anyway, for breaking her heart. That lying son-of-a-lawyer was the real bad guy.

Kirk thought: *She's not a kid anymore. Maybe I should tell her the truth.* He said, "Mary Lou isn't just anybody."

"But she's not the woman that's got you so allfired hot and bothered and speculating about her every look and twitch the way Felicity does."

"Have you been talking to Blackie?"

"I'm not blind, you know. But, no. I'm not in on his hot little bet."

"*His hot little bet?* I told that no-good snake I'd fire him if he—"

"Since when did you ever do a mean-hearted, nasty thing like that, big brother?"

Kirk was swigging a final gulp of cola, when the vision of those thickly bundled envelopes in that drawer of his rose up to haunt him. Suddenly some of his cola went up and some went down. The upshot was that cola spewed everywhere. He was strangling, spitting and choking even after Sierra jumped up and pounded him on the back. When she was through, and he could swallow and actually breathe again without feeling as if he was drowning or being beaten half to death, he looked her in the eye and hoped his hot face wasn't a guilty shade of red.

He thought: *You might be surprised at just how mean-hearted and nasty I can be, little sister.*

He said, "Whaddaya say we get back in the saddle?"

He thought: *I did it for your own damned good.*

He knew: if she ever finds I kept her letters, that pounding she just gave me will be nothing to the whacking she'll give me.

Cattle lowed in the pens to Kirk's right, a hundred head ready to ship. As the hauler opened his trailer, Kirk shouted orders to his riders to get into position. He needed two men at the chute to keep the cattle moving once they started up the ramp. Sierra was in position.

"So, where the hell is Blackie?"

"He went up to the house. Said he forgot he promised Felicity he'd do something," Sierra shouted so she could be heard over the cattle.

"Felicity? Who does that withered runt think he's working for, anyway?" With a quick flash of his quirt, Kirk had the roan in a hard gallop. A minute later as he was about to dismount, he caught sight of Felicity around back in the rose garden, hovering over Blackie who was hauling two huge boxes from the garage to the garden for her. Kirk remembered Sierra telling him that Felicity had ordered some new rose cuttings and was hell-bent on planting them.

Kirk's anger toward Blackie lessened when he saw that at least she could get the rascal to work. It was obvious from the dirt on him that Blackie had been busy mixing compost and rotted manure into the soil to fill planting holes for more of her roses. Watching what Blackie and Felicity were doing with rapt attention were that no-good Fred and that worthless stray cat she'd brought home from Whitehorn last week.

Felicity sure was a pretty sight with the sun shining in her dark hair, with a gleam of golden light shimmering down the side of her slim neck and nose. Unable to take his eyes off her, Kirk stood rooted where he was. He didn't much care if she looked up and found him. In her own special way, she was a beautiful woman. The other hands looked at her, too. Why couldn't he? He wished...

Hell.

Still, he went on watching the wind and the sun blow in her hair. Funny, how even if a woman never spoke to or looked at a man, a man could still learn her odd little habits if he took a mind to.

Thus, Kirk knew that Felicity had trouble sleeping these days. Or, rather, these nights. He'd had the same problem himself ever since she'd moved into the ranch house. Sometimes she'd pace back and forth on the long veranda. Sometimes she burned the midnight oil up in the attic where she pored over books and papers till her back ached. He knew she got up as early as he did, because her bedroom light was always on when he met with the hands right after dawn and told them what to do.

He knew she loved gardening, and she could cook as well as a professional chef. She'd had Sierra and Blackie to dinner a time or two. He knew she could play the piano like a concert pianist even if she stopped the minute she suspected he was anywhere around. And she always did seem to sense him, even when he was as quiet as a mouse. It was as if she had a special radar that was tuned just to him. She had an imagination, too, because once he'd come upon her trailing about in a musty, yellowed, turn-of-the-century wedding gown that she'd blushingly claimed she'd dug out of an attic trunk.

"You could pass for a young Miss Havisham."

"Why, you're far more literary than I suspected, Mr. Conroy," she'd said.

"Dickens was required reading in high school."

"Still, he left an impression on you."

He saw no reason to disillusion by admitting all he'd read was a page or two before hightailing to get himself a set of *Cliffs Notes*.

Kirk knew Felicity had a way with animals, especially the no-good variety. Hell, Fred practically lived with her now. And that mangy mother cat. What sort of fool woman grew up rich and then went grocery shopping and brought home the ugliest orange cat in three counties and then doted on it as if it was something special?

Kitty Mother, as she called the she-devil, had a litter in her belly to boot. Kirk had just about lost all respect for Fred since the hound had taken up with the cat, too. A dog with a lick of sense should know better. All it had taken was a well-placed claw bloodying his nose, and his hound that had scars from coyote battles now shared his porch, his water bowl and his dog food with a cat.

Kirk knew Felicity ate vegetables. Even inedible ones like squash. The first time she'd gone shopping, she'd bought extra turnips for him, excusing her blunder by saying she'd figured he'd forgotten to put them on his list.

"I don't eat vegetables," he'd said in her kitchen that day as she'd opened a big jar of pickles.

"Unhealthy habits aren't something to be so proud of."

"Except for french fries."

"Which don't count," she'd said in that superior tone women always use when they talk about vegetables. Then she'd bitten into a big, juicy pickle.

Kirk didn't feel like debating the wisdom of attaching moral values to anything as disgusting as turnips. "There's never been a cat around here before," he'd said to change the subject.

"Louise Derringer had a cat. She wrote about it in her diary."

"Who's Louise?"

"You know. She built this house and got the rose garden started."

He didn't know, and if he ever had, it hadn't interested him enough to remember. He said, "Right. Old Louise."

"A lamp fell over. Her cat woke her up and they were able to put the fire out and save the house."

"The durn cat probably knocked the lamp over in the first place," Kirk couldn't resist saying.

"You would think the worst of a poor, defenseless animal."

"How's that any different than you always thinking the worst of me?"

"And why do you always think everything is about you?"

"You're changing the subject. I know you don't hate me as much as you pretend."

"And just how do you know that?"

"Because I've seen you walking out toward my house when I have Mary Lou over for an evening."

Felicity had set her half-eaten pickle down on the counter. "For your in-for-ma-tion..." She had spoken that word with humiliating precision. "I take walks. Every night. Without the slightest consideration to you or your love life. In fact, I never give you a thought."

Something had come over him. "Well, that's about to change," he'd whispered, inspired.

Then he had stalked over toward the counter, involuntarily forcing her to back up against it.

"What...what do you think you're doing?" she'd squeaked, all her cool reserve gone.

Her question had made him wonder the same thing.

He stopped inches away from her. He savored the heat of her and the smell of her even as the look of fear on her face made him writhe inside.

"Don't you have enough girls chasing you? Do you have to add me to your list of conquests?"

He'd wanted to snap something cool and hateful back at her, but the haunted look in her eyes stopped him cold.

"You're not a conquest," he said softly.

"Good. Because I don't think you and I have much in common!"

"What's that supposed to mean?"

"I like good books and cats and flowers and...and..."

"All the finer more civilized things in life," he suggested helpfully. "Like poetry."

"Exactly."

"While I'm crude and rude and into wild living. You probably think my idea of poetry is men's-room graffiti."

"Exactly," she snapped.

"You probably miss a lot if your nose is always stuck between the pages of a book."

"I'm more experienced in life than you might think," she snapped.

Her cheeks turned red, and he suddenly got curious. But she offered no more.

"How come you like my sister so much then when everybody's always said we're as alike as two peas in a pod?"

"I guess because you're a man, Mr. Conroy."

"That's pretty sexist...for an intellectual lady like yourself. But I'm glad that you, at least, noticed my sex."

That last brought even more color to her already colorful face. He felt pleased with himself that he could affect her so powerfully.

"We both like Fred," he said. "We have that no-account, disloyal, cat-loving hound in common."

She took a deep breath, and that made her breasts rise. He watched them too pointedly and then stepped back from her to let her pass.

But as soon as she got to the door, she couldn't leave without getting in one more lick. "Kirk Conroy, I've had enough romance to last me a lifetime. So, do us both a favor and leave me alone."

Then she stalked into the back of the house. A minute later a door had slammed upstairs. Then another. As if she were banging them for good measure.

He went out and eased his own door shut as silently as a whisper.

So, she wouldn't know for sure he'd gone.

So, she'd keep wondering about him.

Chapter 3

The mountain air was cool and crisp and sparkling.

One moment Felicity was laughing at Blackie's grumblings and reveling in the near-magical, floral colors and odors of the purple irises and lilacs.

In the next she felt that dangerous prickle of awareness tracing up and down her slender spine.

Ignore him. And maybe he'll go away.

Heavy boot heels crunched behind her and then came to a determined standstill. She could almost hear Kirk's thick heels digging into the soft earth behind her—as if he were planting himself there permanently.

"Sorry to interrupt your little project, Felicity—"

Nobody, at least no man, not even Patrick, had ever managed to make her feel quite so warm and fluttery...by just saying her name. His tone was deep and dark and yet as soft as sheered velvet.

Brows knit, spade fiercely clutched in her muddy gardening glove, she whirled.

As usual a wide grin broke across his handsome face, and she knew he wasn't sorry at all.

"I'm afraid I need to borrow Blackie," he said.

His sharp look toward Blackie snapped the skinnier man to his feet and had him sprinting toward the corral as fast as his springy frame could carry him.

For a long moment Kirk didn't speak. Instead he watched two elegant black mourning cloak butterflies flitting near her roses. Then Kitty Mother leapt, batting orange paws at the butterflies, and Fred began barking and jumping friskily.

"Something sure smells mighty good in your kitchen. And you sure do look as pretty as a picture this morning, Felicity." Kirk gave her another smile.

"I made a chocolate cake. Sierra's eating supper with me tonight."

"Sierra is always saying you're a real good cook."

"It's a hobby of mine," she managed to reply with a nonchalant air even though her own smile was brittle at the edges.

"How did you know chocolate cake is my very favorite?"

"I didn't." She pretended an indifference she was far from feeling. Oh, why could this man make her feel so intensely?

His blue eyes were as hot as lasers. Didn't he have work to do? Was he trying to make her feel guilty for not inviting him to dinner?

She did feel guilty, too. Which was ridiculous, considering he probably had a month's wages staked on how soon he'd bed her.

Oh, why did just the thought of white cotton sheets and hot brown skin make her feel warmer than the sunshine? She wanted him gone. Just as she was about to tell him so, it hit her that despite his friendly pose, he seemed undeniably tense around her, too. Was he worried about losing his precious bet, for Sierra had told her he was careful and clever about money? Or did she make him as nervous as he made her?

Sierra had told her he'd asked about her, said they were involved. Whatever had he meant by that remark? Why had his saying it stuck with her for days? And for nights, too?

She felt involved, so involved she'd had to constantly remind herself about his bet and his reputation.

Just as she was trying to think of something to say, the telephone rang. So, all she said was, "Gotta go."

"Oh, me, too," he said just as tightly, just as nervously.

She thought she was rid of him till the man on the phone said he wouldn't hang up till he talked to Kirk.

Kirk was already mounted when she ran out onto the front porch, and the sight of him sitting so tall on that large, skittish roan of his made her stomach flutter again.

His lazy gaze found hers, and she registered a wealth of unsettling emotions in his warm, blue eyes.

"It's for you," she whispered.

She raced inside, moving faster than she usually did these days.

As he took two long steps past the threshold, she found herself staring at the caked mud on his boots and the trail of little black bits behind him.

He got her message without her nagging him and stopped, extending his hand toward hers apologetically as she handed him the cordless. Holding it, he stepped outside and carefully wiped his boots on the mat. He didn't say much, just listened mostly, but when he hung up, his easy smile was gone.

"That was Hugh Dayton from the next ranch. Says a drifter assaulted and robbed a neighbor's wife on the highway outside Whitehorn when she broke down. Took her truck which has been found abandoned out at the Laughing Horse Reservation."

"So?"

"So—we've got to be more careful. Especially you. So—I'll be driving you in to town...for a while."

"The last thing I need is you watching over me. I'd rather Blackie drove me."

"That's because you've never been his passenger. He can't see too well, and he drives like a bat out of hell. He's a coward, too. If there was trouble, he'd run for help and leave you to the drifter."

She put her hands on her hips.

"Miss Evans, I hate to sound pushy, but I *am* the

boss around here, least till Chayce gets back. He asked me to protect you—"

"Which he had no right to do—"

"Still, he'd blame me if anything happens to you. So, maybe I don't like this any better than you, but I say who drives you. And who doesn't. You just stick to your librarying."

"Li-bra-ry work. Research. Librarying isn't a word." Why was she arguing with this caveman in a cowboy hat?

"Li-bra-ry work," he mimicked easily, smiling that beguiling smile that made her feel like a girl again. "You can correct me anytime. I kinda like it. It's a form of attention." He paused. "How's it going, by the way?"

"What?"

"Your li-bra-ry work? Louise and her cat? Etcetera."

The way he mimicked her pronunciation annoyed her so much that she snatched the cordless out of his big brown hand.

"Have a nice day, Mr. Conroy." She latched the hook of the screen door. "I'll get back to my gardening, that is, if you don't mind."

"The garden's out here."

"I'm waiting till *you* leave."

Still, he just stood there on the porch, ignoring even that broad hint.

"The house looks nice. I'm sorry about the mud. I'll run around back and get a broom—"

"No. I'll sweep. Look, I'm sure we both have better things to do than stand here and make small talk.''

"I do have plenty to do, but before I get back to it, I'm gonna tell you something, Miss Evans. Maybe I don't have a master's degree from some fancy university. Maybe I didn't grow up in some big mansion and know famous people. Maybe I don't spend a lot of my time in li-bra-ries. But I do know a thing or two about manners. Are you always this rude to everybody? Or do you have a special grudge against me?''

She *had* singled him out.

Because of his dangerous appeal.

Not that she was about to admit *that* to the conceited likes of him! Not when he was gambling she was an easy lay.

"Goodbye, Mr. Conroy!" she said very firmly. "I'd much rather sweep...than have you here... underfoot...pestering me.''

The garden had its dayside and its nightside.

Felicity had never walked in the garden at night, but she chose to do so this particular evening—to avoid the path that led too near Kirk's cabin.

The chilly air had her shivering, or was it that with the moon behind a cloud, the garden seemed to be huge masses of ghostly flowers, nameless in the velvet dark. As she walked down the pebbly path, a rose softly brushed her cheek. She inhaled its perfume with a heady gasp. Then a gigantic lily shape loomed against a wall of black shadows. A vivid trail of light at her feet told her where the bed of white roses lay where once the tiny blossoms in Abby's bridal bouquet had bloomed.

"Beautiful," she whispered in a tone of utter reverence.

"Yes," agreed a deep husky voice behind her. "Very beautiful."

"You!" she gasped, jerking to a halt. "I—I thought I was alone. You were so still in those shadows."

"I saw you come out," he murmured. "I didn't want to disturb you. Or...pester you."

She would never have come out; she would never have abandoned herself so eagerly to the night beauty of the garden had she suspected he was there.

"Do you mind if I join you?" he asked.

"It's always been my habit to walk alone."

"Mine, too," he countered easily. "But I'm in the mood for company."

The moon came out from its cloud, and its golden light transformed the garden path, which ended at the gurgling fountain beside Abby's roses. The moon painted his hair with highlights of gold.

"You and me..." he began in that deep, resonant tone that made her pulse quicken.

"There is no you and me."

But her voice came breathily. And the perfume of the roses seemed to cast a magic spell as did his voice and his presence.

"Exactly. See, out here we're stuck with each other," he persisted. "And I'm the kind of guy who usually likes everybody. What do you think? Maybe we could start over and be friends.''

"Mr. Conroy, please... I'm sure you have plenty to think about around here besides me. I suggest you do it.''

"You've become a burr under my saddle blanket so to speak. What are you running so hard from, Miss Evans? I mean...besides me?''

His question was soft. His sincere tone pulled at her heart.

She'd been running and hiding ever since her mother had died. There hadn't ever really been anybody she could talk to since then. Except for Abby, and she'd even kept a lot from Abby. She'd been carefully taught that the less said, the less that could turn up in tabloids.

Don't trust him. Don't trust any man.

"How many times are you going to ask me questions like that?''

"Maybe till you answer them. I'm mighty curious, you know. It's a failing of mine.''

"Of which you have many?''

"Don't we all?'' His eyes gleamed. "I'll bet you're not as lily-white as you pretend?''

She flushed guiltily.

"Well, don't you worry about it. I haven't yet known anybody who was perfect. I am curious about your particular story, though.''

He *did* have a curious nature. If she'd given him answers in the beginning, maybe things would never have gone so far.

"See, I think about you," he persisted, his voice as honeyed as the garden darkness. "I don't know why I do, but I think about you a lot. I have the craziest thoughts. Like now. You know without those big glasses... How come you don't wear them all the time?" he asked absently.

"Contacts." She caught his clean, male scent. Oh, why did she let him slide his hands against her cheeks and remove her glasses?

"And with your hair down," he rasped, his voice beguilingly unsteady as his big brown hand fumbled in the silken mass, expertly undoing the clip so that soon the long, thick waves swirled in loose, chocolate curls around her shoulders.

All the needs she'd been fighting ever since she'd met him rose up fresh and strong and made her feel young and free and...sexy.

She wanted the same thing he wanted.

He saw it, too.

His powerful arm circled her waist and scooped her close.

"Why do you want to make this so complicated, Felicity?"

She caught no more than a shuddering glimpse of his lean, hard features and beautiful mouth before he kissed her once, very gently, and then very hard.

After that she only felt and ached and sighed. Oh, and how she ached and sighed. Every single atom in her being did a somersault.

Feelings!

Heat flowed through her—lava hot. She reveled in

the warmth of his tongue tracing inside. She felt a wild exhilaration. Her arms curled around his neck.

In the next instant, though, she was shoving her balled fists at his chest, breaking free of the drugging heat of his mouth and embrace. When his work-roughened fingertips gently brushed her cheek, she lowered her head and trembled.

"There... You got what you came for," she whispered. "Are you satisfied?"

"Not by a long shot. And you aren't, either."

"I want you to go."

"Part of you does," he agreed. "But you're shaking like a leaf."

"Because I'm so scared."

"Your skin's as hot as a campfire, and your heart's racing just like mine." He caught her hand and held it against his chest so she could feel the mad thumping of his own pulse. "There's nothing to be scared of. There's only you and me."

She was easy. Too easy. For a man like him.

"I hate you. Leave me alone."

"Oh, it's not me you hate, honey. It's somebody else. You liked me kissing you. You liked it a lot. That's what's got your goat. You know something— I liked it, too, way more than I wanted to. I've never known anybody like you. Chilly and frosty on the outside but fiery underneath. You may think I'm all wrong for you, but you're just as wrong for me. I didn't want to like you, either."

"Why don't you ever, ever just go when I ask you?" she whispered frantically.

"Maybe I'm ready to face my demons."

"Well, maybe I'm not."

"They won't ever go away, honey, unless you do."

He let her go, so she could run inside.

Slouched against a tall cottonwood tree, Kirk watched the house for what seemed like hours. He saw lights go on and off in every room. The way those rectangles of light kept snapping everywhere made it obvious she didn't feel settled. Any more than he did.

Every time he remembered the way she'd clung to him for that split second or two, the way her tongue had flitted halfway inside his mouth, the way she'd wanted to give way to what she'd felt for him, but had stopped herself, he burned from the memory of her.

Suddenly her bedroom light went out. He was about to head for home when the screen door opened, and she stepped out onto the porch. Her shoulders were stooped. He felt an ache of remorse when she sank down on the swing and buried her face in her hands.

She was crying.

Because of him.

It took him a spell to get his nerve up to call to her softly.

All he said was her name.

But it snapped her white face out of her palms. Her eyes were huge and bright.

He was on the porch by the time she jumped up from the swing.

"Hold it," he whispered. Before you go inside, I want you to know that I feel bad about what happened. And I'm sorry."

"Not nearly as sorry as I am."

"I'm not going to bother, er, pester you anymore. I'll do things... *your* way. I'll let that yella-bellied Blackie drive you into town since you want him to. From now on, I'll leave you strictly alone. Unless... you come to me... and tell me you want it otherwise."

"That's not very likely."

Her words and her sad, determined look cut him to the quick, but he forced a smile. "Whatever you say, honey." He waved goodbye to her and hid his feelings as best he could.

But he wasn't nearly as good at it as she was.

Chapter 4

Funny, how when a man does exactly what a girl tells him she wants him to do, it often isn't what she wants at all.

Funny, how it doesn't feel one bit funny, either.

It felt lonely.

Ever since Kirk had given her his word as a gentleman to avoid her, he'd done just that with such an overabundance of zeal that Felicity had spent the most miserable week she could remember. She felt a thousand times lonelier than she had as a solitary child roaming the gilt-edged, high-ceilinged rooms of her uncle's mansion or playing outside alone on the vast, perfectly manicured green lawns where she hadn't even been allowed to keep a pet or touch a flower.

It had been salt into her open wound that Kirk had

so easily consoled himself by having the beautiful Mary Lou over to his cabin every single night, too.

Why, the very next night after he'd sworn to avoid Felicity, Felicity had come upon him cooking filet mignon out by a campfire and serenading Mary Lou while he strummed his guitar.

When Felicity had heard his singing and his date's quiet laughter, she'd tried to sneak away.

But Kirk had the ears of a lynx. "Whoa!" he'd cried. "Who goes there?"

"It's just me. I was out walking.... I didn't realize—"

"Have a nice walk—"

She'd tried to think of something casual and friendly to say, but her throat had tightened. Some intense emotion had welled up and almost choked her.

For several days after that, Felicity had stuck closer to the house. Then one pretty night, she couldn't resist another walk. Again, as if fatally drawn, she ended up too near Kirk's house. This time he'd come running outside onto his porch with a burning pot.

Felicity burst out laughing at his clumsincss.

He set the pot down and came toward her, a gentle smile on his rugged face. "That's the first time I've seen you do that. At least around me."

"Do what?"

"Laugh like any normal young woman." His voice had changed to velvet.

Images of his dark face so near hers in the garden

flew before her eyes. Again, she felt his warm, solid body against hers, his arms locked around her waist. She willed him to hold her again. To kiss her. Had he thought of their kiss again? She had. Over and over again, she'd replayed it like a tune she couldn't get out of her head.

But Mary Lou came outside in a pale lace dress, and it was she who put her arms around his waist and drew him near enough for a kiss.

Felicity stiffened. But even though he stayed glued to Mary Lou, Felicity felt he was drawn to her.

Why? Why did she care about him so much? What was happening to them?

Why did her longing for him stay with her for the rest of the night? She even dreamed of being with him in the garden, only in her dream he wasn't satisfied with a kiss. And the next morning when she got up, she felt shivery with an odd new restlessness that made her know she wasn't about to quit thinking about him.

She didn't like the way he'd gotten such a grip on her imagination. Finally she decided that if she wanted his attention, and she did, she was going to have to actively seek it. Every time she thought of him running out with that burning pot, she smiled. Just as every time she thought of Mary Lou holding him, she burned with other feelings she didn't want.

Finally her obsession overpowered her good sense. It was nearly noon when she put aside her research and went to the kitchen and began baking a chocolate cake.

Maybe the way to fight fire was with fire. Maybe if she spent some time with him, he'd lose his hold. Maybe she should have a little fun with him and the hands, especially Blackie who'd made such sport of her. It would serve all of them right if she acted as if she *was* interested in Kirk. Not that she intended to let their relationship get out of hand. So, right after lunch, after her cake had cooled, she iced it and took it down to the pens.

The cowboys were sitting around a table under a tin shed, drinking coffee.

Only Kirk wasn't there.

Blackie and Sierra and two other hands, who had taken a break from vaccinating calves, stared at her—thunderstruck—as if they could see straight through her.

"This is mighty nice of you," Sierra said as Blackie seized the cake.

"It sure is," Blackie said.

"Save a piece for Kirk," Felicity whispered, lingering, blushing.

Blackie grinned at that, and Sierra stared at her in disbelief.

"Sure, I'll tell him," Blackie said conspiratorially. "Chocolate is his favorite, you know."

Oh, yes, she knew.

Not that she said so.

Sierra's gaze narrowed on her new friend too thoughtfully.

In the darkness the ranch house looked all closed up and forbidding. Kirk studied the sprawling shape of it against the cottonwoods awhile, listening to the soft tinkle of piano music and wondering what she'd meant by bringing the cake out to the hands. Blackie had sworn Felicity had worn her hair down and that she'd specifically ordered them to save him a piece. Sierra had acted as if he was too conceited for words when he'd asked her if she thought Felicity was after him.

"She's always cooking—you know that. That's because the kitchen was the one room her aunt would let her play in as a little girl. The kindly cook felt sorry for her, too."

A man could hope, couldn't he?

When Kirk finally mustered up enough gumption to knock on the front door, he knew his hopes were justified because her hair *was* down, and when she saw him, she smiled. Then she whispered in a slightly breathless voice, "Hi."

"I brought your crystal cake plate back."

She took it from him, and he noticed how her eyes sparked and her cheeks brightened when her hands brushed his.

"Did they save you a piece?" she asked.

"Not much of one. But what I had... was...delicious."

"Thank you."

"No. Thank you," he said. "Felicity, I stood outside awhile just then...listening to you play the piano. It was the first time I ever heard you play a whole song through 'cause you always stop when I'm anywhere near. I like the way you play."

"I like the way you sing."

"I stayed away. Just like you asked me to. And only because you asked me to. It wasn't easy."

"Do you think it was...any easier for me...." She stammered to a halt.

"Honey, you're surprising me at every turn today."

"I'm surprising me, too." Her eyes were huge and luminous. "Kirk...I can't have feelings for you...or for any man right now. Can you understand that?"

"Maybe I could...if you'd tell me why."

"I—I can't. Not right now. Please, try to understand."

She was shaking. She looked scared to death. He fought the urge to demand what was wrong. But he guessed if she wanted to tell him, she would. He was too direct, too impatient sometimes. He had to quit rushing her. Her trust was something he'd have to earn.

"I can try," he whispered.

"You'd better go."

"Okay, but before I do, Felicity, something's happened. Something that I came down here to talk to you about. It doesn't have anything to do with you and me. Gus, the rancher next to us, called and said his wife, Lou, had a scare this evening."

"What...what happened to her?"

"A drifter came up to their house. Said he wanted a cup of coffee. He looked so strange, Lou told him to go out to the barn and find Gus. But the stranger pulled the screen door off the frame and went inside.

Lou ran out the back door and barely got away from him. I'm wondering if I shouldn't stay up here with you till they catch this guy. There's no telling what he's after. I could sleep on the couch.''

She sucked in a startled breath. Her cheeks paled. ''I don't think that would be such a good idea. I mean not right now.'' Her quiet voice held a tinge of nervousness. He caught the sweet smell of her.

''Okay. You're probably right. But if you get scared or hear the slightest sound…that makes you nervous… You call me, and I'll come check it out.''

A shutter banging in the wind woke Felicity a few hours later, and after that she couldn't sleep. She got up and played the piano for a while. She played the same prelude she'd played earlier when she'd known Kirk had been standing outside listening to her. As she played it, she imagined him listening. As she did so, she imagined him out there in the dark. Just the vision got her shivery. She thought of ten good reasons why she most definitely shouldn't call him and say she was scared. But the main reason was that her wanting him had nothing to do with the drifter and everything to do with him.

Kirk watched Felicity methodically make up the couch in the living room. He'd offered to do it himself, but she'd insisted. Probably so she could keep busy and wouldn't have to look at him.

When she was done plumping the pillow and smoothing the white cotton sheets with those slim fingers he couldn't quit watching, the bed she'd created made for an air of intimacy and expectation between them.

"I shouldn't have called you," she said.

"Not to worry."

"Funny, how I don't feel sleepy or scared now."

"Why don't you just do whatever you feel like then?"

"It's 2:00 a.m. You probably have a hard day tomorrow—"

"Most likely." He stared at the piano. "You could play."

To his surprise, she sat down at the piano. He watched her long, slender fingers settle on the keys and listened to the soft notes in the shadowy lamplight. But most of all, he observed how the music softened her face. The music or maybe her nearness or maybe just her acceptance of his being there softened something inside him, too. He got a taste, his first, of how good it might feel if she ever relaxed around him.

"How'd you learn to play like that?" he whispered when her hands fell away from the keys a little later and she lifted her foot from the pedal.

"Oh, I had lessons. But I can't remember when I couldn't read music. I was a very small child. My mother was always playing. Everybody was amazed when I just sat down and started playing. I even taught myself to read. It's a gift, I suppose. My mother had it, too."

Her mother who had died. He wondered if Tina would have played if she'd lived.

"You should do something with it," he said.

"That's what everybody says. But I don't want it to become work. I enjoy it."

"I guess that counts, too."

He got up and went to her. Instead of touching her, he ran his hands over the smooth walnut of the instrument, and she watched his hands flow against the warm, shiny wood, as if she sensed how much he wanted to touch her skin the same way.

"You play the guitar."

"I never took lessons. I just learned 'cause somebody told me it was a way to get girls."

"You're incorrigible."

Her eyes without glasses were extremely dark and very sparkly up close. "That's better than some things I've been called."

"I like the way you sing."

He stared at her mouth and then drew a long breath. "Maybe someday I'll sing to you, then. But, I warn you, when I'm inspired, I can be a ham."

"Maybe you could sing…just generally now…not to me I mean…and I could play." Her fingers returned to the keys.

The sleek, wet-looking texture of her lips made him ache to kiss her. "Okay," he said.

She played "This is My Sunshine" and he sang.

Afterward, no sooner did the last shared notes die, than they turned and stared at each other again.

"That's a favorite of mine," she said.

"Mine, too. See there. We do have something in common."

"Not enough." But her eyes shone with an uncommon brightness.

Again, the music, her voice, her nearness had stirred him.

"I want you," he whispered simply.

"You're supposed to be protecting me."

"I can do two things at once."

"Maybe…some things." Her voice was soft and teasing as he bent closer. "But the last thing you could ever be is my bodyguard."

His fingers pulled her chin closer. "Oh, Felicity… Honey…"

"Don't," she breathed. "Please… You're way too charming for a girl to…"

Inspired because she'd called him charming, he coiled his other hand in her hair, and using it like a silken tether, he drew her toward him.

"Don't be scared anymore, Felicity. Not of me. I don't want to hurt you. I just want to love you."

Chapter 5

In that split second before he kissed her, Felicity's eyes met his and clung questioningly while the moment of white-hot intensity spun between them.

Don't be scared, he'd said.

She was petrified.

Maybe he didn't intend to, but he could hurt her so badly.

They had so much working against them. Everything. They were too different. He was emotional, unafraid, honest, in ways she wasn't sure she could ever be. He had no idea that all she could ever give him was tonight. This moment.

She was crazy, crazy not to run.

But desire spun its hot, enticing web all around her.

There'd be a time for running and hiding, and soon, she supposed.

"Kiss me, Felicity," came his deep-throated appeal. "Honey, I've thought over and over about that night in the garden."

She let him draw her halfway across the piano bench, his lips meeting hers with the kiss she'd been so afraid of all night and yet aching to have.

His mouth was hard, expert. His tongue came inside her parted lips instantly, sleek, needy, devouring her like a destroying flame. Only with him, all the sensual wildness that had already gotten her into so much trouble was a thousand times wilder.

Why couldn't she have met him first?

It wouldn't have mattered.

When he deepened the kiss, her heart raced.

But no faster than his.

When he drew away from her a long time later, his eyes were blazing. "I think we'd better stop," he murmured, toying with a strand of her long brown hair. "...if we're going to stop."

"Oh, we are," she whispered, not wanting to.

Why had she baked that cake? Called him? She had only meant to play at love, not to be swept away by it. This was only a bet to him. While she had so much more than herself at stake.

"You're dating Mary Lou...."

"I'll stop. I don't ever think about anybody but you. I just brought her out here...to try not to think about you after you told me to stay away."

"This is all happening too fast. I can't believe—"

"I know what you mean. I've never felt this way

for any other woman," he whispered. "I've never come close—"

Was he telling her the truth? Or was he just so practiced and good at making love that he would say anything to get the woman of the moment into his bed?

It was difficult for Felicity to think with her pulses and emotions racing. He had only to smile, to stroke, to make her crave him so much more.

All her life she had wanted to be loved, to be special to someone. She'd imagined an intellectual who loved to read as she did, who shared her scholarly interests in history and culture. Not a rugged outdoorsman. But never, till now, had anyone from her own world come close to making her feel what she had always wanted to feel with a man.

"I'm wondering if I can believe anything you say," she said.

"Sure you can."

"I'm wondering if you've just got a line...that works with all the women you meet. Is that deep, sexy, sugarcoated voice of yours sincere or just practiced?"

He tensed; the lines of his handsome face hardened. "You're special to me, Felicity," he rasped. "Don't you know that yet?"

"I had to say that," she said pleadingly because he was angry. "It's very hard for me to trust...men after..."

"Damn it. Why?"

"I—I can't tell you."

"I may be falling in love with you, and you won't even answer a simple question."

"Because it's not so simple."

"Somebody used you and moved on...and you're afraid I'll do the same."

"That much is true, but there's more to it." *So much more.* "I'm all mixed-up, Kirk."

"Okay. I won't ask questions. I'll even go if you want me to."

She couldn't answer. Something outside herself seemed to take charge of her in that dazzling, lamplit moment. Maybe it was his virile nearness or maybe just his warm pirate's smile. Maybe it was the white-hot flare of his gorgeous blue eyes. Whatever. All her reason and sanity simply melted away.

He made her feel alive and desired and loved. At the same time, she was terrified of him.

As he knelt closer to kiss her neck, she shivered as she caught the spicy scent of his aftershave. He brushed her jaw with his lips, and her eyelids with their long, curled lashes drifted closed. For the space of a heartbeat, his mouth hovered above hers.

She didn't want an affair.

He wouldn't want her at all when she finally confided in him.

So—what was she doing here, with him like this, tonight?

Whatever it was, she couldn't stop herself. It was as if she were suddenly caught in a riptide of sensual excitement.

His long fingers threaded through her hair and

found the zipper at the back of her dress. With a deft movement the thin material peeled away revealing her slim bare back. He ran a hand down the length of her slender spine. In the next instant he had unhooked her bra. He stripped his own shirt off.

Then his hands were all over her smooth skin, lifting her and laying her beneath himself on the rug.

Body to body.

He stared down at her, adoring her with those intense, hot eyes. Beneath him she felt small and deliciously feminine; he seemed huge and powerful, and yet he was infinitely gentle.

She slid her own hands through his midnight black hair, savoring the springiness as well as the silky texture. Then her fingertips glided down his muscular neck, over his furred, brown chest.

"You're perfect," he whispered.

"So are you."

"I think I'm falling in love with you," he said.

Before he could kiss her again, she remembered Blackie's bet. Did he mean that? Or was this sex and nothing more?

"Does this mean you'll win your little bet?"

He paused, clearly puzzled. His head came up. "What little bet?"

"The one with Blackie and all the hands? About how soon you'll get me into your bed. Does the floor count?"

"Oh God." His groan was heavy with shame and genuine anguish. "You knew about that?"

"All along."

"Well, no wonder you were so dead set against me." A new tension made his voice tight. He wasn't as unaffected as she'd thought he'd be.

"I baked that cake to sort of tease all of you. I didn't mean for things to go this far."

"So, you were just teasing me tonight?" His smile was tight. "When did you stop teasing?"

"I got kinda carried away."

"Kinda," he said, but more tenderly. "Look, I never had anything to do with Blackie's bet. He lost all his money in Vegas. His wife kicked him out. They've got two kids. Sheila made me swear I'd fire him if he so much as bet a nickel on anything. Then Sierra told me his bet, but I didn't have the heart to do anything about it since he put on such a show of working so hard any time I ever saw him. But that was before I knew you knew. Honey, if that's all that's been worrying you about me— Why, I'll get dressed right now and bring him up here and get him to confess. I'll fire the skunk—"

She turned away. "No."

"Felicity, you matter to me. *You.* I don't know why, but you do."

Do it now. Tell him now.

"That isn't...all," she whispered. "I've got other problems...responsibilities that have nothing to do with you." Hot tears gathered behind her eyes.

"Maybe I could help you with them."

Macho cowboys were hardly an enlightened breed. Her own uncle would probably disown her. "You probably won't want to."

"Honey, what's wrong? Why can't you trust me just a little?"

Show. Don't tell.

She'd been protecting herself so hard, she hadn't thought about his feelings at all. Maybe…it was time…. "You'll find out," she said. "And soon. Very soon. But, let me tell you in my own way."

"All right."

Self-consciously she put his hands on her breasts and moved them slowly down her thickening body. Since he didn't suspect her intention, since he thought this was loveplay, her taking the initiative merely inflamed his ardor.

Every kiss swept them with the realization of how much they wanted each other, of how much pleasure they could find in each other. When his mouth suckled each of her nipples, one at a time, Felicity's body shimmered in glowing response. She lost her fear of his touching her. Heat gathered inside her, knotted, and she felt an urgent need for him to enter her and take her. Almost, almost, she forgot her purpose.

"I can't believe you're letting me do this," he whispered. "After the way you made me keep my distance." He wrapped her tight in his arms, jubilant in his possession of her.

She hugged him back for a long time before reluctantly forcing his broad palms to resume their exploration. When his callused hands came to her rounded stomach, she kept them there, forcing him to concentrate on the slight swelling there. His stalled fingertips began to burn her flesh.

He sucked in his breath. She felt him tense as his searing eyes widened and raced from her face down her body.

Then without a word, he froze, yanking his hands off her stomach.

"Well...now you know," she said quietly, falling back limply on the rug, tears dampening her lashes, slightly ashamed that he knew. She couldn't see his face too clearly for the dark, so she just lay there, imagining his feelings, her attitude more than slightly cautious.

He lay down beside her with a terrible patience that frightened her. Suddenly his still, muscular frame seemed larger and far more dangerous than it ever had before. Oh, how she wanted to hide.

"I'm expecting a baby," she said, stating the obvious. "Is that so terrible?"

"Would you just give me a minute?" he whispered in a stunned, tormented tone she scarcely recognized. "I don't think I can talk about this right now. It's a helluva shock, you know. I thought we were about to make love. I didn't know it was show-and-tell hour."

She felt crushed, shut out by him for the first time, and yet she'd been equally upset when her doctor had told her that, no, she didn't have a stomach virus, that she was pregnant. She had been stunned because Patrick had always been so obsessive about contraception. Then that very same night, before she could tell Patrick about their baby, he'd taken her to dinner and told her that his wife had come home.

"*Your wife?* You never told me you were married." She'd known then that she would never ever tell him about their baby.

He'd taken her hands and said he was sorry he hadn't told her he was married before, but he hadn't thought it was important since he'd been separated nearly a year. But then Andrea had come back. She'd been in therapy. She didn't blame him for everything anymore. She'd lost weight, and she wasn't so angry now. She was the girl he'd grown up with and fallen in love with. She was his history. He'd realized how sacred their marriage was and how much he'd wanted to try again especially since Andrea had invested so much in her therapy!

Felicity had begun to cry. She'd thought: *What about us? What about our child?*

Instead she'd sobbed brokenly, and Patrick had said she was making a scene—as if that was what mattered. She'd cried louder, and he'd said he was sorry—as if an apology could repair the damage. He'd grown impatient, and she'd known it was over. Not just for him, but for her, too.

Aloud to Kirk, Felicity said, "I see now I shouldn't have trusted you. I don't know why I did— It...isn't like me.... But you were so *curious.*"

"Damn it. None of that garbage is the issue. By the way, who's the happy father."

"He's out of the picture."

"Oh, really?"

She didn't like the strained, sarcastic edge in his

voice, but what she said was, "I don't want to talk about him."

"So, what is he—some low-class jerk? Or some dumb cowboy like me...who's not good enough or smart enough...to marry you?"

Why was he taking this so personally and getting so defensive? "How can you think such a thing?"

"Maybe because you never tell me anything, and I don't know a damn thing about you. Does he even know?"

"No."

"So, you didn't tell him?"

"Why does *he* matter so much to you? Why do you assume I'm mistreating him?"

"Why do you always ask why? I don't sit around analyzing my every thought the way you seem to. *He* matters. That's all. I'm half in love with you, but you're carrying *his* child. We nearly had sex. What would he think about that?"

"I don't care what he thinks! About anything!" She pressed a hand to her mouth. "I had a very good reason for not telling him."

"Oh, God. Here we go. So, what are you going to do now, alone?"

"I'm doing it. Chayce and Abby said I could stay here till I thought this thing through. I didn't want to tell anybody about this. I certainly didn't want to involve you."

"Obviously."

"I knew you were the last kind of man..."

"What the hell is that supposed to mean?"

"You're always running around with all those girls. I knew you wouldn't be seriously interested in a woman who is going to have a baby."

"Oh, I guess I'm supposed to be a real bastard…as bad as you think the father of your baby is. You even said you enticed me…as a joke…and you say I'm insincere."

"I'm sorry. I'm not sure I mean half the things I'm saying. You're not the only one who's upset. I know this is an unexpected complication."

"You can say that again, sister."

Raw, confused emotions tore at her. She was going to lose control in another second or two. "Look. Just forget about me."

"Oh, like that's real easy! Maybe it is for you."

"Be glad this didn't go any further."

He levered himself off the floor and began yanking on his jeans. "I'm going to have to think about this."

"Of course. I understand."

"I doubt that. You haven't figured one damn thing right about me yet."

I knew you couldn't take my being pregnant, she thought wildly. He'd been open about his feelings when it came to the little stuff, but now— So, he wasn't any different, after all.

"Good night," she whispered.

She thought: *So, it's over.*

"I'll be back," he said.

"Sure."

She lay in the dark, terrified of the aloneness. She began to sob, and once she started, she couldn't stop.

Chapter 6

Looking as fresh as a new rose in the bright sun-shine and way more rested than she felt, Felicity was sitting in the garden. She was proud of her hard-won control. Kitty Mother was purring trustingly on her lap when a tight-lipped Kirk strode around the back of the house and informed her rather tersely that he intended to spend the day in Whitehorn.

"Probably most of the night, too," he said. "Blackie can look after you."

"The night, too?" she asked, jerking her head away from him.

She'd cried her eyes out last night. She knew it was over. So, why did it still hurt so much when he confirmed it?

"That's what I said...in plain English, isn't it?"

There was a new awkwardness between them. He

was more formal, and she more terrified. His tone was clipped, his stance rigid. He wouldn't even look at her when she got up the nerve to look at him. Thus, if she glanced up while he was explaining something, he tilted his chin and stared over her head at the mountains.

Did he think she was some low, scarlet woman?

"I thought I loved *him*," she whispered brokenly.

She thought: *I don't owe Kirk Conroy an explanation.*

"I don't want to hear about him," he said.

"I wouldn't have told you if I hadn't thought you could handle it."

"I am handling it."

"So, that's what you call this?"

"This?" he queried innocently, as if he didn't know what she was talking about.

"What you're doing. The way you're talking. Or rather not talking. This…this…*attitude*."

He stared at her.

She said, "You're being positively hateful." *Oh! That felt good!*

"Sorry. Maybe you shouldn't pry so hard."

"I thought—"

This time he did continue to stare at her, but his eyes were so hot and angry she wished he'd look elsewhere.

"Are you going into Whitehorn to see Mary Lou?" she whispered.

"You're pregnant…with another man's child… you won't even tell me who *he* is…then you say you thought you loved him...and *you're* jealous?''

"Maybe." To admit such a vulnerable, indefensible emotional reality was a first for her.

His eyes flamed blue. They were a perfect match with the sky. "You want the truth. All right. I'm taking the day off. The whole damn day, and I intend to do whatever I feel like doing. I'll see whoever I feel like seeing. Mary Lou... Whoever... I'm not married. I don't have to answer to anybody. Or to *you.*"

"Which is the way you like it, I'll bet."

"No. It's the way it is. I intend to enjoy myself, too."

"Doing what?" She paused, trying to restrain herself. "Getting somebody pregnant?"

"No! But if I did, I'd marry her, damn you."

"That's easy to say!" she shouted.

"I would!"

He looked so smugly self-righteous she wanted to slap him. All the guilt and shame brought back the black desolation that had driven her to seek Abby's comfort. And then Kirk's understanding. Always, always Felicity had wanted kindness, friendship and love. Only she had no idea how to get it. What she had found instead was the most shattering disillusionment.

"Oh! You think you're perfect. And that life's a neat, simple process...that you know all the answers all the time. Well, you don't. All my life I was this protected little princess. I lived in a bubble. Then I

got out into the real world, and I made a mistake...about a man. I admit that.''

"A damn big mistake.''

"One I'll have to live with for the rest of my life,
but I intend to make the best of it, too. *I want this
baby! More than I've ever wanted anything!* I don't
care who you see or what you do! Just go! Stay away
forever, for all I care!''

"I don't need your permission to live my life,''
he yelled.

"I was right about you,'' she said. "You're just
like *him.*''

"No, missy. I *did* get a girl pregnant. But I married
her!''

"What happened?''

"It's a long...tragic story.'' His voice was deeper,
gruffer. His eyes held a sadness reaching far beyond
sympathy. "Not one of my favorites, either.'' She
studied the grooves running from his handsome nose
to his lips. "What good are regrets?'' he murmured.
His tone was suddenly cautious, suspicious, vulnerable. "Why should I tell you a damn thing, when
you won't give me the time of day?''

Her eyes clung to his, but his face seemed made
of stone, set against her. He gave her nothing more.

She felt her control slipping. So, bunching Kitty
Mother in her arms, Felicity rose to her full height
and then fled the garden and him for the attic with
its dormer windows where she began reading that
section in Louise's diary that dealt with the arduous
making of her wedding gown. Later she came to a

section where Louise described packing her gown away in a trunk so that it could be worn by her daughter. But Louise had had five robust sons and not one daughter. Had no one ever worn the gown again—until that day she'd found it and tried it on?

Only later when Felicity had finished that particular diary, and she knew for sure Kirk had gone, did she and Kitty Mother venture outside again. Then Blackie was there, skinny as ever, dirty in his gardening outfit, saying Kirk had sent him to do anything she might want, to lift anything heavy, to vacuum the house even.

"Like I hired on to be a lady's maid," he grumbled.

"I have a mind to set you to dusting all the living-room knickknacks," she teased. "Abby'd kill you if you broke one."

He shuddered.

Part of Felicity wanted to send the old reprobate packing—if only because Kirk had sent him. But part of her welcomed his irreverent, lazy company. If Kirk's prime failing was his curiosity, it was a failing she shared. She had questions about Kirk, and she suspected Blackie could supply the answers.

Thus, she offered him a beer, knowing he had a weakness for the brew, and hoping it would loosen his tongue. And later as they pruned and treated the roses to an all-organic top-dressing of chicken manure, blood meal, unbleached bonemeal and green sand, she asked Blackie all the questions that had been festering in her mind, ever since Kirk had said he'd conceived a child and married the mother.

"You've known Kirk awhile—"

Blackie chuckled. "Since he was no more'n knee high."

"How come he never went to college or settled down?"

"Oh, he did—both them things." He shot her a long perceptive look. "Had a talent for 'em, too." He paused to scratch his head. "You know I'm feeling a might thirsty...after all this hard work out here in the sun—"

He hadn't worked more than ten minutes, and most of that in the shade.

She ignored his hint. "So, he did go to college?"

"On college loans 'cause his grades were so good, but then his girl back home got herself into trouble. Hey—what's this blood meal for? It's heavy as lead. My back's gonna go out if I carry one more sack."

"It's an excellent nitrogen source." Felicity wrinkled her brows when he dumped too much out, and dust flew everywhere. "You were telling me about Kirk."

Blackie shot her a sly glance. "You know, Felicity, my throat's plum parched. Kirk might not take to me talking about his personal—"

"Why don't I just run in and get you another beer while you empty that sack?"

Blackie beamed at her. "Took you long enough to take a hint. And while you're up, why don't you bring two? Keep you from having to run back for a third.''

"I—I won't be a second," she promised. Then she dashed into the kitchen, returning almost instantly with one bottle.

"Just one?" He took it grumpily.

"You were saying Kirk went to college—"

"I was saying he doesn't like me gossiping about him."

"Why? I won't tell."

Blackie took a long, regretful swig. "You're mighty stingy with your beers."

"You're mighty stingy answering my questions."

"Oh, all right," he agreed, still miffed. "You're just like my Sheila. You're gonna keep pecking at me till I talk, I reckon. So, here goes... Her parents were wealthy, see? Thought he wasn't good enough. Did everything to break them up. Then when she got pregnant, they wanted her to get an abortion."

Felicity's hand went protectively to her stomach. "Oh, dear—"

"But Kirk dropped out of college and convinced Lisa to marry him. She was pretty as a picture but so young. She wasn't ready for motherhood or marriage. Neither was he. Well, Kirk married her anyway. Somehow he worked and took care of the baby, but she was just too young for married life, and it wasn't too long before she got herself a boyfriend."

"Oh—"

"Lisa wanted the kind of life she was used to. One

thing led to another till they were hollering at each other all the time.''

"That's no good.''

"After the divorce, her father saw to it that Lisa got the baby. I think she wanted it just 'cause Kirk did. Then she and the baby were killed in a car accident at an unmarked railroad crossing. Kirk was so devastated by the loss of his daughter that he told me over and over he never wanted to love anybody or anything so much again. You should see that child's grave. There's a stone dollhouse just like the one he built her to play with. Stone lambs because she loved her stuffed lambs so much. And the inscription he had carved still brings tears to my eyes, and I ain't sentimental.''

"Oh…''

"He didn't go back to college. He didn't do much of anything for a while but live wild and bad like he was mad at the world. Sometimes, like on her birthdays, he'd lie out on top that child's grave all night long.''

Felicity remembered her mother's grave. She'd wanted to die, too, and maybe a part of her had. Till…she'd met Kirk.

"He's recovered on the surface, but he's worked damned hard not to care too deeply for anybody again. Those deaths marked him, though, made him a soft touch.''

Felicity stared at a glistening dewdrop that looked like a tear in the velvet center of a soft Bourbon rose. Her baby was already so precious to her; she couldn't imagine the pain of losing a child. And yet she could. The fear of it haunted her in the dead of the night. Sometimes it even caught her by surprise in the middle of the day.

"I guess he sees love—real love—as a trap. I can't say I blame him. I saw what it did to him. That's why he's so hell-bent on chasing lots of girls, so nobody's ever special. But you know, he's not nearly so irresponsible in other areas of his life. He's got a lotta money. Invested, too. In the market, land, bonds, I don't know what all. He's smart that way. Reads about that boring stuff all the time. Never gambles, either. Won't touch cards. He lives in that cabin 'cause he prefers a simple life out here. Not because he can't afford a bigger house in town."

He'd married the girl who'd had his baby. He'd loved his daughter with his whole being. He'd been running from his feelings just like she had. Only he'd hidden his pain behind a smile and flirtatious manner.

She'd been wrong about him.

Maybe she was book-smart, but she wasn't too talented at figuring men.

It was closing time at Susie's, but Kirk wasn't near ready to go. The dimly lit bar was way more fun than he remembered, he thought blearily.

Cowboy hats hung on wall pegs and on the back of every chair. Good thing, too. He hadn't been in the rough bar five minutes before three bikers with big purple spiders stitched into the backs of their dirty leather jackets had swaggered up to him, kicked his chair and then threatened to break his legs if he didn't give them his table.

"Be my guest, boys," he'd taunted with the jaunty grin that had gotten him into a lot of fights without half trying. "Sit down! Or move your ugly asses. You're blocking my view of the ladies." Kirk leaned back in his spindly chair, daring them to kick it out from under him. "I bet I got more friends in here than you do. Don't I, cowboys?" he hollered to nobody in particular, not caring much whether anybody answered.

"Yo, Kirk!" the nearest table of out-of-work cowboys yelled back in assent. "He's with us," they yelled meaningfully, issuing a threat to the mean-looking trio in black leather.

"You guys must be new to Susie's," Kirk said, beaming up at the fiercesome threesome, cockier now that he knew for sure the cavalry would be coming. He'd fired at least two members of the cavalry for rustling. Good thing they were too drunk to remember their grudge against him.

When the trio got bored with him and shuffled toward a table in the corner, Kirk started eyeing the ladies again. They were prettier and way friendlier than Kirk remembered. Especially Susie, who looked big and soft and all woman in her tight-knit, black top. Or maybe the girls just seemed prettier because he'd gotten drunk so fast and worked so hard to stay that way.

Had he spent the past two nights here? Or just tonight? Hell. Time was a most perverse thing to figure even sober. It went slow when you wanted it to go fast and fast when you'd have liked slow better. What difference did it make anyway? He didn't have to answer to a living soul. And he hadn't, either. Not since Tina had died.

No more difficult highbrows for him he thought fuzzily as he lifted his beer mockingly in a salute at a neon-lit beer sign that kept blinking off and on as if it had a short.

Especially no more pregnant ones, he vowed silently to those same blue strips of light. The female mind was none too logical at the best of times; the pregnant female didn't think. She was driven by her hormones.

Then Susie walked by him in slinky black jeans and that stretchy top, and he made a slow, assessing sweep of her figure. She made a little shriek when he grabbed her and shouted at the weary group of bearded musicians who were packing their instruments, ordering them to play one more rock song.

"They're through for the night. I already paid 'em, honey." Susie's low purr had the raspy quality of a contented cat.

"Sugar, you promised to save the last dance for me."

A smile edged the corners of her glossily painted lips. Her face was exotic, feline, somehow, like her voice. "Your drunken mind is playing tricks on you again. You haven't been here in a spell. Then you come and drink me out of house and home. You flirt and dance with every girl— I nearly had to throw

you out for picking two fights— Naughty.
Naughty—''

"Is a lecture any way to show appreciation to your
best customer?"

"I'm closin', and you're in no condition to drive.
Could I call someone?"

One of the bikers in spider garb guffawed.

"Hell, our Susie's turning into one of them coffee
cup psychologists."

"Our mommy, too," another taunted.

"I don't drink coffee!" Susie snapped, wriggling
free of Kirk. "I'll have you know I read women's
magazines! I ain't nobody's mother either."

"Sor-reee!" said a cowboy who belonged to the
cavalry. "If it was up to me, I'd say Conroy's just
back to being his wild, fun-loving, old self."

"Damn right I am," Kirk bellowed as he pulled
Susie out onto the dance floor. "Now you tell 'em
to play our song."

"I'm calling you a ride. That's what I'm gonna
do."

"How about you driving me to your place,
sugar?"

She studied him as appraisingly as he'd studied
her. "Now there's an idea," her smoky voice teased.

Then somebody put a quarter in the jukebox and
heavy rock music assaulted them, throbbing in Kirk's
blood along with the alcohol.

They danced, if you could call it that, for they just
stood still, holding each other very tightly, swaying

in time to the beat, as cowboys and bikers stomped in time and cheered loudly.

"Get on a table, Susie," somebody yelled.

One of the guys dressed in a spider jacket said, "Take it off. Take it all off!"

"Let's git," Susie said, seizing Kirk's hand.

It was late—2:00 a.m. But Felicity was up—reading, or rather flipping pages of Louise Derringer's diary.

Kirk had been gone two days and most of tonight. Where was he?

When she saw headlights at the gate flash against her window shade, she arose. When those headlights slowly veered at the fork, turning toward his cabin, she got up and walked hurriedly downstairs. From the porch she raced toward his house.

The night was dark and cool. By the time she reached the truck, her heart was beating rapidly and she was shivering.

When he didn't get out, she grew more worried. She went to the driver's side and pulled the door open.

"Kirk—"

"Well, hello there—" a woman with indecently bright red hair purred. "You his welcoming committee, honey? Or are you the reason he's in this sorry condition?"

"I—I—"

"Well, come on. It's gonna take two of us to get him into his house and into his bed."

Felicity recoiled in embarrassment. "I—I'm not supposed to lift anything heavy."

As she leaned closer once again, the stench of cheap booze and cigarettes that filled his cab made her slightly nauseous.

Felicity had a confused impression of Kirk's black head resting too familiarly at an odd angle against the woman's bosom. And was that glossy stuff on his dark cheek lipstick?

"Kirk—"

"Felicity, honey—" he grumbled, smiling at her drunkenly. "What are you doing in Susie's?"

He appeared to be in a semiconscious state at best.

"Look..." Felicity's expression turned guarded and uncertain. "I—I didn't realize he was with—"

"My being here doesn't mean anything."

"Maybe not to him...or to you... But..." Felicity's unhappy voice trailed away as she began backing toward the house.

It was over.

He was as bad as she'd thought he was.

Maybe worse.

Chapter 7

Felicity started in her bed at the click of hard, cowboy boot heels climbing the stairs outside and stomping purposefully across her front porch. When a huge, male fist slammed hard against the solid door frame, she jumped. Next her doorbell chimed. Again and again. When she didn't answer, a deep, familiar voice started hollering.

"Open up, Felicity!"

"Go away," she whispered, cowering under her cotton sheets a while longer.

"Damn your hide, girl, open the door!"

His screaming and banging on her front door caused a mighty tension to form between her shoulder blades.

She went to her window and raised the sash. "Go away!" she called down to him.

When her gentle command only made him bang his fist drunkenly and repeatedly against the door, she removed one of Chayce's golf clubs from the bag in her closet and scampered downstairs.

"You're going to wake the whole ranch up, you hear!" she snapped from her side of the door.

"So be it!" he hollered back, jamming and flattening his dark, handsome face into a ludicrous shape against her windowpane.

"I've got a golf club!" she threatened.

His drunken smile was lopsided. "What the hell for, honey?"

They fell silent for a spell, but neither retreated.

Finally she cautiously cracked the door. "So, where's your redheaded girlfriend?"

Kirk swore silently as he ran a hand over the crown of his glossy, black head. "Oh, Felicity, she's not my... Hell, honey, what are you planning to do with that thing—brain me?" He took the golf club and set it inside the door. "Susie's gone home where she belongs. She owns a bar. All she did was drive me here. Designated driver...so I wouldn't kill somebody. Hell, I told her I drive better under the influence." He grinned again. "Now, I'll have to get my truck back tomorrow."

"You're drunk."

Their eyes clashed for long, charged seconds.

"Yes, very," he admitted ruefully. "I'm sorry. It's not something I do on a regular basis."

"You'd better go somewhere now. And sleep it off."

"How about right here, honey?"

Her foolish heart started clamoring. The heat in his gaze told her how much he still wanted her. "I don't think that's such a good idea—"

"Well, maybe I do." He pushed against the door, and she backed farther inside, allowing him to come in. "And maybe I'm gonna have my way for a change."

"Kirk Conroy—"

"It's what we both want, isn't it, honey?"

He grabbed her and pulled her close. She managed to wedge a hand against his chest, but he was so strong he held her effortlessly no matter how she pushed and tugged to get loose. "You're so damned beautiful. Why do you have to be so damned beautiful?" he whispered.

Why, oh, why did the agonized hunger in his passionate, low voice have to stir her so?

"I wasn't with that girl, honey. Not like you want to think. The fact is I haven't been much of a man that way since you got here. Not that I haven't tried. Made a fool of myself, too. There were girls enough at Susie's. Pretty ones. But none of them turned me on...not the way you do. They sensed it, too."

"Oh, so that's my prime talent. You make what you feel for me sound so cheap."

"You've got way more schooling than me. Maybe you'd better start polishing my lines, so we'll get along better. All I know is what I feel for you. It's hot. And it's intense. You've about driven me crazy, girl. I want you all the time."

"Then how come you stayed away two days."

"So, you were keeping count?"

She looked away.

"Well, so was I. And I couldn't stay away more'n two, or I would've. I swore a long time ago I'd never have anything to do with another kid. They get to me in a way nothing else can. But it wasn't just your kid. I stayed away 'cause I wanted to forget you, too. But I wanted you so bad, I didn't even care all that much if you're pregnant with another man's child. I'm willing to try to understand how you got in this mess. I even want to help you. That's why they scare me. As I see it, maybe I've been a coward too damned long. What kind of man runs from what he wants most? I accused you of running. Well, I've been running, too. Maybe there's only one solution for you and your baby…and for me."

"What is it?"

"It's pretty desperate."

"So?"

"Marry me."

"Just like that?"

"You probably want me on bended knee with a velvet black box—"

"No. I'd rather you were sober and thinking clearly. This is all too complicated—"

"No. Smart people…people who read books all the time the way you do like to make everyday stuff complicated. The fact is you want me and I want you and you're expecting a baby. Your baby would be better off if I was in the picture."

"Look, nobody's forcing—"

"That's right. I want you. And I'm asking you to marry me. I'll love your baby as much as any baby you and I ever have."

"You're drunk."

"Honey, we settled that point. You're repeating yourself unnecessarily."

"You don't know the first thing about me—"

"Whose fault is that? I've been trying as hard as I know how to get to know you. What do you say…to my honorable proposition?"

"Proposal," she said, correcting him.

"Well?"

"Ask me again in the morning."

"That's better than a no." He managed a charming grin despite his inebriated state. "You gonna allow your fi-an-cé to sleep over?"

"You're not my fiancé…not yet anyway."

His voice turned a shade silkier. "Well—are you…gonna let me stay?"

"Yes."

"Now that sure beats a no by a long shot."

Her heart raced when he lowered his mouth to hers. It didn't matter that his breath tasted of beer or that his skin and hair smelled of cigarettes. His mouth was hot, eager, demanding more of her than she had given any man.

He crushed her closer, his mouth traveling through her thick, brown hair, down her cheek. She closed her eyes on a muted sigh when he began to suck gently at the base of her neck. She was finding way too much pleasure in his thrilling kisses and in the hard, needy way he pressed her against the wall so that she intimately felt how aroused he was.

This was crazy.

But it felt wonderful, too.

He slid a bold, denim-clad thigh between her legs.

"It would be nice if you kissed me back for a change," he said, "since it's very likely you'll be my fiancée by morning."

"Oh, it would?"

But when she complied, he jolted back against the front door, trembling so violently she smiled dreamily, feeling very powerful and desirable, indeed, to have shocked him so. "We'd better stop," he said tersely. "Unless you have a mind to go further—"

Her eyes snapped open. "I never thought a man like you would suggest we stop—"

"You're important to me, honey." Gently he cradled her face in his hands. "I asked you to marry me, didn't I? I said I'd be a daddy again. Some man hurt you real bad. Well, I know what it's like to be hurt. I don't want to hurt you the same way he did. I'm willing to go slow— I'll do anything...to win you."

She was touched, more than she wanted him to know. Her feelings scared her because if their relationship didn't work, she was going to lose a big piece of herself in this wide-open rangeland of Montana.

"I think you're right. I think we should slow things down."

Reluctantly she led him up the stairs and opened the door to a guest bedroom. At his door, he gathered her close again, but this time he kept his mouth and touch gentle as he kissed her good-night. And his willingness to let her go, only made her want to stay with him all the more. The hardest thing she ever did was to close that door while he stood there watching her with those hot, dark eyes of his.

In her own room, she slid between her cool cotton sheets and stretched out. She closed her long-lashed eyes and tried not to think of Kirk in the next room. But as she lay in the shadowy dark, sleep didn't come. Instead her desire for him flamed more wildly. Her blood pulsed like a lava flow, and she began to hope against hope that he would forget himself and his gentlemanly stance as she was forgetting herself, that he would come to her, strip her, and pull her close. She wanted to surrender to this throbbing madness that seeped from her womb to every cell in her body, to this fierce urgency that made her shiver even though she was burning up beneath her covers.

She wanted his tongue, hot and seeking inside her mouth, just as she wanted the impossible sensual pleasure of his long, lean body covering hers and plunging deeply into her again and again until they were both sated and could lie together limp and warm, tangled in each other's arms and legs.

Finally she drifted to sleep, but even then she dreamed of him. Then some sound outside awoke her. Fred tore around the side of the house, toenails ripping into the wooden porch, barking loud and long, and she jumped up from her bed. Was it instinct, fear or desire that sent her running on light, bare feet straight to his room?

Kirk started expectantly the very instant she opened his door, as if he'd been dreaming of her, too, wanting her.

"Felicity—"

The raw, velvety way he said her name in the gilded dark made her ache with desire. Then she was flying across the room, and he was folding her into his hard, warm arms, covering her with his blankets. His skin was hot. His mouth was immediately on hers, his tongue inside, coaxing hers into a mating dance with his. He had brushed his teeth, and the clean minty flavor of toothpaste now mingled with that of beer. He had showered, and his warm skin smelled deliciously of soap.

He kissed her face, her throat. Then his mouth and tongue trailed everywhere until she felt herself glowing inside and out, until she felt as fierily radiant beneath his mouth as a living coal. His every kiss, his lightest breath just fanned her hotter. She said his name in that velvet dark, and he said hers in a breathless way that made it sound so infinitely precious.

When he finally entered her, he stopped and grew still deep inside her, and she sensed a rightness in their union she had never felt before. He made her forget every man and every love that had gone before him. His lovemaking was expert and yet tender, violent and yet gentle, erasing all past loves and lovers. She grew hotter and hotter, and they came together, exploding at the same moment in a mutually shocking eruption of exquisite, erotic pleasure.

Afterward she lay quietly in his arms, burning with wonder and a lingering afterglow of emotion. She felt alive in a way she'd never felt before. When he fell asleep, sated, she lay in the dark admiring the inky blackness of his brows, the glossiness of his hair, and the utter perfection of his muscular body.

She awoke at dawn and found him sleeping still. She smiled, remembering the wild abandoned things he'd done to her, the intimacies they'd shared that she'd never shared in exactly the same way with another. Slowly she arose. She hoped she was not being a fool again, but for the life of her she could not keep herself from loving him.

Pulling on a robe she went downstairs, first to the kitchen, nearly stumbling over Fred. Then she stepped out onto the porch. She had only a moment to admire the fiery dawn and maroon sky as the sun peeped over the mountains. Then a rough arm snaked out of the shrubbery by the porch and roughly circled her throat. "Morning, ma'am. I'd sure like a cup of coffee—"

The drifter!

Panic knifed through her.

Where was that worthless Fred? Then she remembered—the kitchen. Would Kirk be sober or alert enough to defend her if she screamed?

She wished she had a gun or that golf club, but since she didn't, she did what any sensible, unarmed, pregnant woman under such circumstances would do—she bit the blue-and-green dragon tattooed on that lean arm that choked her, gagging on the man's unclean, hairy flesh. When he roared in pain and flung her hard against the swing, she screamed in mortal terror that he might have hurt the baby.

"I'm pregnant!" she whispered.

"Witch!" He lunged toward her, too furious to care, but just as he leapt, something orange and furry flew in front of him, tripping him.

"Bastard!" Kirk yelled, storming naked out of the house with a golf club raised over his head just as Felicity pushed the swing with all her might.

The drifter's eyes bulged as he fell forward into the fast-moving swing. Staggering, he grabbed the railing, pulled himself back on his feet and ran as if he'd seen an apparition from hell, and since Kirk didn't have a stitch on, and the morning was a chilly one, he didn't give chase.

Instead he pulled Felicity into his arms. "You okay?"

"He scared me pretty badly, but I'm okay."

"I think we scared him pretty bad, too. I don't think he's coming back anytime soon."

"If Kitty Mother hadn't made him trip—"

"I'm the hero!" Kirk bellowed. "Not that mangy cat!"

"Of course you are, darling!" She kissed his cheek. "Why, if you hadn't come out—"

"That cat!" he grumbled, still upset to have been upstaged even for a second. "Where is that no-good Fred?"

"Fast asleep in the kitchen," she said. "I guess we'd better call the law."

"Not till I make love to you again. Holding you close again has got my adrenaline pumping."

Her gaze fell, and she smiled. "More than your adrenaline, I'd say."

"Last night was fun," he murmured.

"For me, too."

Then he started kissing her.

"I think we'd better get inside," she said, "before somebody sees you and gets scared or figures out how pretty you think I am first thing on a cold morning."

He laughed.

They didn't make it to the bedroom, but their sex was even hotter than the night before. When she told him so, he laughed conceitedly, taking full credit. "It'll get better and better, I promise you."

Then he went upstairs and fell asleep, but Felicity couldn't sleep. So, she got up and dressed and went back downstairs where she found Blackie on her porch, with a worrisomely eager gleam in his eyes as if he were chock-full of embarrassing news to impart.

"I'll be collecting a fat reward," he said. "Two thousand bucks! Enough to get my truck out of hock."

"For what?"

Blackie seemed to be eyeing the golf club by the door with an unusual amount of interest. The look he gave her after that made her blush.

"Why, for catching that drifter and turning him over to the law. The jerk ran straight into me—so hard he knocked himself out when he pitched over headfirst."

Felicity stared at him.

"Now you won't believe the tale that worthless individual started telling the law just as soon as he came to—"

Oh, dear. Her cheeks flamed when Blackie lifted the club and began to run his hand up and down it as if it was a cat and he was stroking it.

He gave her another sly look. "Why, he says a naked man ran out of this house and chased him with a golf club. Described him as being about Kirk's height with black hair. Described the most intimate parts of the man's anatomý with amazin' detail. Said the fella has a mole right by his—"

She snatched the club. "Now why would the fool go and make up something crazy like that?"

Blackie shook his head, but his eyes sparked. "He said the naked man had blue eyes. Now who do we know that fits that description?"

She made a low, choked sound.

"Kirk wouldn't be here, by chance? This here wouldn't be that golf club—"

"Just exactly what do you want? I'm sure you've got something better to do than stand around here telling me some drifter's lies and asking me silly questions."

Blackie looked dubious. "Yes, ma'am. But *if* you

do see Kirk, would you tell him I'm looking for him?''

She scowled at the impudent skunk, an appellation she'd hadn't thought fit...till that moment. ''Sure— *If* I see him—''

''*If*'ll do, ma'am.'' Blackie waved goodbye and gave her a toothy, too-friendly smile.

Chapter 8

Felicity heard the crew laughing from the other side
of the tall cottonwoods. It was their noon camp, the
herd was grazing in the pasture to the west of the
house. The hands had set coolers out under the trees,
and the scent of hot coffee and smoke and fresh beef
wafted in the air.

The men were eating and chatting in the deep
shade of the trees. Thus, they didn't see her approaching in her pale, pastel dress, carrying a platter
of deviled eggs, tuna sandwiches and freshly baked
chocolate chip cookies. When Kirk had awakened,
and she'd blushingly told him that Blackie was looking for him and telling tales, he'd sworn softly. Then
he'd kissed her, saying he'd better handle that rascal
promptly and promising that he'd be back to propose
to her on bended knee when he finished work.

When she got close enough to hear the men ribbing one another good-naturedly, she smiled, intending to call to them. But before she could do so, she heard Blackie rasp her own name suggestively in the same lewd breath he snickered Kirk's.

Felicity stopped dead still and sank to her knees, holding her breath while the men laughed derisively.

"Naked? You've got to be kiddin'? With a golf club?" More rounds of crude laughter followed. "That's funny as hell!"

Felicity's heartbeat accelerated. Her grip on the platter weakened, and her deviled eggs slipped precariously toward the sandwiches and cookies.

"I ain't even got to the good part, boys. Don't you see that this means Conroy bedded her? I seen her face, this morning, too. Ever time I picked up that golf club, she turned as purple as a beet. Ain't seen any woman ever look or smile like she was more satisfied. You owe me, boys. So, pay up."

The noon air was brisk and crystal clear. Maybe that was why it pierced like icy-sharp needles against Felicity's hot, damp cheeks. The sunlight was shimmering in the leaves. Maybe that was why everything seemed to go blurry, and she had to blink back tears to see.

Beyond the trees, the land rolled before her in an undulating expanse of dips and swells toward the faraway mountains. Yet suddenly the brightness had gone out of the pretty day and the beauty out of the wondrous landscape. Felicity felt as trapped and pitiful as a wounded animal, as dolefully imprisoned as a caged coyote—and just as lost. Why couldn't she ever learn that her aunt and uncle had known what they were talking about? She should have stayed in the east and stuck to her own kind.

"When'd Conroy have time to bed her last night, you old fool?" Ryan demanded. "What makes you think he'd even want to? Why, he was picking fights with bikers and chasing every skirt at Susie's last night. He was liquored up pretty tight, and Susie was on his lap more'n she was tending bar. He went home with Susie, old fella."

"Why, any man would take Susie over Felicity," another hand said, pure envy in his awed, young voice as he conjured Susie's ample charms.

Perspiration rolled down Felicity's face and burned her eyes. Those weren't tears! They weren't!

Forgetting the platter, she let her hands fall to her sides. Sandwiches, deviled eggs and cookies rained down in an avalanche onto the long, dewy grasses. She threw the platter down on top the mess.

"Hey, Conroy!" one of the braver cowboys shouted. "Who'd you bed last night? Susie or Felicity? Or both?"

"You creep!" she wanted to scream. "How can you let them joke...about me...about us...." She imagined him sprawled before them as proud of his conquest of her as a male peacock, strutting before them, showing off. She imagined his wide, conceited grin, that could make her melt. And she felt fury and pain. So much pain.

Felicity never heard Kirk's murderous curse as he

sprang up, fist raised, faster than the speed of lightning. She never knew that his balled hand slammed into the other man's jaw and sent him reeling backward, and that even when three of his men jumped him and held him, he threatened everybody else with more of the same if they ever even thought of making light of Felicity's name again. Nor did she know that in the next breath he swore he'd marry her or die trying.

By the time he got to that last part, her hot tears were blinding her, and she was running headlong toward the house. She ran even after she got a stitch in her side. Ignorant of Kirk's rage and instant defense of her honor, she thought herself foolish to have believed even for a second, that their souls had blended as well as their bodies when they'd made love.

She stumbled several times, but always she picked herself up. She knew she wouldn't stop running till she got as far away as she possibly could from Montana and Kirk Conroy.

The evening stillness was broken by the clatter of the roan's hooves on the concrete barn floor. Kirk dismounted with a frown and tossed his reins toward Ryan.

Kirk hadn't finished work till six-thirty. He'd just found the platter and a few cookie crumbs on his way back and had grown anxious. Even though he stank of dust and leather and horses, he headed straight for the house to find out why she hadn't shown up for lunch.

He thought of Felicity and how she'd looked with her face aglow and her eyes shining with love in the early morning—before, during and after he'd made love to her. At the thought of returning to her, visions of her running to the door, hurling herself into his arms, feeling her hands close tightly around his neck as she stretched onto her tiptoes, her lips parting so he could kiss her.

But she didn't answer when he knocked. Nor did she come running when he pounded louder and hollered. When he finally got up the nerve to open the door, the house was as empty as a tomb. Odd, how he suddenly had the same sinking feeling in his gut as he'd had the day he'd come home and found Lisa and the baby gone.

Women! Men were such simple creatures compared to women. A man could leave a woman with a smile on her face in the morning and she could get sulky by nightfall, harboring some new grudge her wild imagination had manufactured against him. Why did a woman's mind fester when a man was off going about his business as innocently as a lamb?

Kirk knew she was gone, that the picture was black and bleak.

Still, he strode through the rooms, hoping against hope, shouting Felicity's name, determined to find her.

The shades in her bedroom were drawn. Everything was ominously neat and tidy.

Then he opened her closet and saw only empty hangers.

Downstairs on the freshly waxed kitchen table he found two envelopes. One had Abby's name on it. On the second he saw his own. She'd written Abby's, but she'd typed his.

He tore into his envelope and ripped out a thin sheet of paper covered in tiny, cramped swirls of blue ink.

Kirk

I've come to my senses since last night. I imagine you have, too. I won't hold you to promises made when you'd had too much to drink and I came into your bedroom and practically threw myself into your arms.

I always knew you weren't a one woman man—

He frowned. What the hell was that supposed to mean? He was damned tired of her assuming the worst about him.

So, don't worry about me.

I'm a big girl.

My mother left me a trust fund that's enough for me to live on the rest of my life and raise a dozen children.

Money! When would he ever learn? Rich people always put money before everything else. Didn't she know how much he'd love her and that baby? Didn't that matter at all? He wanted to build a life with her, to take care of her, to give her all the things her damned money couldn't buy!

So, don't worry about me or the baby. We'll do just fine on our own.

Felicity.

But what about him?

Her words were so cold. Kirk's face went as hard as stone as he shredded the letter and dropped the bits into the nearest wastebasket. Again, he remembered the long empty years after Lisa had left him and his dear little Tina had died.

Dear God.

How many long, dark nights had he lain awake or drunk himself into oblivion because he'd dreaded the next empty day? How many months, years even, had he simply existed. Then without warning Felicity had taught him to care again. She had no idea how afraid he'd been of falling in love. No idea of the desolate hell she'd plunged him back into by leaving him without even saying goodbye.

As if he were nothing to her.

Would he survive a second time?

There wasn't going to be a second time.

He had to find her.

But where would he look?

He didn't have the slightest idea where she might be.

He wondered if Abby knew.

Even if she did, he wasn't at all sure she'd tell him.

Chapter 9

Seven months.

The autumn had been brief, chilly, the winter long and bleak.

Even now that it was March, the days were still icy cold. Not that the storms were as long or as severe. The snow was thawing, and the days were getting longer and warmer. Miraculously emotions that Kirk had believed dead forever, like hope, had begun to burn brighter.

At first after Felicity had gone, Kirk had been bitterly angry and too deeply hurt to think clearly. Slowly, however, his love for her had conquered his utter, dark hopelessness. After all, she wasn't dead. He had only to find her.

He began to hope that Felicity might relent and phone him. He began to believe that if he could just talk to her, everything would be all right.

But she hadn't called.

He'd told himself that in time he'd quit missing her.

But he hadn't.

Abby and Chayce had been furious at him at first, blaming him for Felicity's disappearance. But finally when they saw how miserable he was, Abby took pity on him and gave him the only address she knew, that of Felicity's aunt and uncle in D.C.

"Not that it'll do you any good to see them," Abby had warned. "They'd be dead set against someone like you."

Somebody like him.

He'd remembered Lisa's parents humiliating him.

How right Abby had been.

He had resisted the impulse to bolt for Washington, but in the end, he'd made the trip. The ten minutes he'd stood outside their mansion staring at their verdant lawn gathering his courage had felt like a century. Finally he'd rung the bell, and after a long time Felicity's uncle had opened their grand door. The man's troubled frown had only gotten colder and darker after Kirk introduced himself.

The uncle had neither introduced himself nor shaken his hand. Instead, he'd led him silently down a long hall past a series of museum-quality rooms to some sort of formal sitting room and ordered him to sit down on a spindly, antique chair. The uncle sat down and stared at him, letting the silence lengthen in an unfriendly way.

The frail-looking aunt, whom the uncle had summoned from the back of the house, had had an equally imperious look, with thick silver hair, and parchment-pale skin. She had a habit of touching her forehead and wrinkling her brow as if she had a splitting headache whenever something unpleasant was said.

The uncle had begun the interview on a note of sharp impatience that had brought the aunt's thin hand fluttering to her knitted brow.

"You wasted your time coming here. I don't know where Felicity is, and I don't care to know. Oh, she came here at the end of last summer...told us all about the baby...as if she hoped we'd condone that sort of thing and take her in. She said she was thrilled. I threw her out, of course. She was *her* sister's child."

Again the aunt's thin fingers pressed themselves between her now-closed eyes. The gesture had held genuine agony.

"Just tell me where Felicity is, and I'll go."

"I'm sure," the uncle said, disbelieving him. "You're here, pretending you want to do the honorable thing. Well, I don't believe that for a minute. You probably got her pregnant on purpose, so you could get at her money. I've dealt with gold diggers like you before. Your kind never has the slightest guilt about what they do. You've ruined her. She'll never be able to hold up her head in her world again."

"Her world?"

"He means our world," said the aunt in a low,

cultured voice. The large-knuckled, age-spotted hand at the forehead was shuddering visibly.

"*The only* world that matters," the uncle said.

"Is that so?" Kirk had stood up and stared wearily at the ornate room and its fabulous furnishings and original oil paintings. "This place feels dead. You people seem dead."

Despite the sadness Kirk felt, he was glad he'd come, for only now could he understand that sad, lost loneliness that had been at Felicity's center. Only now did he realize how much she needed him and how completely and irrevocably in love he was with her.

He *had* to find her.

"If you change your mind, give her this." Kirk pulled an envelope with a letter in it from his suit jacket pocket. "I love her, and I want to marry her." Before he could hand his letter to the worried aunt, the uncle snatched it, tore it in two and pitched the twin halves forcefully toward a gilt trash receptacle.

Then the uncle stepped between him and the can. "I suggest that when you leave my house today you never think of this family or my niece again. I invite you, however, to stop by my office at the end of the hall before you go, where I will write you a check. I think that the sum of, say, one hundred thousand dollars, should be a satisfactory compensation for your role as a sperm donor."

The aunt's eyes popped open at this insult. Hot, angry blood rushed into Kirk's cheeks, and he took a step toward the man. It was on the tip of his tongue to yell at him what he could do with his money. Only with the greatest effort did he restrain himself.

"I don't want your money, mister," he said quietly. "All I want is Felicity."

"You may think you're holding out for higher stakes," the older man sneered. "If you walk out of here with nothing, that's all you'll ever get."

"So be it then." On a note of dark, suppressed rage, Kirk stood up. "You stupid bastards. Can't you see, you're turning your back on the only person who might really ever give a damn about you? Felicity and the baby need you. All the money and position in the world can't give you half as much joy as she and that baby might."

The aunt's hand fluttered again, but they said nothing.

Kirk strode out of the room, down the long hall and out of the mansion.

Where the hell was Felicity?

Would he ever be able to find her again?

When Kirk hired a private detective, and the man failed to find her after a month of trying, Kirk felt near the end of his rope. Then, only three days later, Abby received a letter from Manhattan. Blackie, who had carried the mail from the box to the house every afternoon, had raced eagerly to Kirk's cabin.

Kirk had just burned his supper so badly Kitty Mother, her half-grown kittens and Fred hadn't even bothered to sniff the pot when he set it on the floor.

"She finally wrote her," Blackie said without pre-amble.

Kirk whirled. "What the hell are you talking about?"

"Felicity—"

Kirk grabbed his hat from the peg and pushed past him.

"Ain't you gonna stay and have a beer—"

"No! And don't you help yourself to one, either! You're the cause of this, old man! You and your lousy bet! Don't think I haven't thought this thing out and come to the conclusion that Felicity was coming out to see me for lunch when she dropped that platter. She heard what you said about collecting that bet! She heard the men laugh. She was shamed and humiliated to the core."

For once Blackie had the decency to look shame-faced. "Women have no right to be so dad-burned sensitive and difficult about sex. She's even worse than Sheila. I didn't mean nothin'. Neither did the other boys."

"You never mean nothin', you old fool. But you sure do cause trouble. It's bad enough how you've messed up Sheila's life, but if you're smart, you'll stop meddling in my affairs."

"Where is she, Abby?" Kirk pleaded.

"She told me very specifically not to tell you."

"So, she did mention me?"

"Only in a negative way."

Well, that was something. "Show me her letter."

"It was addressed to me."

"Show me!"

"Doing that might cost me my best friend."

"Don't you want her to be happy?"

"What kind of question is that? You broke her heart."

"I didn't do any such thing. There was a simple misunderstanding."

"She mentioned that bet again. Her handwriting shook. Like she's still not over that."

"Damn Blackie. I never was in on that."

"If you hurt her like that again, ever, I swear, I'll kill you."

"I love her. I want her to be my wife."

"Tell *her*. Not me."

"I would. If I knew where she was. Now are you going to show me that letter—"

"She told me she never wanted to see you again."

Like all women, she was determined to drag out the moment when she held power.

"She told me that she would raise her little girl without a father."

"So, she has a little girl?" For an instant he remembered the wild, thrilling joy he'd felt at Tina's birth. If only he could have been with Felicity. If only he could have helped her when she brought the baby home. "What's her name?" he whispered.

"Jackie. She named her after her mother who died when she was a little girl—Jacqueline. She has dark hair like Felicity and like her mother. And long fingers, too, just like they had."

In his mind's eye Kirk had a vision of a tiny little feminine creature with soft dark curls bundled in a pink blanket in Felicity's arms.

"How long are you going to torture me like this, Abby? Where is she?"

Still, Abby held him in suspense. "I wouldn't tell you where she is now...if I couldn't hear the misery underneath her bright wordy sentences or if I hadn't watched you mope around and act so miserable all winter. Chayce says you're not worth killing as a foreman."

"Damn it, Abby! Are you going to lecture me, or are you going to tell me where the hell she is?"

"I'm not going to tell you. I'm going to take you there myself because I don't entirely trust you even yet, even if you have adopted Kitty Mother and her litter."

"Damn."

What did a man have to do?

Whatever it was, he'd do it.

Chapter 10

Felicity's pied-à-terre was on the fashionable Upper East Side in New York's prestigious Carlyle Hotel. At first Kirk was put off by the stately, forty-story, brick-and-limestone tower with its 1930s glamour and by the lobby's black-and-ivory-marble floors and creamy classical decor.

"Relax," Abby whispered after she'd talked to Felicity. "She's not going to lynch you."

Their flight had been long and bumpy. Fatigue drained Kirk's muscles. He felt heavy and tired. The glamour of the building added to his discomfort because he felt like a fish out of water in his jeans and cotton shirt. Especially when everybody else looked so cosmopolitan.

He was too tired to argue, so Abby said, "Here's the plan. She thinks I'm coming up. You go up instead."

"All by myself?"

"You're a big boy. She isn't going to physically hurt you."

"But—"

"Just knock on the door. Only not as hard as you usually do. Then let Mother Nature take her course."

"Mother Nature?"

"Kiss her, you big idiot! What could be easier?"

All the light went out of Felicity's eyes and smile the moment she saw him. First their gazes clashed. Then her gentle features froze in inchoate pain.

He hated startling her and scaring her like this. At the same time he felt drawn by the unusual mingling of strength and vulnerability in her delicate features.

"I love you," he whispered. "So much. Do you have any idea what you've put me through these past hellish months?"

She breathed in sharply. "What I've put *you* through? You always think everything is about you."

"No.... I've gone mad...worrying about you."

He saw the tears in her eyes as she tried to slam the door. Quick as a flash, he jammed his boot against the door frame.

"There's no reason not to hear me out, Felicity. I'll go in a minute or two, if you still want me to. I swear I will."

He went cold inside when he said that. Yet his fear heightened his senses and strengthened his resolve.

She lifted her shoulders in a defeated shrug, turned

with a cool indifference, and let him follow her inside.

She was slimmer, lovelier, but her apartment was
too cosmopolitan for his taste with its ebonized floors
and high black baseboards, crisp white walls, mir-
rors, modern art and antiques. The immaculate
kitchen had been done in stainless steel and granite.
He thought of his messy cabin with its views of the
mountains, with that cat and her kittens and Fred
swarming all over his porch.

This place reeked of old money and bone-deep
style. And yet in its own way, it felt even colder than
her aunt and uncle's mansion.

Hell, why had he come?

Suddenly he felt too far away from Montana and
its wide-open spaces. He almost missed her cat.

"Where's Abby?" she demanded.

"Downstairs." He forced the word through the
constricted muscles in his throat.

"I don't know why you bothered to come. You
got what you wanted." Felicity's voice broke.

"Oh, no, I didn't, honey."

Her eyes filled with tears. "You humiliated me."

"I'm sorry you were hurt. I don't like what those
guys said about us any more than you do. I took care
of it."

"You took care of it?" She averted her white face.
"What's that supposed to mean?"

Her fear restored a fraction of his male confidence
and cowboy swagger. Suddenly his mind cleared and
he remembered Abby's plan.

Kiss her, Conroy. That's your best hope. And the sooner, the better.

"Forget what they said. I love you," he whispered raggedly, torn by his desire and love for her and his terror of losing her.

Show her, Conroy. Quit trying to tell her.

Before she could protest, he had her in his arms, crushed against the solid wall of his chest.

She stiffened, but even so, she lifted her mouth to his. Even so her flesh melted against the hard feel of his body.

"Don't," she murmured, but her moist lips parted invitingly.

Her hands fluttered against his chest, to push him away, he thought. Instead they slowly curled into his collar and tugged him closer as if she wanted him and yet feared him.

As always, his hunger was a physical ache. Her perfume filled his nostrils. Abby had told him to kiss Felicity boldly and forcefully, to overpower her will to resist him.

Instead he ran his hands slowly through her silky, dark hair as if she were infinitely precious to him. He placed soft kisses on her eyelids, her cheek, her throat. Everything he did was tender and sweet. And, finally, slowly, oh, so slowly he kissed the corner of her mouth, waiting for her to invite him to do more.

"Why did you run from me?" he whispered on a breathless, agonized note. "Why did you leave me?"

"I—I didn't want to," she admitted huskily.

"Don't ever leave me again. You don't know what

I've been through in the past...how much that hurts.''

"Okay. I won't."

Their lips were so close. Their need grew so that the wanting inside him pounded like thunder. She placed her hands on either side of his face. Then she kissed him as boldly and as recklessly as Abby had commanded him to kiss her.

Waves of fire went through him when she arched her body to his. Then he was lost.

In no time at all they were naked on her sofa. She opened her body to his, and he sank down, down into her coiling heat, melting, dying. Then they stiffened and called out each other's names. And after those long months of suffering, their lovemaking forged anew their soul-deep bond.

Afterward she said, "My aunt sent me your letter. That's why I wrote Abby. I—I wanted you to come."

"Why didn't you write or call me?"

"Because I'm not too good at this. I don't chase—"

"Honey, we aren't playing a game. You're going to be my wife."

"You'll have to teach me how to make you happy."

"You're off to a rip-roaring good start. But...just tell me you love me."

"I love you."

"Tell me every single day for the rest of our lives."

"I promise. I love you. I love you. Anything else?"

"Now...kiss me again...and...and touch me... down there." He guided her hand between his legs.

A fierce pleasure burned in her eyes as she searched the hard planes of his face and saw that he wanted her more than he'd ever wanted her.

When she touched him again, a shock went through him. He had wanted to make love to her slowly, reverently. But he found he couldn't go as slowly as he'd wanted to. It was as if he was desperate, as if he were starved and had to make up for the last seven months of doing without.

Afterward, when they were both spent and sighing, she curled up against his chest. They slept and then they showered. She showed him the baby who looked just as cute in her pink blankets as he'd imagined.

"I wish I could have been with you when you gave birth," he said.

"Next time," she promised tenderly.

Then Jackie cried, and he picked her and her trailing pink blankets up and began to pace in the elegant apartment.

"Are you sure you want to leave all this?" he asked because he was no longer afraid of Felicity's answer.

"I love you. All I ever want is to be with you," Felicity said. "Forever."

"I'll make you happy, Felicity." Then he bent his face closer to the baby's. "You, too, my little darling."

Jackie squealed back at him as if she agreed.

Epilogue

Everybody was screaming for the beautiful, dark-haired bride to throw her bouquet.

Everybody except Blackie and Sierra and the bride's aunt and uncle.

Blackie was standing in a corner holding the bride's baby.

The bride's aunt was hovering over the infant because she didn't trust Blackie as far as she could throw him.

The bride's uncle stared at the crowd of rough Montanans with the stony expression of a man who felt very ill at ease. But he'd given the bride away at the altar, which had made Felicity very happy. And when no one was watching, he took quite an interest in the baby. He'd even offered the guest cottage behind his mansion to the bride and groom for their honeymoon.

Sierra stood beside Blackie, a frown on her pretty, tanned face even though the baby was cooing at her. Sierra had agreed to be a bridesmaid, if reluctantly. Not that she'd been a good sport about having her dark blond hair curled and piled on top of her head. And she'd complained quite loudly and colorfully at having to be laced into a corset and then stuffed into a tight, old-fashioned, green ruffled dress with scratchy lace ruffles. The gown was too short to boot, and Sierra kept scratching at her neck in a most unladylike fashion, saying that the ruffles tickled her chin.

Not that Felicity felt much sympathy for her. She, too, had had to squeeze herself into an antique gown, for she'd chosen to wear the one she'd found in Louise Derringer's trunk.

The bride and groom stood together on the stairs. Slowly Felicity lifted the bouquet to smell the tiny roses one last time before she tossed them to the waiting throng of women beneath her. Smilingly she remembered the last wedding when she was handed the bouquet and then fainted in Kirk's arms.

She'd been terrified of him that day.

How she loved him today.

And, oh, how he loved her.

She had been so terrified of his feelings and hers.

But, oh, how she gloried in those feelings now.

If only…she could throw the bouquet to the one girl who was as lonely and needed love as much as she had. If only the bouquet could bring equal magic into that girl's life.

Staring down at the pretty Mary Lou, Felicity raised her arm. But just before she tossed the bouquet, Kirk whispered a name in her ear and she hesitated.

They laughed together, sharing a secret.

Then she threw the bouquet.

Her aim was true.

Everybody cheered.

Everybody, that is, except the tomboy bridesmaid in green ruffles who caught the bouquet and ran.

Everybody, that is, except the bride and groom. They smiled at each other adoringly and then, unable to wait till they could be alone, their mouths and bodies melted together.

Kirk hugged Felicity to him.

He had told her how much he wanted her to be his wife, how much he wanted to be a daddy again, how this time he wasn't going to fail.

Their mouths clung.

They wanted to kiss each other endlessly.

And they could.

Because marriage meant forever.

COWGIRL BRIDE

Susan Mallery

Chapter 1

Sierra Conroy wasn't sure if it was the sharp cry or the flash of movement that caught her attention and she didn't much care. Before her mind finished registering what had happened, she'd already grabbed the rope hooked to her saddle and started racing toward the corral. The milling steers spelled trouble as clearly as a neon sign.

With an instinct honed by years spent on a ranch and in the rodeo, she dived into the melee of sharp horns and hooves. Someone called frantically from outside the corral, but she ignored that voice. Weaving between the annoyed animals, she searched until she saw something other than muscular shoulders, flashing tails and dust-covered hides. Her brief glimpse of jean-clad legs was enough to send her in that direction. She pushed her way through the corral.

"Steady," she said, speaking in a low voice designed to calm. Unfortunately whoever was in the pen with her wasn't equally at home with the restless steers. She felt the animals' growing tension.

Something flat and powerful butted her in the center of her back. She stumbled forward and bumped into a steer that bellowed in protest.

"Stay still!" Sierra called out. "I can't find you if you keep moving around."

More animals lowed in annoyance.

"Help me!" Terror laced the cry.

Sierra swore under breath. The steer next to her lowered its horned head to charge. She quickly ducked to the left, around another animal and saw a young boy being pushed and shoved by the unsettled herd.

"It's all right," she told him, reminding herself to smile, even as she felt the danger grow. "You're going to be just fine."

By God, that had better be true. She'd spent her entire life around big, ill-tempered animals and she refused to be trampled in a corral. The cowboys gave her enough grief about being a woman. When she received the bouquet at her brother's wedding a few weeks back, the men had tormented her for weeks. She wouldn't allow them the satisfaction of smirking at her funeral. Of course if she was dead would their attitudes really matter?

Before she could work that problem out, several of the steers shifted, giving her a clear path to the boy. She jogged to his side and wrapped her arms around him.

"Let's get going, kid," she said.

Out of the corner of her eye, she saw an arc of movement. Instinct again took over. She turned, shielding the child's slight body with her own. Pain exploded against her upper arm, sending both her and the child staggering. She ignored the bone-jarring jolt, the sick feeling in her stomach and the instant wet heat that told her she was bleeding. Steers had kicked her before, although it had been a long time. She'd nearly forgotten how badly it hurt. Of course the stitches wouldn't be much better. Why on earth had she thought this job would be fun?

"He kicked you," the kid told her.

"I figured that out already."

She continued to use her body as a shield while they made their way to the edge of the corral. One last steer lowered its head for a final charge. Sierra saw a man standing on the other side of the fence. Refusing to give in to the weakness creeping up her left arm, she bent over and grabbed the boy.

"Catch," she yelled and tossed him toward safety. At the last second possible, she spun on her heel and narrowly avoided a head-on collision with several hundred pounds of annoyed steak-on-the-hoof.

She staggered the last couple of feet and climbed out between wooden slats. Her legs gave way as soon as she reached safety. She leaned against a fence post and slid to the ground. When her butt hit packed earth, new blood trickled down her arm and she bit her tongue. The hell of it was, the morning wasn't even half over.

All she wanted to do was sit there until the aching stopped, but that wasn't an option. She had to check the cut on her arm. Maybe she wouldn't need stitches.

She nearly smiled at that one. There was too much blood for the wound to be small and shallow. One more scar for her collection.

She pulled her flannel shirt free of jeans and began unbuttoning it. She drew it back over her shoulders and released her right arm first. The spring morning was chilly and goose bumps erupted on her tanned arms. Teeth clenched, she winced as she peeled the blood-soaked left sleeve down her arm. A shiver racked her. The thin cotton tank top she wore underneath might accommodate her modesty but it wasn't worth spit for warmth.

She didn't want to look. Looking at an injury always made it hurt a whole lot worse. Still she had to. Sierra forced herself to stare at her arm. The hoof-print formed a perfect half circle about four inches wide. The bleeding cut was on top, the area below was covered with blood. No doubt it was already swelling.

"Stitches and a bruise. Guess this just isn't my day."

"Sierra, I don't know how to thank you. If you hadn't rescued Rory, he might have…" The male voice trailed off, then the man swore sharply. "You're hurt."

She opened her mouth to make a sarcastic response. Sarcasm and pretending not to give a damn were often her only defenses in this male world she inhabited. But she couldn't speak. Not because of what he'd said, but because of the sound of the man's voice. Her mind didn't want to believe. She *refused* to remember. But her heart knew—and recognized. It thundered in her chest, then jumped to lodge in her throat.

She tilted her head back so she could stare up at the intruder, stare and convince herself it wasn't true. The morning sun was in her eyes. She had to raise her right hand to shield her eyes, vaguely aware she'd lost her hat in the corral. It would be trampled now. She loved that hat. After five years it fit perfectly. Damn it, why'd she have to go and lose her best hat?

The distraction nearly worked. Worrying about the hat was almost enough not to notice the man's strength, his broad shoulders and the familiar set of his head. She could try to convince herself that Fate wasn't playing a cruel trick on her, that her past hadn't shown up to bite her on the butt with a nip that was a lot more startling and painful than the kick to her arm.

Then he knelt down to inspect her injury. He was nearly eye level and without the sun blinding her, there was no reason not to see him. To see him and remember.

"Dylan McLaine," she breathed, too stunned to feel his hands as he gently probed her arm. She hadn't seen him for a lifetime. If he hadn't been here right this minute, she might have been able to convince herself she'd forgotten all about him. But she hadn't.

Without closing her eyes, she remembered Dylan—loving Dylan had been the best part of who she was. When he'd left her—when he'd betrayed her and walked out of her life—she'd not only lost the man of her dreams, but she also lost herself.

"You're bleeding," he said, reaching for her flannel shirt. "I didn't see Rory fall into the pen, but when I heard the cry, I knew what had happened. Then you tore in after him. I knew if anyone could save him, you could. But I sure didn't want you to get hurt."

He took a knife from his jeans' pocket and notched the flannel, then tore it into strips. Two he folded into square pads and pressed against her arm to stop the bleeding, the rest he wrapped tightly to secure the pads in place. It was only when he'd knotted the ends together and sat back on his heels that she realized two things. First, his hands were shaking and second, she'd stopped feeling the pain.

He looked at her. "How can I thank you?"

By growing old, she thought to herself. By being ugly and hard and not anything like the boy she remembered. Unfortunately he'd done none of those things. Oh, there were a few lines by his eyes and his lips didn't automatically turn up in the soul-stirring smile she remembered so well. He'd become a man in the ten years they'd been apart. Still handsome, still strong, still...Dylan. All the years and miles hadn't been enough to make her forget, or allow her to recover.

"Sierra?"

He spoke her name as if it still mattered. Almost wistfully. The way he'd spoken it a hundred—a thousand—times before. The pain returned with a nearly audible crash. She winced as her heart twisted painfully, still bruised from the loss she'd suffered all those years ago.

She deliberately closed her eyes. "Go away."

"I can't. Not until I thank you for saving my son."

The steer's kick had been like the brush of a feather when compared to the impact of Dylan's words. His son. She remembered the slight boy she'd hustled out of the corral. Forcing herself to face the inevitable, she opened her eyes and looked past the man still kneeling beside her. Her gaze settled on the skinny kid in black jeans and an orange-and-white University of Texas sweatshirt.

His son. The boy looked to be about nine or ten, with reddish brown hair and blue eyes. He was slight, with a sweet, earnest expression that made him impossible to hate. Not that she'd planned on hating him—he hadn't done anything wrong. The circumstances around his birth were unfortunate. At least Sierra had always thought so. But that was never the child's fault.

Dylan held out a hand to the boy. "Rory, come and say thank you to the lady who saved your life."

Sierra noticed Dylan's fingers trembled slightly.

She wanted to think he was as affected by their re-
union as she was, but that wasn't it at all. He was
still recovering from the shock of Rory falling into
the pen with the steers. The natural reaction of a
parent when a beloved child was in mortal danger.

As Rory approached, she looked at him closely,
trying to find some resemblance to the man in front
of her. She didn't see much, although there was
something familiar about the way his mouth tilted up
at the corners and the shape of his eyes. But those
characteristics didn't come from Dylan. They belonged to Claire—Rory's mother.

She hadn't thought more pain was possible, yet a
new wave crashed over her, taking away rational
thought and the ability to breathe. All she could do
was feel. Not just the agony of this moment, but all
that she'd suffered ten years ago. It was as if the time
between had never passed. She remembered standing
in front of Dylan, listening in disbelief as he swore
to her nothing had happened that night. That he and
Claire had only been friends. That he still loved
her—Sierra.

She'd wanted to believe him, had needed him to
be speaking the truth, because anything else was too
unthinkable. If Dylan had betrayed her, there was
nowhere for her to run and hide. He was her world.
So she'd believed because it was easier than facing
the truth. But she couldn't keep believing. Not when
the truth stood directly in front of her. Truth in the
shape of a nine-year-old boy.

As Rory stopped at his side, Dylan placed a hand

on the boy's shoulder. "Son, this is Sierra Conroy. You and I are going to have a talk about following instructions, but first I want you to thank her. She risked her life to save you, and got a bad cut in the process. That steer could have killed you both."

Rory didn't seem to appreciate the gravity of the situation. His face split into a broad grin as his eyes widened. "You're a real superhero! Just like on TV."

"A superhero?" Sierra asked, feeling more like roadkill than anything larger-than-life. "That's a lot nicer than a few other names I've been called."

"You made me fly."

"I tossed you out of the pen, kid. There's a difference."

The boy moved closer to her and grinned. "It felt like flying."

"I'll bet it did."

His gaze swept over her before settling on the makeshift bandage around her arm. His humor faded. "I'm real sorry you got kicked. Does it hurt bad?"

When compared with the shock she was feeling? Hardly at all. But that wasn't what he was asking. "I'll recover," she said. "I've had much worse."

"Really? When? Do you have scars? Can I see them?"

"Rory." His father spoke in a stern voice. "You're missing the point, son."

Rory glanced at his dad and nodded. His chin lowered as he stared at the ground. "I'm real sorry for what happened, Miss Conroy. I didn't mean to fall in with the steers. I was just sorta watching them, but I couldn't see anything so I climbed on the fence to get a better look. Then I guess I slipped.''

While she didn't blame the child for his part in destroying her life, she certainly hadn't expected to like him. Yet there was something appealing about Rory's big blue eyes and engaging smile. "Have you been on a ranch before?" she asked.

"Sure." He grinned. "Sorta. My dad just bought a ranch. We've got horses and steers, like this one. And the house is real big, but it's kinda dark inside."

A ranch? Sierra tried to imagine the ever-perfect Claire in a ranch setting. It was beyond her mental abilities. "A ranch can be a lot of fun," she told the boy. "But it can also be dangerous. If I hadn't come along, there's no telling what would have happened to you."

"My dad would have saved me," he said confidently.

Sierra didn't voice her private thoughts about what a citified lawyer would do in a corral full of restless cattle. She didn't doubt that Dylan would have risked his life to save his son, but she doubted either of them would have survived the resulting chaos.

"And if your dad hadn't heard you calling?" she asked.

Rory thought about that for a second. His mouth twisted and he shoved his hands into his jeans pockets. "Oh."

"Yeah. Oh. Do you think you could have made it out on your own?"

"No, ma'am."

"You think you weigh enough to push back those steers?"

"No, ma'am." His voice got a little softer and smaller.

"You think your parents would like finding you after you'd been trampled?"

This time he just shook his head.

"You think you're going to remember all this the next time you want to climb a fence you shouldn't be climbing?"

"Yes."

She could barely hear the word. "Good. You've learned an important lesson. I want you to know that even though it was stupid to climb the fence, you did the right thing when you called out for help. And when I was looking for you, you kept your head. You followed instructions very well. That made a difference. You're a smart boy. Good for you."

He grinned. "Yeah? Thanks, Miss Conroy."

"You can call me Sierra."

He looked at his father, who nodded at the unspoken question. Sierra felt her heart contract. For those few minutes, she'd been able to forget Dylan was right next to her. Now she was forced to acknowledge him, even if just to herself. She swore silently. Why couldn't she have forgotten all about him?

She didn't bother waiting for an answer. If there was one, she wasn't going to like it anyway. If only he would go away. But the way he was looking at her, as if seeing her was the bright spot in an otherwise dull day, that wasn't going to happen anytime soon. Seemed as if she was going to have to be the one to end the conversation.

"I'd better get this looked at," she said, and motioned to her arm.

She braced her right hand on the fence behind her and started to push herself into a standing position. Dylan leaned forward and grasped her around her waist. "Let me help."

"I don't need—"

But it was too late. He was already helping. She found herself caught up against him, her breasts brushing his upper arm, her body close enough to absorb his heat. Memories flooded her. Memories of how good they'd been together, of how he'd always made her feel so alive just by being near her. She didn't want to remember any of that. She wanted to forget the past and pretend it had never happened. She wanted the scars to fade, too.

Even as she tried to pretend she wasn't affected, she inhaled the familiar scent of him. That combination of masculinity and temptation. It wasn't cologne or even sweat. Just some chemical reaction in his skin, a faint, delicious essence that set her nervous system on fire. A shudder rippled through her from her scalp to her toes.

"Are you all right?" he asked. "Do you feel faint?"

His impersonal concern was insulting. She wrenched free of his embrace and stepped to one side. "I'm fine. Couldn't be better. Now, if you'll excuse me—" She turned to leave.

"Sierra, wait. We have to talk."

Such simple words. They shouldn't have had any power over her, but they did. The power to wound and maul.

We have to talk. He'd said that to her all those years ago, right before he'd told her he was marrying someone else. She vaguely recalled an apology, something about him not wanting it to be like that. She couldn't remember exactly—the shock had been too great.

She wanted to scream at him. To tell him it was too late to talk about anything. He'd destroyed all her dreams when he'd left her. While she might not have recovered, she'd learned to get on with her life. Maybe that wasn't perfect, but it was all she had. Damn him. Damn them both.

Without wanting to, she glanced at him over her shoulder. He was dressed casually. Jeans, boots, a shirt. Just like most cowboys. But she knew the difference. His watch was expensive, as were his boots. Expensive as in they cost more than she'd made the previous month. The unfamiliar truck by the barn was new and equally pricey. She might not be the naive young woman he'd left ten years ago, but all the growing up in the world wasn't going to strengthen the branches on her family tree. The Conroys were good people—good, *poor,* people. Dylan came from another world, one where ancestors mattered and class was a trait, not something one attended while in school.

From all appearances, he was the successful lawyer he'd always wanted to be. He'd achieved his dreams. Funny, he'd once told her that none of that would matter if he didn't have her. Guess he'd changed his mind.

"No," she told him. "We don't have to talk. There's nothing left to say."

Chapter 2

Sierra Conroy had grown up but she was still beautiful enough to make a man wonder how he could survive without her. The years apart had allowed Dylan to forget that. Now, staring into her flashing hazel eyes, he realized that he might have forced himself to get on with his life and leave the past alone, but a part of him had never been able to let *her* go.

She stood tall and proud, a strong woman, facing him down, despite the shock of seeing him and the obvious pain from her injury. He wanted to believe her air of calm hid an inner turmoil. He wanted to believe that she'd never forgotten him, either. That she was as affected by this meeting. He had to believe that because one look at her was all it had taken for him. It was as if the ten years they'd been apart had never happened. Back then, he'd been willing to turn away from his family and their dreams for his future, just to be with Sierra. Here he was, ready and willing to do it again.

Only it wasn't going to be that simple. They'd both changed. There were complications, explanations, not to mention a nine-year-old boy between them. Dylan's feelings might not have changed, but both he and Sierra had. He knew she wasn't going to welcome him with open arms. He was lucky she hadn't already decked him.

"It's not what you think," he told her, wishing he had the perfect words to make her understand. Ironically he was a lawyer and words were his stock-in-trade. Yet at this—possibly the most important moment of his life—he couldn't think of anything to say. Anything except the truth—that she was lovely with her dark blond hair pulled back into a braid. With her tanned skin, her full lips, her muscles and her work-roughened hands. She might not fit the traditional definition of womanhood, but she'd always epitomized femininity to him.

"I suppose you're not a successful lawyer," she said contemptuously. "You're not here to flaunt all you've become."

He eyed her arm. "Maybe I should take you to the hospital."

She dismissed him with a scowl. "Yeah, right. Don't try to avoid the question."

"I'm a lawyer," he said. "I'm not here to flaunt anything. I'm here because I bought a ranch."

That startled her. Her eyes widened slightly as she

continued to glare at him. Her only concession to her injury was the gentle way she cradled her left arm in her right. "What do you mean? You bought a ranch around here?"

Dylan put his hand on his son's shoulder, then smiled down at the boy. "It's something we've talked about for a long time, right?"

Rory grinned. "Yup. We're gonna be cowboys. Just us guys."

Sierra frowned. "Us guys?"

Dylan hesitated. He hadn't wanted to tell her this way. Not that there was a good time and place to discuss the state of his marriage—make that his former marriage. Sierra had the most at stake in wishing his relationship with Claire failed, yet he didn't think she would be happy they'd divorced. In her mind, he'd abandoned her for another woman. Knowing her the way he did, he knew she would have expected him to at least have had the common decency to leave her for someone he would stay with for a lifetime.

"Claire and I are divorced," he said quietly.

Sierra's frown faded. Her expression turned neutral. "I'm sorry," she said, in a polite tone that was supposed to tell him the news had no meaning for her. Was that true? Had he come back for nothing?

Not nothing, he reminded himself. With or without Sierra, he wanted the ranch. It would be a place to which he could retreat. A place where his son could grow up surrounded by horses, cattle and wide-open spaces. What could be better?

"The ranch is going to be my new base of operations," he told her.

"You'll practice law from there?" she asked.

"No. I'll have an office in town. But I am going to be involved with the ranch as well. The buildings are in good shape, but the herd needs work. I want to start a breeding program. That's why I'm here."

Sierra shrugged. "I don't know what's for sale. You'll have to talk to the boss about that. I'm just one of the hired hands."

"I know. Don't you ever want more than that?"

Her gaze turned icy again. "No one here is interested in your opinion of my life." She glanced at Rory and closed her mouth. He knew that if his son hadn't been standing there, listening to everything being said, she would have had a lot more to tell him.

"You're good, Sierra. You've lived on ranches, you understand what has to be done. I'm not here to buy livestock. I need a foreman. I'd like to offer you that job."

Something flickered in her hazel eyes. A flash of longing maybe—or was it regret? He couldn't tell. Then the light faded and her lips curved into a bitter smile. "Gee, thanks. That would really be a move up for me. I'm a fair judge of livestock, but I've never been much of a judge when it came to men. Still, even those of us who are slow learners eventually catch on. Thanks, Dylan, but I'll pass."

"I know what you're thinking but it's not true,"

he said quickly. "There were extenuating circumstances. There's a lot you don't know."

"I know enough." She raised her chin in a proud gesture he remembered so well. Deep in his chest, his heart tightened painfully. He would sell his soul to go back in time to change what had happened—but that wasn't an option. And she didn't know enough. But this wasn't the time to convince her of that.

"Dad says you're a barrel racer," Rory said and grinned. "That you're pretty good—for a girl."

She raised her eyebrows. "I went from being a superhero to just a girl in the space of ten minutes. Talk about fickle. I wonder where you get that trait from."

"What's fickle?" Rory asked.

Dylan ignored Sierra's dig and answered his son. "Fickle means not being able to make up your mind about someone. Liking them and then not liking them."

"I like you," Rory said instantly to Sierra. "I think you're great. Dad promised that I could learn how to ride, but I haven't started lessons yet. Can you teach me?"

"Me?" Sierra shook her head. "Look, kid, I've got a lot of responsibilities around the ranch and not a whole lot of free time. I..."

Rory's slight body seemed to shrink. His shoulders fell forward and his mouth drooped at the corners. "Yeah. Okay. You're too busy. I understand."

Dylan silently cursed his ex-wife. The woman had

never worked a day in her life. She'd had a live-in housekeeper and a nanny, and she'd still managed to make her son believe she was too busy to deal with him. Rory had learned early on that his mother considered him a burden. Dylan continued to work hard to make the boy feel special and wanted, but he knew that nothing he would ever do could make up for the maternal rejection. The boy had translated that into an expectation of rejection from all women.

"I'll teach you," Dylan said and was rewarded with a slight smile.

"Really?"

He nodded. "Assuming I remember how. It's been a long time since I've been on a horse. I guess we can fall on our rears together."

Rory laughed at the thought.

Sierra rolled her eyes. "Don't be ridiculous. You were never much of a horseman, Dylan. You'll hurt yourself and do Lord knows what to your son." She glanced at Rory. "All right, pip-squeak, I'll teach you to ride. But there's more to it than just taking a wild gallop. You're going to have to take care of your horse. That means feeding it and cleaning up after it. If you think a dog makes a mess in the back-yard, wait until you see what a horse can do."

Rory grinned broadly. "I promise to do everything you say."

"You're going to, whether you promise or not. I'm a tough teacher, but you'll learn."

"When can we start?" Rory asked.

Sierra nodded to her arm. "Give me a couple of

days to heal. I'll be in touch." Before Rory could ask, she crouched down so they were eye to eye. "I promise," she told the boy. "I won't forget."

Rory flung his arms around her. Sierra didn't respond to the impulsive hug and when the child released her, she stood up and cleared her throat.

"About the foreman job," Dylan began.

Sierra didn't bother saying goodbye. She spun on her heel and headed for the barn. He stared after her for a long moment, wondering how long it was going to take to convince her that he wasn't one of the bad guys. What would happen if he couldn't?

"Is Sierra mad at you?" Rory asked.

"Not exactly," he answered, then ruffled the boy's hair. "So you'd rather she taught you to ride than your old man?"

"Yeah!" Rory grinned. "She's cool."

"That she is." He took his keys from his jeans pocket and handed them to his son. "Let's go."

Rory raced to the truck and carefully unlocked the passenger's door. Dylan followed more slowly, wondering what his next move should be. He could give Sierra a few days to get used to the idea of him being back in her life. After all, he had the advantage—she was going to be coming to his ranch to teach his son to ride. There were possibilities in that.

"Lost, McLaine?" a low male voice asked.

He turned toward the sound and squinted into the sunlight. The man moved out of the shadow of the barn and as he did, memories put a name to the face. Kirk Conroy—Sierra's older brother.

"Or are you just checking to see how the other half lives?" Conroy said, his tone as unwelcoming as his expression.

"Neither." Dylan glanced at the truck and saw Rory sitting on the front seat. He held a couple of plastic action figures in his hands and was obviously oblivious to Kirk's presence. "I wanted to talk to Sierra."

"She doesn't have anything to say to you."

"You don't know that."

Conroy moved a few steps closer, his posture challenging. They were about the same size. Talk about an even contest, Dylan thought, standing his ground.

"She didn't need you all those years ago, and she doesn't need you now."

"How can you be so sure?"

Kirk's eyes darkened. "Because I held her while she cried after you ran off and married Claire. You didn't stay around long enough to watch her heart break, but I did."

Dylan hated that he'd hurt her. That wasn't supposed to have happened. "There are things she didn't understand. I tried to explain..." His voice trailed off. Even to his own ears, his excuse sounded lame. At the time the right course had been so clear. In a choice between honor and love, he'd done what he'd thought was right. Now— Now he could only look back and wonder.

"But she never answered your letters, did she?" Conroy said with grim satisfaction.

His success in the courtroom was often based on

a feeling in his gut. He'd learned to pay attention to what his body was trying to tell him. At this moment, it was practically screaming a question. So he asked it. "How did you know I sent her letters?"

Kirk shifted uncomfortably. It wasn't much, but it was all Dylan needed. Several missing pieces clicked into place. He hadn't believed it when she'd never written him back. Despite what he'd done, they'd loved each other. He thought he'd been a fool for caring about her when she'd responded with silence. That wasn't it at all.

"She never got my letters," he said, knowing it was true. "You had no right to keep them from her."

"I had every right." Kirk pointed at him. "You promised to love her forever. You promised to stand against your family and marry her. You let her dream. But in the end, you turned your back on her and how she felt about you. You married another woman and never gave Sierra a second thought. That damn well gives me the right. She's my sister and I'm going to make sure you don't get a second chance to destroy her."

There were so many things he could tell the other man, Dylan thought to himself. But the truth wasn't always as simple as one might like. A thousand thoughts flooded his brain, a thousand images from the past. A thousand second guesses. In the end, he didn't even bother.

"You're wrong," he said quietly. "About me, about why I did what I did, and about me not giving her a second thought. I never stopped loving your sister."

Kirk's angry stance never wavered. "That must have made you a poor excuse for a husband."

"That's what my wife said the day she left. Goodbye, Kirk. Don't think you've seen the last of me because I'll be around. I'm going to do my damnedest to explain everything to Sierra. I owe her that."

"The only thing you owe her is to stay the hell out of her life."

"You're probably right. But I can't." Dylan headed for the car.

Kirk let him go without saying a word. As he turned the truck, he saw the other man still watching him. Would Kirk report the conversation to Sierra? What about the letters? Did he still have them? Would he ever tell his sister about them? Would Sierra believe Dylan if he told her about their existence?

Too many questions, he thought as they rolled onto the highway and headed back to their ranch.

"Dad?" Rory asked.

He glanced at his son. "What?"

"Is Sierra that lady? The one Mom always talked about?"

Dylan grimaced. Claire hadn't cared who could hear her when she was in the mood to scream about something. He didn't like to think about all the things his son had heard over the years.

"Yes," he said. "She is." Only Claire hadn't referred to Sierra as a ''lady.'' Instead she'd been ''that cowgirl bitch you can't forget.''

''You still love her?'' his son asked.

How like a child to cut to the heart of the matter. ''I'm not sure,'' he said, going for easy instead of honest.

''Well, *I* like her,'' Rory announced and relaxed into his seat. ''I think she's cool.''

Dylan smiled, and for the first time since deciding to move to the ranch and look up Sierra, he thought there just might be hope for all of them.

Chapter 3

Sierra kicked at the wooden fence post that was sunk deep in the ground, then tugged on the wires. The twisted metal was taut against her fingers. Although this portion of the fence was older, it was still in decent shape and wouldn't need replacement for a few years. She pulled a small notebook from her jacket pocket, removed her right glove and made a notation.

Riding the line was a time-honored tradition on a ranch. The boring job was necessary to insure the cattle stayed where they were supposed to. Sierra was always willing to take her turn, but she never volunteered for the duty unless she needed to think. Which was why she'd been out checking fences for the past two days.

In the space of a heartbeat, everything had

changed. Her world, while not perfect, had been comfortable and familiar. Now she couldn't look around at the lush pastures and grazing cattle without another image superimposing itself on the scene. An image of a man's face. Dylan.

She'd actually reached the point where she could go weeks without thinking about him. When he'd first left, she'd barely been able to take a breath without recalling him. Then she'd been able to forget him for minutes at a time. Going an entire day without wondering about him had happened after a year or so. Gradually, though, time had healed…or so she'd thought. Apparently the scar wasn't more than a superficial covering. One look into his brown eyes and she'd felt herself ripped open again.

She put the notebook away, pulled back on her glove, then walked to the next fence post and kicked at it. As she tugged on the wire, she felt a twinge in her left arm. Neat stitches held skin together. The swelling had finally started to go down, but she was going to carry a bruise for a few weeks. In addition to giving her time to think, riding the fence lines also gave her time to heal. She would rather take light duty than use a sick day. Sick days implied a weakness she didn't dare show around the ranch.

Sierra sighed softly. It was time to move on. She knew that now. She'd proved herself in a man's world and she was tired of it. Tired of having to be smarter, faster and better than everyone else, simply because she was a woman. She was tired of the teasing, the not-so-subtle joking, the occasional resentment. She wanted more.

Dylan had offered her a job as foreman. If anyone else had dangled that carrot in front of her, she would have snatched it up in a heartbeat. She had the skills and the experience. But working for him wasn't an option. So where did that leave her? The rodeo circuit had lost its appeal. She didn't want to travel anymore, she wanted roots. A place to call home. Someone to love.

Love. She pulled her borrowed hat off her head and turned it over in her hands. Except for Dylan, the emotion had always eluded her. There had been a few men she'd cared about. Good men, strong and caring. She'd tried to fall in love with them, to feel the same bone-stirring heat, the same fluttering breathlessness, the same passion. It hadn't happened. Love didn't occur on demand. A voice deep inside whispered it might be because she was a one-man-woman. And Dylan was that man.

What if he was the only one she could love? Where did that leave her? She grimaced. She was so damn tough on the outside, but so scared on the inside.

A faint sound caught her attention. As she recognized the rumble of a truck engine, she glanced at her horse to make sure the animal was secure. She settled her hat back on her head and wondered what her boss wanted with her that couldn't wait until she returned to the barn. And then she knew. With a sureness that defied explanation, she knew the man driving to see her was Dylan.

The fence line was set at the top of a small rise. She wasn't that far from her horse. She could easily mount up and be halfway across the field before he cleared the hill. But instead of running, she stood her ground, telling herself that eventually seeing him would get easier. It would have to. It sure as hell couldn't get harder.

He was in the same four-wheel-drive truck he'd had a couple of days ago. As he stepped from the driver's side, she tried not to notice how his jeans emphasized his long legs. The denim was soft and worn, settling around his lower half with easy familiarity. A navy down vest hung open, exposing the gray-and-cream plaid flannel shirt below. All he needed was a hat and he could pass for a cowboy. At least on the outside.

"Hello, Sierra."

His voice was low and raked against her skin like fine sand. She shivered involuntarily. Her mouth went dry. "What do you want?" she asked, knowing she sounded rude and not caring.

One dark eyebrow raised slightly. "You haven't called Rory. Did you change your mind about giving him riding lessons?"

She turned her attention to the fence post she'd already checked. Moving deliberately, she squatted down and examined the base. "I've been busy. But I haven't forgotten. I'll call tonight."

"He's really looking forward to it. If you'd rather not—"

She raised her head to glare at him. "I said I would teach him and I will. I don't break my word."

He didn't even have the courtesy to flinch at her not-so-subtle accusation. "Good. He's had enough disappointment recently."

"I won't add to that." She slowly rose to her feet. A thousand questions circled through her mind. But more important than any of them was the idea that if she thought she could leave without looking as if she were running away, she would be on her horse in a hot second.

"He likes you," Dylan told her, and took a step closer.

Sierra had to consciously not back up an equal amount. "He seems like a good kid." She paused. "Are you and Claire really divorced?" She hated herself for asking, but she had to know.

He nodded.

Why? What had happened? But she only thought the questions.

He read her mind. "I'll tell you anything you want to know."

She shrugged, trying to convince both of them she didn't care. Dylan obviously took that as permission to speak.

"Claire and I never cared enough about each other," he said and shoved his hands into his jeans pockets. "I was willing to try and make the marriage work, but she got tired of me being in love with someone else."

Sierra's stomach convulsed once as the words sank in. The still-broken pieces of her heart quivered and she had to force herself to relax. It would be so easy to believe him, but she'd already been lied to once. "Not very original," she said. "I would have thought you'd have a better line."

"It's the truth."

"Lawyers are supposed to be more polished with their words. If you really want to make it in politics, you'd better get yourself a good speechwriter."

The second the words left her lips, she knew she'd made a mistake. Dylan's expression was triumphant. "You've been checking up on me," he said.

"Don't be stupid. We might all live on ranches around here, but at heart, this is a small town. Everyone knows everyone else's business." She damned her fair skin and hoped her tan was dark enough to prevent him from noticing the blush stealing up her cheeks. She hadn't been asking—exactly. She'd been listening. There was a difference. "You've always been an object of interest."

His mouth straightened. "How much did they talk when I ran off with Claire?"

Sierra swallowed. She didn't want to recall that time. The whispered comments, the pitying stares, the endless days with nothing to do but get through the pain. "It was a long time ago. I don't remember," she lied. If only she'd been able to forget. If only she could forget now.

She turned to leave. It no longer mattered if he thought she was running away. Better to run and be whole than stay and risk more hurt.

"Sierra, wait."

She hurried to her horse, but he caught up with her before she reached the animal. He grabbed her right arm in a grip that neither bruised nor offered any chance of escape.

"Did you think about my job offer?" he asked. "I was serious. I want you to be the foreman on my ranch."

She lost herself in his face. In the handsome lines that had been etched into her brain. She noticed new lines fanning out by his dark eyes and the first few hints of gray at his temples. He'd grown up some, but she would have known him anywhere. This was the face she'd thought she would wake up to for the rest of her life. The face that had haunted her for ten years. There was no going back and the only way to go forward was to go on without him.

"I don't want your job," she told him. "I'm not interested in working for you."

"We've always been good together. We could help each other."

"I don't need your help."

"Yes, you do. There's a lot you need and I'm just the man to provide it."

She shook her head. Talk about arrogance. "I learned my lesson a long time ago. You're an unfaithful bastard, Dylan McLaine, and I don't want anything to do with you."

"You're wrong about that, too."

If she'd known what he was going to do, she would have fought harder. Or maybe she would have acquiesced more quickly. As it was, there wasn't time. One minute he was holding her arm, the next he tugged her toward him. The unexpected action made her momentarily lose her balance. She stumbled, nearly falling into him. He took advantage of the situation and pulled her hard against him. When they touched from shoulder to thigh, he knocked her hat to the ground, then lowered his head and kissed her.

It was like being inside a firecracker. She heard a faint sizzling sound buzzing in her brain. Everything went dark for a second, before the world exploded into a thousand blinding lights. Nerve endings fired up as messages were flashed to her brain. She didn't know what to feel—what to notice—first.

His body was hard. Taut male planes pressed against her curves. His thighs like rock, his chest broad, his arms unyielding. But his lips were soft. Warm and firm, yet so gentle she wanted to weep.

He brushed his mouth back and forth against hers. The slow, teasing motion eased the tension from her body. Her hands, trapped between their bodies, slowly relaxed and her fingers uncurled. She wished she wasn't wearing gloves so she could feel the heat of him.

The tip of his tongue touched her bottom lip. Instinctively she parted for him. He hesitated long enough for her to silently beg him to enter, then he did, moving with the confidence of a lover who remembers.

She remembered, too. All of it. His sweet, sweet taste, the instant fire that ignited everywhere he stroked. The dance that had been theirs alone. She pressed the tip of her tongue against him and her breasts swelled. He circled her intimately and her thighs began to ache. So much pleasure. She'd forgotten what it was like to feel alive…to see the world in perfect color. To be a part of something that had always been greater than either of them could be alone.

Without wanting to, knowing that she would pay the price later, and not finding it in herself to care, she raised her arms until she could hug him close. She tugged off her gloves and let them fall to the ground, then touched the cool silk of his dark hair. With her other hand, she traced the line of his shoulders and moved down his back. Thick muscles bunched and released under her ministration.

The combination of sensations, his mouth against hers, his tongue, his body so close, left her breathless. When he traced a line down her spine and cupped her rear, she didn't need any urging to arch against him. As her belly nestled against his groin, she felt the hard ridge of his desire. Answering need fluttered inside of her. They had been young and inexperienced. Together they'd learned about the magic and mysteries of love. Despite that inexperience, or perhaps because of it, no one had made her feel what

Dylan had. No one had been able to touch her soul with just a kiss.

He raised his hands and cupped her face. With a groan of pure pleasure, he pulled away from her mouth and trailed his mouth along her jaw to the sensitive spot behind her right ear. She caught her breath as he licked the skin, then bit gently on her lobe.

She had to hold on to his shoulders to maintain her balance. At some point, the world had started to spin. Every cell in her body remembered what it had been like to make love with him, and they cried out in a single voice. She wanted him. She needed him. Despite everything, nothing had changed.

He drew back and gazed into her face. "Sweet Sierra."

"Damn you, Dylan." She didn't want to feel this. She didn't want to feel anything. Going through the motions of life instead of participating was so much easier.

"I've already been in hell," he said. "You can't make it worse by sending me back."

She squeezed her eyes shut, not wanting to risk seeing the truth. Better to believe it was all a lie. Safer...at least for her.

"Tell me you don't want me," he said. "Say the words and I'll go away."

"I don't want you."

He laughed softly. "Liar. Even your mouth betrays you. It quivers right here." He touched a corner. She sucked in a breath. "Yeah. I know what you're feeling. You think I don't feel it, too?"

He traced her lower lip with his finger. Without wanting to, she touched him with the tip of her tongue and tasted his skin. He groaned low in his throat.

"I've never wanted a woman as much as I want you," he said. "That hasn't changed."

The burning in her eyes warned her that tears weren't far behind. She who never cried. She cleared her throat and stared at him. "Everything has changed."

"Not this."

He kissed her again. This time there was no subtlety. He invaded like a conqueror. She met him, planning to do battle, but surrender was so sweet. When his hands settled on her waist, she couldn't find it in herself to protest. Even as strong fingers moved higher, she kissed him back, stealing into his mouth for a small victory of her own.

When his hands touched her breasts, she again saw all the colors in the universe. Fire shot through her as her skin absorbed ecstasy and her nipples tightened until they ached. He brushed his thumbs against the taut peaks and she surged against him, wrapping her arms around him, knowing if she could get close enough to crawl inside, then everything would be all right.

She wanted him. She needed him. Everything else was just an illusion. Second best. It was as if the ten years apart had never existed.

He broke the kiss and rested his forehead against her shoulder. Through her shirt and bra, she felt the warm puff of his breath. "If you knew how many times I'd imagined this," he said.

"Me, too," she breathed, and tensed in anticipation.

Her horse nickered in the distance. Sierra tried to ignore the sound, but somehow it couldn't be pushed away. Slowly, not wanting to, she became conscious of the fact that they were standing in the middle of a field. There was no one else around; she wasn't worried about being seen. But the familiar trees and solid ground reminded her that ten years *had* passed. This was a different time, and she was a different person.

His mouth closed on her nipple. Perfect pleasure shot through her. She squeezed his shoulders, then roughly pushed him away.

"No!" she commanded. "No more."

He stared at her, his chest rising and falling in time with his rapid breathing. She wanted to slap him. She wanted to kick him and beat him until he felt what she'd endured with him gone. She wanted to tear off her clothes and make love with him.

"Don't make me do this," she told him. "Not again."

Chapter 4

Dylan watched the shifting emotions in Sierra's hazel eyes. Passion was the strongest, but anger was a close second. Anger and maybe a little confusion. He couldn't blame her for feeling the latter—he was a little lost himself. Obviously the physical connection between them was as strong as ever. Maybe stronger. He'd remembered wanting her, but he didn't remember craving her the way his lungs craved air.

"I'll never *make* you do anything," he told her.

Her mouth twisted. "Yeah, right. You probably think it's going to be a lot easier than that. A couple of kisses and I'll be ready to fall into your bed."

"Aren't you?"

She raised her head slightly and squared her shoulders. "No."

She'd never been a good liar. But right now he

wasn't as much concerned with her lack of skill as her motivation. Why was she denying the obvious? "Whatever we had before is still very much alive," he told her. "I want you, Sierra. I want you in every way a man can want a woman. You make me feel alive. I'd forgotten what that was like."

She folded her arms over her chest. "Don't go all nostalgic on me. This was a one shot deal. You caught me off guard, that's all. It's not going to happen again."

He reached out to touch her. She flinched, but didn't move back, so he gently tucked a loose strand of hair behind her ear. As usual, she wore her long hair in a neat braid. She'd done the same in high school. When they were alone, she allowed him to take off the rubber band and comb his fingers through the rippling waves. He'd always loved her hair.

"What isn't going to happen?" he asked.

"All of it." She made a sweeping gesture with one hand, then tucked her fingers back under her arm.

"Talking?"

"Whatever."

"Kissing?"

She scowled. "Damn it, Dylan, what do you want from me?"

That was easy. He didn't even have to think about his answer. "A second chance," he said promptly. "There's still something wonderful between us and

I don't want to waste another ten years until we find each other again.''

"There is no us. There's you and there's me. We're separate and we're going to stay that way. As for what we had—'' Her eyes flashed with fire as the anger burned off the last of her passion. "I loved you and you betrayed me. You lied to me about your relationship with Claire and then you left me. It's taken me a long time to forget you, but I finally have. I don't want to remember again.''

He noticed she said forget, but not forgive. She hadn't forgiven him and he couldn't blame her. But where to start? After all this time, would she even believe him?

"It's not what you think,'' he began.

"I know exactly what it is and what it was. You wanted to be successful. Well, glory be, you are. Congratulations, Dylan. You're a hotshot attorney. I hope the money keeps you warm at night because I'm not going to.''

"It's not about the money. It never was.''

She shook her head in disbelief. "It sure wasn't about love, or keeping promises. At least not the ones you made to me.''

Her sharp words were like a knife wound directly to his heart. He held her gaze without flinching— after all he deserved what she was saying.

"I've moved on with my life,'' she continued. "You're of no interest to me.''

"You kiss as if you're really interested. Face it, Sierra. I still turn you on.''

Some instinct warned him and he managed to grab her arm before her palm connected with his cheek. She struggled to continue her forward motion and slap him. When it became obvious he was stronger, she tried to pull away. He didn't let that happen, either.

"Let go of me," she demanded.

"Not until you listen to me."

"You can't say anything I want to hear."

Frustration bubbled inside of him. "You're probably right."

So he did the only sensible thing under the circumstances. He kissed her again.

He hauled her hard against him, pulling her until she was once again flush against his body. He was still aroused and her belly nestled intimately against his groin. He deliberately rotated his hips, making sure she understood what he was doing. The small sound that escaped her parted lips told him she'd figured it out.

He waited a heartbeat, willing to listen to any protests, but there was only the faint whisper of her breathing. So he lowered his head to hers and claimed her mouth.

She'd already parted her lips. He didn't bother with polite inquiries, instead sweeping inside to claim her, like a wild animal claiming its territory. He wanted to taste her and touch her, to be around her and in her, joined in the most intimate way possible.

When he knew he had her complete attention, he

released her arm and rested his hands on her waist. She placed her palms flat against his chest, fingertips lightly scratching at the fabric of his shirt. They belonged together—they always had. Anyone else would be second best...for both of them.

They consumed each other, caught up in the flames of arousal. He lost himself in the heat of her, in the overpowering need. He'd spent a lot of time trying to convince himself being with Sierra wasn't nearly as intense and perfect as he recalled. He knew now that it was more so.

She met him with a passion that matched his. They danced together, the movements sure and familiar—specific touches and motions they'd taught each other all those years ago. He withdrew, allowing her to follow him back so she could tease his lips, his mouth. He lowered one hand to her rear, cupping the curve, squeezing gently. A shudder rippled through her. Her body tightened, her muscles tensing in anticipation. Her hands pressed flat against him.

"No!" Sierra gasped, and pushed away. She staggered a step away and folded her arms across her chest as if she were trying to hold herself together. "No, Dylan. Please don't."

The soft plea worked as nothing else could have. His entire being still on fire for her, he nodded briefly. He had to clear his throat before he could speak. "I won't kiss you again if you promise not to run off," he managed to say at last.

She shook her head. "Let it go. Let me go. There's nothing left to talk about. We have separate lives."

"That doesn't matter."

"Of course it does. It always mattered." Her smile was bitter. "I never figured out what you saw in me back in high school. I dressed in jeans and shirts, not those pretty dresses the rich girls pranced around in. I wasn't especially smart or funny or anything that you would have wanted."

"I loved you."

Hazel eyes darkened. "Why?"

At last an easy question. "Because you made me laugh," he said, remembering all the fun they'd had together. "I liked how you think, how well we got along. I enjoyed your company, your way of looking at the things. I liked looking at you, being with you. Loving you was the best part of my world, Sierra. I was a better man when I was with you. We understood each other. We wanted the same things. I could imagine growing old with you." He shrugged. "None of that has changed. At least not for me."

She dropped her gaze to the ground. "I asked," she muttered quietly. "I only have myself to blame for your answer."

They were both silent for a few minutes. Dylan tried to figure out how to convince her that this time would be different. This time he was a grown-up, not a kid trying to act like an adult.

"Find someone appropriate," she said, still not looking at him.

"You're appropriate."

"Hardly. I'm not domestic. My idea of gourmet cooking is taking the frozen entrée out of the plastic container before eating it. I can't make small talk. I don't decorate, I'm not interested in chic charity work. I'd be a lousy mother. Besides, look at how I'm dressed.'' She motioned to her shirt and jeans. ''What would your friends say?''

''They'd adore you.''

''Yeah, right. Think they want to shake hands with me?'' She held her hands out in front of her. The skin was rough and tanned. Several cuts and scars formed an erratic pattern on her palms. She turned them over. Her nails were short, but she had long, lovely fingers. They might not look right in an ad for nail polish, but he'd felt them on his body and to him, they were perfection.

He stepped forward and took her fingers in his. ''You're beautiful. Everything about you is exactly as I want it to be. Why can't you believe me?''

''Because you're not being realistic. Our worlds are too different.''

''You're just afraid.''

She met his gaze. He watched her expression harden and she pulled free of his grasp. ''Do you blame me?''

And then he knew. Whatever he'd suffered when he'd left her, it wasn't close to what she'd gone through in being left. He'd gone away, with a wife and a child. She'd stayed behind in a small town that thrived on gossip. In doing the right thing, he'd destroyed the only woman he'd ever loved.

''I'm so sorry,'' he said softly. ''I can't tell you how sorry.''

"It's too late for apologies. They can't fix anything now. It's not important anymore. We've changed. Let the past be, Dylan. Let me be."

"I don't believe that's what you really want."

"Why? Because it's not what *you* want?" She planted her hands on her hips. "I'm not the same person you left behind. You don't know me anymore. Don't presume to think you understand anything about me."

"Fair enough. We've both changed. But some things have stayed the same." He drew in a breath to steady himself. Maybe it was too early to play this card, but he wasn't sure he had a choice. "I still love you."

She froze like a small creature catching the scent of an approaching enemy. Her eyes widened and her lips parted. Color fled her cheeks leaving her oddly pale, despite her tan. Her hands slipped down her hips and hung loosely at her sides.

"No," she said, the word more shadow than sound.

"Yes," he told her firmly.

"No." She shook her head. "You're just saying that. It can't be true."

"Why is it so impossible to believe?"

She closed her eyes and half turned away. An unexpected pain shot through him as he wondered if she was going to cry. Torn between giving her space in which to compose herself and wanting to go to her and hold her close, he did nothing. After a moment, she turned back toward him, her expression neutral.

"You just disappeared," she said, her voice resigned. "You'd made me promises about being together forever, and then one day you were gone. You took everything. My hopes, my dreams. I didn't know how to exist in a world without you. I didn't know how to get over the lies."

"I didn't lie to you."

"What would you call Rory if not a lie? You swore you h-hadn't—" Her voice cracked. She straightened her shoulders. "You swore to me you hadn't slept with Claire, yet the proof that you did is your nine-year-old son."

There were dozens of things he could tell her. The truth for one. But the stiffness in her body warned him she wasn't prepared to listen. Not now. He shouldn't have told her he loved her. He should have waited a little so she could get used to having him around.

"I didn't just disappear," he said, deciding to pursue a safer topic. "I wrote you several letters. You're the one who didn't write back."

Her mouth twisted. "I never got any letters."

"I know. Maybe you should ask your brother about that."

"What are you talking about?"

He shrugged. "Take it up with Kirk."

"You're saying my brother kept your letters from me?" Her tone highlighted her disbelief. "You're going to have to do better than that."

"All it takes is one question, Sierra. Why would I lie about something so easy to check?"

Her eyebrows drew together. He desperately wanted to pull her into his arms and hold her again. He needed to feel her body against his. Only when they were together did he know he'd finally come home.

But he didn't bother trying to hold her or kiss her. She'd erected fences and signs warning him to Keep Out. He would listen...for now.

He stood by his truck until she'd ridden away. When she disappeared over a rise, he slowly opened the vehicle's door and stepped up into the driver's seat. His parents had taught him he could do anything he set his mind to. In all his attempts, he'd only failed once—he'd let Sierra down. But he wasn't an impressionable kid anymore. He couldn't be manipulated by well-meaning adults or one determined young woman.

All that stood between him and what he wanted was a little information and a few demonstrations that the fire was still burning bright between them. He knew he still loved Sierra and he was willing to bet everything he had that she still had feelings for him, too. All he had to do was convince her of that.

He thought about kissing her and holding her— and about the incredible thrill of making love with her. They belonged together. He would use everything in his power to make her see that. He'd lost her once—he wasn't going to lose her again.

Chapter 5

"**I**'m ridin', Sierra. Look at me!" Rory grinned from his perch on the small gelding.

Sierra couldn't help smiling back. "You're doing a great job, too. Don't forget, keep your back straight and your heels down." She scanned the boy's posture and nodded approvingly. "Perfect. You're a real natural at this. We're going to have you out herding cattle in no time."

"I'm a cowboy. Dad, look at me."

"I see, son. I guess if you're one of the working cowboys, I'm going to have to raise your allowance."

Sierra tried not to let the sound of Dylan's voice have an effect on her. It was tough enough to concentrate just knowing he was standing by the corral railing, watching her. Not watching her, she amended quickly. Watching his son. She was just the instructor.

Or so she kept telling herself. But she didn't believe those words any more now than she had when she'd first arrived and Dylan had greeted her. There was no denying the man still had the power to get to her.

At least he hadn't tried to make small talk. She wasn't sure she could have suffered through that. She was still recovering from everything he'd told her last week—about still being in love with her.

Don't go there, a voice in her head warned. *Dylan McLaine is nothing but trouble.*

She forced her attention back to Rory. "That's it," she said, turning in place as she stood in the center of the ring so she could keep the boy in view. "Relax your hands." She walked toward him.

"Whoa, Chet. That's it. Pull back gently to bring him to a stop, Rory. But gently." She patted the elderly gelding on his shoulder, then smiled at the boy. "Remember these reins are connected to a piece of metal in Chet's mouth. If you tug hard or keep pulling, you're going to hurt him."

Rory frowned. "I don't wanna hurt him." He leaned over and peered at the horse. "You okay, Chet?"

Chet snorted.

"He's fine," Sierra said. "Just think about having braces and someone attaching a string to them. You wouldn't want that person jerking your head around, right?"

Rory drew his eyebrows together in fierce concentration. "Okay, Sierra. I'll remember."

"You're really good," she said. "You're learning fast. I'm impressed."

Another grin split his face. Freckles dotted his nose and cheeks. He was a sweet kid and she couldn't help feeling drawn to him.

"Really?" he asked.

She reached up and tapped his nose. "Really." She stepped back and slapped Chet's rump. "Go ahead. Start walking."

Rory gave an exaggerated squeeze with his knees. Chet obligingly took a step forward. As she turned, she made the mistake of glancing up and found Dylan watching her. She was too far away to know what he was thinking, which was just as well. Just the sight of him leaning casually against the fence railing was enough to make her heart beat faster.

But she was determined to pretend he didn't matter. So instead of returning to her place in the center of the ring, she sauntered over to where he was standing. Although she was willing to let him think she was immune, she wasn't foolish enough to put herself in actual danger. She made sure she was well out of touching range.

"He's a natural," she said and leaned against the wooden railing. Not only did her stance make her appear casual, but it also had the added advantage of allowing her to watch Rory's progress without having to look at his father.

"He looks great on a horse. I really appreciate you taking the time to help him."

She shrugged. "I don't mind. It's a fun change for me." She paused, then decided the truth wouldn't be so bad—this one time. "He's a good kid, Dylan. You've done well raising him."

"I think Rory gets all the credit."

He continued to speak about his son, but she couldn't concentrate on his words. Her body betrayed her, shivering slightly in anticipation of his touch, even though she'd positioned herself so that wouldn't happen. Her mind, still reeling from all he'd said the last time they'd spoken, replayed his unbelievable statement—*I never stopped loving you.*

Had he really said it? Had she imagined the words because she wanted them to be true? Did she want them to be true?

It didn't matter, she reminded herself. He couldn't still love her. Not after all this time. And based on all that had happened when he left, she wasn't sure he'd ever cared. But why would he lie about that? Was he trying to trick her into trusting him again? To what end?

"Back straight," she called as the boy continued to ride around the ring. "Very good. Try to feel Chet's movements and sway with him, not against him." Rory moved back and forth in an exaggerated mimic of the horse's slow gait. "Excellent. Just like that."

"You're very patient," Dylan said.

"It's not difficult to be patient with one bright

child. But I don't think I'd do well with a ring full
of nine-year-olds.''

"You'd be fine."

She made a fatal error in judgment and glanced at
him. His dark gaze was warm and affectionate. Instantly her toes curled in her worn boots and she felt
her heart begin to pick up its pace. Without wanting
to, she leaned toward him.

Get a grip, she told herself and quickly straightened.

She turned her attention back to the child on the
horse, grateful for the distraction. While she watched
Rory, she searched her mind for a neutral topic of
conversation. Something that would distract them
from—she wasn't sure what, but they needed dis-
tracting.

"Have you found someone you want for the foreman job?" she asked.

"Sure."

His easy answer made her stomach tighten in an
involuntary flinch. He'd only asked her a couple of
days ago. Foolishly she'd thought he'd meant the job
offer. "Really?" She was pleased her voice sounded
calm. "Who?"

"You."

She turned toward him. "I said no."

"I'm going to keep asking until you say yes.
You're the right person. I can be very stubborn when
I need to be."

He gave her a slow smile. A smile she remembered from her past. A smile designed to make her

want him all over again. Damn him, it worked. She felt her resolve melting and if he'd asked her again, right then, she might have found herself saying yes.

"You're destined to be disappointed on this one," she told him, hoping her face didn't betray her inner thoughts.

"Life has taught me a couple of lessons. I'm no longer willing to give up things that are important to me. I've learned the value of hanging on, no matter what other people might think."

She knew he was trying to tell her something, trying to explain a moment from their past. She didn't want to know what it was. Enough time had passed that she was no longer troubled by those memories, but that didn't mean she wanted to relive them.

Before she could figure out how to answer him, he pushed off the railing. "I nearly forgot. I have something for you. It's in the truck." He turned and walked toward his barn.

Sierra watched him go, then returned her attention to Rory. She called out a few more instructions. Today he was simply getting the feel of being on the back of a horse. Next time they would work on staying in the saddle during a trot.

Her gaze moved past the boy and she took in the wide-open spaces around the main buildings. Despite a few years of neglect, Dylan's newly purchased ranch was impressive. There was plenty of acreage, a huge three-story house, three barns, houses for the ranch hands, along with several thousand head of cattle. Once again she regretted the fact that he was the one offering her the job. If it had been anyone else, she would have jumped at the chance to run a place like this. The potential, the challenges, even the long hours of work all appealed to her. She could have made something of this place.

She heard footsteps behind her and angled toward him. He handed her a large, round box with a familiar logo on the top.

Sierra raised her eyebrows. "You bought me a hat?"

"Yours got trampled when you rescued Rory. It was the least I could do." He shifted his weight as if he were uneasy. "I hope you like it."

Sierra hesitated before opening the lid. While she appreciated the gesture, a hat was a very personal item. She wasn't sure what he would have bought, or if she would like it. If she didn't, she would have to act polite. If she did, well, she didn't want to think about that. A good hat lasted for years. Could she wear one Dylan had bought her without being forced to think about him? Would the hat make a difference? Now that he'd reentered her world, she doubted she was going to be able to find a way to forget him.

She pulled off the top and drew out a black hat. A simple leather braid encircled the crown. She fingered the thick felt and she turned it over in her hands. The shape was familiar.

She looked at him. "This is just like my old hat."

"I know. When I went to the shop, Harvey told me he'd shaped your last one, so I asked him to make this one just the same. You always were real particular about your hats."

She wasn't sure which touched her more. That he'd gone to all the trouble to have this done, or that he remembered something so insignificant about her. Maybe both.

"I don't know what to say," she murmured and set the hat on her head. It was a little new and stiff, but it still felt right. "You shouldn't have."

"You saved my son," he reminded her. "Besides, I wanted to give you something you would like."

"I do like it. Thank you."

Rory waved a hand. "Dad gave you the hat. Isn't it cool? I helped him pick it out."

"Thanks. I love it."

Rory beamed.

"He likes you," Dylan said and leaned against the railing.

Sierra set the box on the ground outside the fence and leaned against the wooden structure, careful to stay far enough from Dylan so they didn't accidentally touch. She might be able to speak with him about incidental things, but she wasn't ready to physically go another round with him. Their hot, passionate kisses had left her weak and hungry for him. She didn't have to be told twice that it was better for both of them if she kept her distance.

"I like him," she said. "He's very good-natured." Something he got from his father, she thought grimly, remembering Claire as being very demanding and not a pleasant person.

"He's lonely for female attention. I try to do the best I can, but I'm not enough to keep him from missing his mother." Dylan grimaced. "Not that Claire was much of a parent."

"What do you mean?"

"Let's just say she had more important things to do than worry about Rory."

Sierra swallowed a sigh of regret. She didn't think she was going to ever have the chance to settle down and start a family of her own. So far she'd failed miserably at the game of love. She wasn't sure she had what it took to be a good mother, but she would very much like to have tried. Maybe with a strong man at her side she would have found the courage and the wisdom to do it right.

"Is that why you have custody?" she asked.

"Yes. It wasn't a battle. When she walked out, she left him behind."

Sierra looked at the child riding Chet. The boy sat tall and proud, his freckled face glowing with happiness. She wanted to gather him close and hug him until he squirmed to be released. The intensity of her feelings surprised her. How could anyone have walked away from Rory?

"How often does she see him?"

"She doesn't." There was no mistaking the bitterness in his voice. "It's been nearly a year and she's flown in twice. The last time was six months ago."

"You've been divorced for a year?" she asked, surprised it had been that long.

"We've been living apart that long. The divorce has been final a couple of months. If you're asking why I waited this long to come back, it's because I wanted to be sure I was free of her."

"I didn't ask."

"Then I'm telling you."

"I see." It took every ounce of willpower to keep her gaze fixed firmly on Rory. From the corner of her eye she saw movement, but she didn't dare look. She didn't want to know what Dylan was doing, or what he was thinking. It was too scary. She refused to believe he'd come back for her. That she still mattered to him. She wasn't going to get her heart broken a second time.

Overhead, puffy clouds chased each other across a brilliant blue sky. She inhaled the scent of grass and blooming flowers, and a darker, spice fragrance that was unique to the man standing next to her.

"Have you talked to Kirk?" he asked.

His question pricked her, causing her good mood to drain away like air out of a balloon. "There's nothing to ask him."

"You don't believe I sent you letters." He didn't ask a question.

"I don't think my brother kept anything from me."

"So I'm lying."

"I didn't say that."

"You didn't have to. Damn it, Sierra, why would I lie about that? Just ask him."

She found herself turning toward him. Anger

danced in his eyes. He glared at her. "It's important."

"For who?" she asked. "It was a long time ago."

"It matters to both of us. We still care about each other."

"Speak for yourself."

"Deny it all you want, but I was there when you kissed me back the other day. You wanted me just as much as I wanted you. Nothing has changed."

Frustration bubbled inside of her. It had always been like this with him. He had the ability to make her feel, to want. It wasn't fair. She liked having her life simple. So what if there was no intense pleasure? There was no soul-destroying pain, either.

"Everything has changed," she told him. "We're two different people. I don't want to go back to what we were."

"I don't, either. I want to go forward. But you won't let me do that because of the past. Don't turn your back on this. Please. Once we were wonderful together. We can be again. Do you want to spend the rest of your life wondering what it would have been like if only you weren't too stubborn to give me a second chance?"

He made it sound so easy. As if all she had to do was say yes. In truth, she wondered about the letters. Dylan sounded so confident about their existence. Had he really sent them and had her brother kept them from her? At the time, she'd been in so much pain. He might have thought it was an act of kindness. It would be easy enough to ask. But if the letters existed, she wasn't sure she was strong enough to read them.

"Dylan, I—"

He held up his hand to stop her. "Don't say anything yet. Rory's tenth birthday is next week. We'd both like you to come."

She blinked at the change in topic. "Um, I don't think that's a good idea."

"He really likes you and it would mean a lot to him." Dylan smiled bitterly. "To be honest, I want you to be there so he has something to distract him."

"From what?"

"From the fact that Claire isn't going to bother to attend. She's in Paris with her new husband. I've been trying to get a message to her so she'll remember to at least call him, but I'm not sure it's going to happen."

She sucked in a breath. No matter what else had occurred, at least she and Kirk had had loving parents to support them. "Is this his first birthday since you two split up?"

"Yeah. He seems okay most of the time, but I know he's hurting. I want the day to be special for him."

Sierra saw Rory wave at her. She waved back. The world could be a cruel place. It was tough enough to handle as a grown-up. What chance did a child have?

"I'll be there."

"Thanks." He cleared his throat. "There's something else."

She raised her eyebrows.

"I've, ah, planned a party so he could invite a few boys his own age. Sort of give him a chance to get to know the other kids."

"I see. How many boys?"

"Ten."

"Eleven ten-year-olds. You're going to have your hands full."

He shrugged. "I can handle it. But I thought maybe you could come a little early and help me set up."

Sierra figured she should have been annoyed but all she could do was smile. "You're hustling me, McLaine. You just want help with this party."

"I'm willing to admit that."

He reached out and touched her hand. She felt the heat of his fingers and her body instantly sparked to life.

"I'd be really grateful," he told her. "I'll even let you have a corner piece of birthday cake, so you can have extra icing."

She'd always had a weakness for icing. And for this man. She was setting herself up for heartbreak. She knew it. Yet as long as he touched her, she could deny him nothing.

"I'll be there," she said.

Chapter 6

They were a little louder than she'd expected, but other than that, eleven ten-year-old boys weren't any more trouble than a corral filled with eleven calves. Sierra watched as the commando game progressed. The boys had divided into two teams and were busy hunting each other through the large three-story house. Two boys raced down the stairs and skittered to a stop in the foyer.

"Did you see two enemies heading this way?" a blond kid asked seriously. "We heard 'em from upstairs."

Sierra raised her hands in the air. "In this matter, I'm as neutral as Switzerland."

The boys looked momentarily confused, then shrugged and raced off toward the dining room.

"Don't even think about going in there," she

called in a firm voice. "It's set up for cake and ice cream. If you bump the table I'm going to have to make sure you never reach your eleventh birthday."

They slid to a halt and looked back at her. She gave them her best "freeze in your tracks, sucker" look and pointed toward the living room. "Hunt in there."

Without saying a word, they did as she told them.

"Not bad," Dylan said, coming out of the kitchen and nodding approvingly. "Simple, direct and effective. You're a natural."

His compliment made her worry about blushing, which, recently, she seemed to be doing a lot. "They're not so bad once you get used to them. I'm trying to think of them as two-legged cattle and act accordingly."

"It's working."

He gave her one of his best smiles. She hated when he did that. Bad enough he looked gorgeous in jeans and a white long-sleeved shirt rolled up to the elbows. Dark hair tumbled across his forehead. He was a cliché—tall, dark and dangerous. The long talk she'd had with her body, not to mention her hormones, hadn't helped. One smile and her knees shook like a straw house in a stiff breeze.

More boys clattered down the stairs. Without saying anything, Sierra pointed to the living room. There were loud shrieks as the newcomers rounded the threshold. Something heavy crashed into a wall. Dylan didn't even flinch.

"I took out everything breakable this morning,"

he said. "I'm going to tear off the wallpaper anyway, so a few dents don't matter."

She remembered the perfectly decorated house he'd grown up in. All the heavy fabrics and expensive antiques had made her nervous. She'd always worried about accidentally breaking something. "Your mother would not approve."

"Tell me about it. Fortunately my mother couldn't make it today."

Rory led the last band of hunters or soldiers or whatever they were down the stairs. They didn't need directions; the noise from the living room led them toward the battle in progress.

"Why don't you make sure no one kills anyone while I see to the cake," Dylan said.

Sierra raised her eyebrows. "Aren't you domestic?"

"I'm showing you my feminine side. Isn't that what men are supposed to do these days?"

His voice was teasing, but something serious lurked in his eyes. Something that made her want to think about his request for a second chance. Could there be one for them? Could she take that kind of risk? What if he walked out on her again? This time she didn't think she would be able to survive.

But the thought tempted her. As she moved toward the living room, she wondered what it would be like to be a part of something, instead of just another hired hand. To have roots instead of the ability to pack up and be on the road in less than an hour.

The battle had ended by the time she arrived. The

boys had flopped down over the worn hunter green sofas, the gold recliner and on the floor. She and Dylan had decorated the room with balloons bouncing off the ceiling and streamers twisting along the walls. A table in the corner held a pile of presents. Sierra's was tucked under the table. A worn leather saddle that should fit Rory better than the one he was currently using. It wasn't new. The leather was scarred and shaped by many years of riding, but it was reliable. Sierra and her brother had both learned to ride in that saddle and she thought Rory might appreciate that fact more than something impersonal from a store.

"Who won?" she asked as she entered the room.

Rory looked up and grinned. "It was a tie. Do we eat cake soon?"

"In a couple of minutes."

One of the boys, one with bright red hair, eyed her. "Are you Rory's mom?"

"No, I'm a friend of his."

"Sierra works on a ranch," Rory said proudly.

A couple of the boys rolled their eyes. "So what?" one of them asked. "My big brother works on a ranch and my uncle owns one."

Rory's face fell slightly. He glanced at Sierra as if asking for her help. Several unfamiliar emotions filled her chest. The boy was proud of her and trying to show off. Unfortunately in this part of Montana, people working on ranches, even women working on ranches, wasn't that unusual. Although the women still had to prove themselves.

If it hadn't been his birthday, she probably wouldn't have shared the information. After all, it had been a long time and she was rusty. Besides, it was kind of embarrassing. But this was Rory's day and she wanted to make it special for him.

"I, ah, can do a couple of rope tricks," she said before she could stop herself.

Eleven pairs of eyes focused on her.

"Really?" Rory breathed.

Too late for second thoughts, she told herself. "Uh-huh."

"Can we see some?"

It was her own fault for volunteering the information, she reminded herself.

"Sure. I should have a rope in my truck. Be right back."

She returned to the living room. Within a couple of minutes, she had the stiff cord spinning neatly. She stepped in and out of the turning coil, then raised and lowered it over Rory. The other boys lined up to have her do the same with them.

She found herself laughing with them as she tried to show them how to manipulate the rope. "It's a smaller movement than that," she said, when one of the boys sent the rope dancing across the floor.

"Aren't you full of surprises?"

Sierra turned toward the voice and saw Dylan standing in the doorway, grinning at her.

"What other secret talents do you possess?" he asked. Before she could answer, he motioned to the corner. "I think we're ready for the presents."

"All right!" Eleven boys cheered.

Sierra collected her rope. As she walked past him, he reached out and touched her arm. "I'm serious," he told her. "I am impressed with your roping skill. Now I'm curious about other secrets that might be even more intriguing."

She bit her lip, not sure how to take his teasing. And he was teasing, she told herself. Despite the fire lurking in his eyes. Oh, but she wanted to believe it was more.

"I love it," Rory said, fingering the supple leather of the saddle, then racing over and throwing his arms around Sierra.

She hugged him back. "I hope so. Kirk and I learned to ride on that saddle. I wasn't sure if you would like it or if I should pick up something from the toy store."

"No. This is the best."

He didn't let her go for several seconds. His body was small and warm. Sturdy on the outside, but she knew his heart was tender. She felt an odd hollowness inside as she realized how much of her adult life she'd spent alone. The fact that it had been by choice didn't help. All her love had had nowhere to go…no one to care about. In that moment, she ached to love a child. One of her own—or even this child.

It's not possible, she told herself firmly as Rory stepped back. Whatever was happening between Dylan and herself wasn't real. It wasn't about anything except wayward hormones and a few good memories from the past. Second chances and falling in love again were foolish dreams. She knew better.

Make that her head knew better, but her heart wasn't sure it wanted to listen to reason.

"Dad, did you see this?" Rory asked, his voice excited. He stroked the leather saddle again. "Isn't it cool?"

Dylan turned his smoldering gaze on her. "Very cool. And very thoughtful. Thanks, Sierra. I know Rory is really going to enjoy your gift."

She felt as if there was more than one meaning in his words. Or was that wishful thinking?

One of the boys called Rory's name and the moment was broken. The child turned away. Sierra stared after him wondering about possibilities. She'd always thought she didn't have what it took to be a good mother, but maybe she was wrong. Claire hadn't even bothered to call to wish her son a happy birthday. With the time difference between Montana and Europe, it was unlikely she was going to get to it at all today. Sierra figured she might not be the most maternal woman on the planet, but she would be able to do a whole lot better job than Claire. At least she knew how to love and give of herself.

"You guys ready for some cake?" Dylan asked.

There was a chorus of "Yes!"

He motioned for Sierra to lead the way into the dining room. She did, then made sure everyone was seated. Dylan brought in the huge store-bought cake. Ten fat candles sat in the center, flanked by small plastic plants meant to represent the jungle with miniature action figures acting out a fight sequence from a popular afternoon television cartoon.

"Dad, it's great," Rory breathed. "Is it chocolate?"

"Of course. And there's chocolate chip ice cream, too."

The boy glowed. Sierra smiled at him, then caught Dylan's glance as he held out a book of matches. "Why don't you do the honors?"

She nodded instead of speaking, telling herself that the lump in her throat was about too much talking with the boys and not some wayward emotion. Still, her hands shook as she carefully lit the candles and she didn't object when she stepped back and Dylan took her hand.

"Make a wish," he told his son.

"Blow 'em out, hard!" one of the boys said.

Rory grinned. He thought for a second, then nodded, closed his eyes and sucked in a deep breath. He got them in one quick exhale.

Even though it wasn't her birthday, Sierra made a wish of her own. That this afternoon, this magic space of a few hours, could be real. At least for now.

"You want to cut cake, or man the ice-cream scoop?" Dylan asked.

Sierra glanced down at her sleeveless blouse. There were a couple of grass stains from a brief wrestling match earlier in the afternoon, and a smudge from brushing up against her truck door. Dylan's polo shirt and jeans looked as clean as when he'd first put them on that morning.

"I'll take the ice cream," she said. "I don't care if I get dirty."

"Okay." He dropped a light kiss on her cheek. "I promised you a corner piece...one with plenty of icing."

She felt herself nod, but it was beyond her power to actually speak. The kiss was a lot less arousing than the one they'd shared in the pasture and yet it touched her all the way down to her feet. She felt her toes curling inside her worn cowboy boots. How did he do that to her?

Rather than spend a lot of time worrying about the answer, she walked into the kitchen and grabbed the carton of ice cream from the freezer. In a couple of minutes, she was elbow deep in chocolate chip ice cream and dipping the last scoop onto a plate. In the distance, the doorbell rang.

"I'll get that," Dylan said, setting a bowl next to her. In it was a small piece of cake with icing on two sides. Some jungle green lumps of the gooey confection had been dropped into the bowl.

She smiled. "I think you gave me more than enough."

"Just trying to make you happy, darling," he said and headed for the door.

She stared after him, stunned, amazed and barely able to breathe. What was he doing to her? Why was she letting him try?

Figure it out later, she told herself and reached inside the carton to pull out some ice cream. As she did, she heard voices from the hall.

"You should have told us it was your son's birthday," a strange man said. "We could have rescheduled. Mike is going to be here all week."

"The timing is fine," Dylan answered. "Rory is spending the night with a couple of his friends. If you don't mind meeting the kids, we can get started in about an hour. There's plenty of birthday cake."

"I wouldn't say no to that," another man said.

Sierra dropped the ice-cream scoop into the carton and glanced around frantically. She didn't know who the men were, but she sure didn't want to meet them. She had stains on her shirt and jeans, sticky ice cream on her hands, and several crumbs on her face from taking a bite of cake. But there was only one way out of the dining room and she could already hear the men approaching down the hall.

She grabbed a napkin and rubbed her face, then tried to clean up her hands. Maybe Dylan wouldn't bother introducing her. Even as the comforting thought formed, she dismissed it. Of course he was going to introduce her—she just had that kind of luck.

As she tossed the napkin in the trash can beside the table and forced her stiff lips into a false smile, Dylan led three men into the room. They were tall, well dressed and obviously successful. She recognized the fifty-something man in a cowboy hat. He was Ben Radisson, a local power broker in the political scene. The other two were strangers. The cut of their tailored suits and their confident air warned her they were just as important and potentially intimidating as Ben Radisson.

Dylan made a beeline for her and wrapped his arm around her shoulders. "Gentlemen, this is Sierra Conroy. We're old friends from high school."

She resisted the urge to run for cover. At least Dylan hadn't implied a romantic relationship.

"Hello," she said.

"And this is my son, Rory."

At the sound of his name, the boy looked up, then sprang from his seat and hurried to his father's side. Dylan ruffled his hair.

"I'm ten today," Rory said importantly.

"Good for you," the lone blond man in the group said. He was slender and handsome with brilliant blue eyes. "Ten's a great age. Did you get presents?"

Rory beamed at the question. "Bunches." He quickly recounted the list, paying extra attention to Sierra's gift.

She shifted uneasily as their attention turned back to her. If only Dylan would drop his arm so she could make a graceful escape before she said or did something stupid. While she wasn't a complete social misfit, she knew she was definitely out of her element with these men.

Dylan introduced them. She tried to put names with faces. The two unfamiliar men were from Washington. She swallowed hard. So the rumors were true—Dylan was thinking of going into politics. She supposed she shouldn't be surprised, and yet she was.

Maybe because she'd gotten used to thinking of him as just Dylan, but he was so much more than the young man she'd once been in love with.

"What do you do, little lady?" Ben asked as Dylan finally released her and went to get his guests some cake.

"I work on a ranch," she said. "I'm, ah, just here helping with Rory's party. You know, like the hired help." She hoped her smile looked more natural than it felt and that she wasn't going to cause trouble for Dylan. These men wouldn't want to know that she'd once had a relationship with him. She might not know much about politics, but it wasn't hard to figure she wasn't exactly material for a candidate's significant other.

Ben raised his dark, bushy eyebrows. "That's real neighborly of you."

She nodded, not sure what else to say.

Dylan returned and handed the men each a piece of cake. "Did Sierra tell you?" he asked. "We go way back."

"No." Ben raised his eyebrows. "Sounds interesting."

Dylan gave her that grin of his, the one that made her want to believe everything he talked about was possible. "It's true," he said. "We were high school sweethearts." He reached out and, before she could pull back to prevent the action, he touched her cheek. "Sierra's the one who got away."

Her heart sank. While she appreciated his willingness to admit to a previous relationship with her, there was no need to risk his future. Didn't he know what the men thought of her? She was completely wrong for what they had planned for him.

She took a deep breath for courage, then turned to look at Ben. With her spine stiff, she prepared herself to blandly accept the relief in his expression. Instead the wily older man's face was unreadable.

"You're going to have to be smarter than that if you want to get ahead in politics," he said at last and took a bite of cake.

Sierra stared at him without blinking. Had she heard right? Before she could ask, there was a knock at the door. The first of the boys' parents had arrived to take them home.

Fifteen minutes later, Sierra escaped to the kitchen where she began rinsing plates and loading the old dishwasher. Dylan came in and closed the door behind him.

"You all right?" he asked.

She nodded. "Fine. I thought I'd clean up before I headed out."

He took the plate from her and set it back on the counter. "You don't have to do that. I asked you to help me with the party, but I didn't expect you to play at being a maid."

His fingers were warm as he held her hand. Too warm. And his touch was slow and seductive, gentle strokes that ignited need deep in her belly. She wanted to pull back or at least think rationally, but she could only stand there absorbing the sensation of having him close and touching her.

His dark eyes glowed with twin flames. "I have a catering service coming in later," he said. "They'll take care of everything." His words were at odds with the desire on his face and she wasn't sure which to believe.

"Okay. I'll leave the dishes."

"Do you have plans for tonight?"

She bit her lower lip. Was he asking her out? "No."

"Would you please stay for dinner. It might be a little boring, but I would really like you to listen to what they have to say and then tell me your opinion when they've left."

"But—" She glanced around the messy kitchen, then down at her clothes. Stains, a rip, ratty jeans. "Dylan, I'm not dressed for this."

He dismissed her comment with a wave. "That doesn't matter. This means a lot to me and I'd really like you to be here."

She could have refused him if he hadn't looked deep into her eyes. Even though it wasn't real and they were both just stuck in the past, and eventually one or both of them would wake up to that fact, she couldn't help responding to the heat there. Heat and some other lurking emotion that made her heart beat a little faster.

"I, um..." She found herself swaying toward him. "I guess I could go home and change."

He smiled slowly. "Only if you want to. What I care about is you being here." He dropped a quick kiss on her mouth. "Hurry back because I'll miss you."

Less than a minute later, Sierra found herself sliding behind the wheel of her truck, wondering what on earth she'd just agreed to. But her lips still tingled and there was a spark of expectation in her stomach. Maybe Dylan was playing her for a fool. After all, she should know better than to trust him.

But she'd never been able to resist him. Looked as if after all this time, that fact hadn't changed, either.

Chapter 7

Dylan reached for the wine bottle and poured the dark red liquid into Ben's glass. The older man gave him a nod of thanks, but didn't take his attention from Sierra and her description of winning the national barrel racing championship several years before.

As he glanced around the table, Dylan noticed all three of the men were mesmerized by her story. He grinned. No, not the story. While it was funny and interesting, what had these men captured was the woman herself.

A nearly forgotten, warm feeling settled in his chest. Pride. Pride in how beautiful she looked in her soft pink cotton dress, with her hair loose around her shoulders. Pride in how she carried herself, how she met each man's gaze deliberately. Pride in how she didn't hesitate to ask questions if there was something she didn't understand.

With Claire he'd had near physical perfection, superior style and taste, but no substance. Sierra was her own person. She might not always do the expected, but she would always do what was right. She was someone he could respect and admire. If only he could convince her they still belonged together.

Ben made a comment and Sierra laughed. As she turned her head toward the older man, the overhead light reflected on her shiny hair. He longed to reach forward and bury his fingers in the silky strands. She sat close enough for him to touch her, but he resisted the temptation. While he had the desire, he knew he also needed the right. And that had yet to be earned.

There was a time he could have laid claim to her and if he had his way, that time would come again.

Mike leaned back in his chair and smiled. "I didn't realize life out west could be so entertaining." The Washington attorney looked at Dylan and raised his eyebrows. "Is this one of the reasons you've been resisting my offers? All this natural beauty?"

"Offers?" Sierra asked, glancing from one man to the other.

"I've been trying to tempt Dylan into my law firm," Mike said. "So far he's resisted. I couldn't figure out why the promise of money and a partnership weren't working. Now I'm starting to understand."

Sierra looked momentarily confused, then she caught the compliment and blushed. "I'm sure Dylan is very comfortable with his law practice here. You don't have to be in a big city to be successful."

Ben shook his head. "Not if you measure success by money, right, Dylan?"

"Agreed, and don't try changing my mind on that one," Dylan said easily, leaning back in his chair. He liked this. Interesting conversation and someone to share it with. Later, he would ask Sierra what she'd thought of the men she'd met and they could talk about the future. He'd always valued her opinion.

"I don't understand," Sierra said, looking from Ben to him. "Everyone says you're doing very well."

"I am."

Ben snorted and took a drink of wine. "Did you bill even a hundred thousand dollars last year?"

Dylan shrugged. He hadn't. But it didn't matter.

"The last of the good guys," Mike said. "That's our Dylan here." Catching Sierra's frown of confusion, he continued. "Don't you know about his practice?"

"I thought I did."

Ben set down his glass. "So you're keeping quiet about it," he told Dylan. "Mighty interesting."

Dylan smiled reassuringly at Sierra. "It's nothing. What they're hinting at is I don't have a lot of corporate clients to pay the bills."

"He doesn't have anyone to pay the bills," Ben said, and sighed. "Thank God. Think of how that will play with the voters. All those years in law practice and after expenses he barely earns enough to be considered middle class.''

"Who are your clients?" Sierra asked.

The attention was making him faintly uncomfortable. "Some people in town and—"

Ben cut him off with a wave. "Dylan does mostly pro bono work. He deals with several women's shelters and a couple of organizations that aid the homeless. There's no press, no fanfare and no money. That's why my people are so interested in getting him on the ticket.''

Sierra turned her attention to him. Her hazel eyes widened. "Why didn't you tell me this?"

"Would it have made a difference?"

She thought for a moment, then nodded. "I think it might.''

He couldn't dismiss the bolt of pleasure that shot through him. "I'm glad.''

It was as if the rest of the room disappeared. He found himself being pulled into Sierra's gaze, as if her eyes were the perfect place to get lost and never be found again. There was a buzzing in his ears, but he heard her clearly when she spoke.

"I'm glad, too," she said softly.

The night sky was an umbrella of stars as Dylan walked her to her truck. Sierra found herself slowing her pace. Foolishly she didn't want the evening to end. She glanced back at the old three-story house and the lights glowing their welcome from behind curtained windows. It was barely nine, but Dylan and his guests had serious business to discuss, business that as a mere friend, she wasn't privy to.

They came to a stop next to her truck. Dylan took her hand in his and squeezed it gently. "Thanks for joining us for dinner," he said. "I really enjoyed your company."

She smiled, despite the fact that her lips trembled slightly. "I had fun, too." She ducked her head. "I didn't think I would fit in with your guests, but it wasn't so bad."

"You were perfect."

Was it her imagination, or did he step closer? The night air was cool and still. Even though Dylan was expected back inside, she found herself wishing he would take the time to kiss her. She needed to feel his body next to hers, his mouth caressing her, his arms holding her tight. Too much had happened too fast. A couple of weeks ago, she'd convinced herself she barely remembered the man. Now he'd returned and she couldn't think about anything else.

She needed his body to remind her that they belonged together, because her mind still wasn't convinced. It wasn't all about him breaking her heart again. The dinner had been fun, but it had also reminded her of the difference in their positions.

"Tell me about your law practice," she said.

He shrugged. "There's not much to say. I take a lot of cases for battered women and homeless people. It doesn't pay much, but I have money from my family and the work is very satisfying."

She stared at his face. "I figured you'd outgrow your desire to save the world."

"I don't think I'm saving the world." He laced his fingers with hers. "I've affected a couple of lives, but I don't kid myself about my importance...or lack thereof."

"But you turned down a partnership at a prestigious Washington, D.C., law firm. That's pretty impressive."

He smiled. "Good. I want to impress you."

"Why?"

The smile faded and his expression turned serious. "Don't you know by now, Sierra? Don't you know why I'm here and what I want?"

A faint ripple swept through her body. She had to consciously tighten her body to keep from swaying. "I'm not sure. You seem very similar, yet you can't be the same Dylan I remember."

"I am the same," he told her. "Not all good, but not all bad, either. I made mistakes in the past and I'm going to make mistakes in the future. It's a part of being human. But there's one mistake I don't want to make again, and that's losing you. You still mean the world to me."

She tightly closed her eyes, wanting to believe him more than she wanted to draw in her next breath. "I wish—" She paused, not sure what she wished.

"That we could change the past?" he asked softly.

She opened her eyes and stared at his face. At the handsome, familiar planes, at his mouth, at the firm line of his jaw.

"Yes," she whispered. "I want to change the past. I want you to have never left me. I want you to have never broken my heart."

Dylan blew out a long breath, then bent down until his forehead pressed against hers. "I want that, too. If only you knew how much."

"But you can't change the past." It wasn't a question.

"No. I can explain it, but I can't erase it." He released her hand and cupped her face. Long fingers stroked her cheeks. "I still love you, Sierra."

They were so close that his features blurred. Without wanting to, she found herself pressing her palms against his chest. Love. The most perfect and most hurtful word. "Why should I believe you?" she asked. "You told me that before, then you betrayed me and left. How do I know this time is different?"

He touched his lips to hers. The heat ignited instant fire. Flames shot through her chest, then moved quickly to the feminine place at the apex of her thighs. Nipples tightened, breasts swelled and that most special part of her dampened in readiness for their lovemaking. It was as if that one, sweet kiss had joined them again. Inevitably. Irrevocably.

And on the heels of passion came fear. The darker side of love swept through her, battling to put out the fire, seeking a way to keep her doubting. He'd let her down before. He'd left her. How could she trust him again?

But the passion could not be denied. Even though he didn't deepen the kiss—instead merely brushing his mouth against hers—she found herself dismissing the questions and not caring about the past. In the face of being with Dylan again, how could the fear matter?

She pressed her hands against his chest and pushed. He stepped back. His breathing was labored, his gaze bright with desire. "You still don't trust me," he said.

She shook her head. "The wanting is easy," she told him. "It's the rest of it that gets in the way."

"I understand." He glanced at the house, then up at the sky. After a minute he nodded, as if coming to some private conclusion. "You need to know the truth," he said. "I don't know if it's going to help, or make everything worse."

"What are you talking about?"

"What really happened ten years ago. I wrote it all down."

"You mean you kept a journal?"

"No. I sent you several letters. Remember? In them I explained about Claire and Rory, and about why I had to marry her."

A cold fist squeezed her heart. She folded her arms over her chest in a protective gesture. "I don't want to talk about that or read about it."

"Don't you see?" he asked. "We have to talk about it. Until you understand, you won't ever be able to trust me."

"There's nothing to understand."

"That's where you're wrong." He reached out and caught a strand of her hair. "Silk," he murmured, wrapping it around his index finger. "I knew it would be." He released the curl.

"Trust me just a little," he said. "I know I'm asking a lot, but if you ever believed we deserved another chance, if there's even a tiny part of you that can even consider the possibility that the magic still exists between us, then go see your brother. Stop being so afraid of the truth." He held up a hand, silencing her before she could speak. "Please. We can talk after that."

He kissed her cheek. "I meant what I said. I still love you. You're the reason I came back."

With that, he turned and walked toward the house. She watched him go, still standing in the darkness long after he'd disappeared inside. Did he know what he was asking? What if there really were letters? What if he could explain the past? How was she supposed to fight against that? How was she supposed to survive loving—and losing—him again?

Sierra stared at her brother's front door. There were still lights on inside, so she was sure he was up, but she hesitated before knocking. She hated to interrupt. She knew he treasured his evenings with Felicity and the baby. The three of them were so happy together. Besides what was she supposed to say to Kirk? Tell me about the past because Dylan says you're keeping secrets?

The whole situation was insane. She was a fool to even consider believing the man. Yet instead of turning back toward her room in the bunkhouse, she raised her hand and knocked on the door.

The sharp sound was loud in the stillness of the evening. Before she could make an escape, Kirk stuck his head out. "Sierra? What's going on? Are you okay?"

Her throat closed unexpectedly and she could only nod. "Fine," she managed to say. "Do you have a minute?"

His eyes darkened with concern. "Sure. You want to come in?"

"No. Let's talk out here. It won't take long."

"Give me a second." He slipped back inside. She heard murmured conversation, then he walked out and stood next to her at the porch railing. "What's going on?"

Having his full attention didn't make it easier to figure out what to ask. She bit her lower lip, then sucked in a breath. "I was talking to Dylan a little bit ago."

"Damn it, Sierra, when are you going to learn your lesson? That guy's nothing but bad news for you. Or have you forgotten what he did to you?"

"I know." She leaned against the railing and stared out into the night. "I haven't forgotten. He hurt me more than I've ever been hurt in my life. But—"

Kirk cut her off. "But nothing. The man's slime. You're better off without him."

"Am I? Sometimes it's hard being alone. You should remember what that's like."

Kirk placed his hand on her shoulder and squeezed. "I know. But he's not the only guy around. If you would give a few of the others a chance, you could have someone in your life."

"Maybe." The problem was she didn't want "someone," she wanted Dylan. Despite everything, that hadn't changed.

"There's no maybe about it. You're a beautiful woman. You have a lot to offer. Let him go. You gotta trust me on this. He's bad news."

"And if I can't?" she asked, not daring to look at him. "I've never loved anyone else, Kirk. I don't think I know how. He said..." She drew in a breath and turned to face her brother. "He said I should talk to you about the past. That you know something. Do you?"

This time her brother was the one to look away. Sierra stiffened in surprise. "Kirk? Do you know something?"

"Not exactly," he growled. "Damn him for bringing this up again. It doesn't matter, Sierra. It was a long time ago."

She curled her fingers in toward her palms, shock battling with disbelief. "Tell me what you know. Tell me what you've kept from me."

"Nothing." He shrugged. "Okay, technically nothing. Dylan sent you a few letters. You know, back when all that was happening. I don't know what they said because I never read them."

Dylan had told her the truth and she hadn't believed him. "I never got them. I—" The world tilted slightly, then righted itself. "He was right about them." What else had he been right about? "You thought you were protecting me, so you kept them from me," she told her brother.

"I didn't want you hurt more. I figured the bastard would try and talk his way out of the situation. I was afraid you'd get caught up in something ugly. You were pretty in love with him. I was trying to help."

Letters. She didn't want to hope the situation could be explained, yet she found herself praying it was true. That he hadn't betrayed her because he'd wanted to. That there was another explanation. "Do you still have them?"

Kirk nodded. "But I don't think you should read them. What do they matter now?"

"They might not matter at all." Or they might change everything, she added silently. "Still, it's my decision to make. I want to read them."

"Okay." He went into the house.

A few minutes later, he returned with a handful of unopened envelopes. She recognized the handwriting and her heart tightened as a flood of emotions washed over her. Regret, hope, pain and something that just might have been the precursor to love.

He held them out to her. "I did what I thought was right," he said.

She took them. "I know. You love me, big brother. You were looking out for me. I wish you'd given me the chance to decide for myself, but what's done is done." She clutched the letters to her chest. "Thanks." She turned to leave.

"Sierra?" he called after her.

She paused on the stairs and looked at him. He was tall and powerful, a dark silhouette against the light from the house. "Be careful."

"I will," she promised, even though it was a lie. It was already too late to be careful. Somehow Dylan had drawn her back into the past. All she could do was hang on for the ride.

Chapter 8

Sierra set the letters on her dresser and stared at them for several minutes. There were five in all. Unopened, untouched for ten years. She wiped her damp palms against her skirt and wondered if she had the courage to actually read them. She sensed that opening the envelopes meant opening up old wounds from the past. While she'd been wrestling with some feelings from long ago, she hadn't actually reexperienced the horrifying pain of losing Dylan. She wasn't sure she could stand to feel all that again.

But there wasn't a choice. She had to know what had happened. So she undressed and put her clothes away, pulled on an oversize T-shirt, then picked up the letters and crawled into bed.

The lamp from the nightstand cast a warm glow on the small room. As the only female ranch hand, she had private quarters behind the kitchen. The room wasn't big, barely ten by ten, with a single bed, small dresser and a closet. But it was all she really needed. Life had taught her to travel light.

Tonight she was grateful for the confined space. She didn't have to worry about unexplained shadows or sudden sounds. Tonight, with her knees pulled up to her chest and the quilt her mother made warming her bare legs, she could risk going back to a time she hadn't been sure she would survive.

She flipped through the letters, glancing at the postmark. The first one sent was on top, the last on the bottom. Drawing in a deep breath for courage, she opened the first envelope.

The letter was two pages long, the white paper covered with Dylan's familiar scrawl. She'd always loved his casual handwriting, black ink only. Despite her apprehension, she smiled, remembering how no one else had been able to decipher his notes, but she'd had no trouble reading them. Maybe because she'd had no trouble reading the man.

My dearest Sierra,
I know how much you must hate me. No, that's not true. I don't know how much, but I can imagine. I know you think I'm the worst kind of man. That I've betrayed you with another woman. With Claire.

I'm not sure it matters, but I have to tell you what happened that night. You remember. When I took Claire to the dance at the country club. You and I fought about it for two days. I'm sorry. I should have listened to you. I should have done a lot of things.

When I told you about the dance, I mentioned that I owed Claire and this was just a way to repay that debt. Her date had backed out at the last minute. She was a member of the organizing committee and had to go to the dance, but she was too humiliated to go without a date. So I said I would stand in for the guy. It didn't mean anything. Not then, not now. You're the one I love, the one I've always loved.

There was a blank space on the page. Without wanting to, Sierra could imagine Dylan staring into space, trying to figure out what to tell her, searching for the right collection of words to make her believe. She found herself hoping he would be able to do that. Even if the understanding came ten years late, she still wanted to know what had happened, and to finally be convinced that he hadn't betrayed her. At least not on purpose.

Claire knew right away something was wrong. My mistake was in telling her about our fight. I see that now. She was sympathetic and took my side, which I liked because I thought I was right. I thought you were being possessive and demanding for no good reason. But I was wrong.

The party was pretty boring, so we went out

to the stables. Claire had some whiskey in her purse and we started drinking. She kept telling me how you didn't understand me and that I had every right to be angry with you.

Several lines were scratched out. Sierra held the pages to the light and tried to read them, but she couldn't. A lump formed in her throat. She told herself he wasn't going to make her cry—not again. But she knew she was wrong.

I honestly don't remember what happened. I swear, Sierra. I don't remember touching her. I never wanted her, or thought about her that way. You're the one I love, the only one. The next morning I realized she'd set me up. That's when I came to you and told you that you'd been right about Claire. I thought we could put this all behind us. That it would just be a bad dream. But we can't.

Claire's pregnant and we're going to have to get married.

The words were a knife to her heart. Sierra wasn't sure why. Rory was living proof that Claire and Dylan had indeed slept together. She knew that. And yet it was so awful to see it in writing. She supposed that in her heart she'd always wanted there to be another explanation.

She reread the few lines detailing what had happened and Dylan's claim that he didn't remember what they'd done. His lack of memory was a small and cold comfort.

I will always love you. No matter what happens, know that. You don't know how much I wish it could have been different. You are my dream for the future, my only fantasy. I can't believe I messed everything up like this. I wish I hadn't been a fool. I wish I hadn't betrayed you.

I'm so sorry. More than anything, I want to be with you and hold you. I will never love her. I will never forget you. I know that's wrong, but I don't care. I know you won't forgive me, and I'm almost glad. As long as you hate me, you'll be thinking of me. Right now, that's the best I can hope for.

All my love,
Dylan

The ache in her belly made her pull her knees closer to her chest, but it didn't help the pain at all. A thousand questions swirled through her head. What had really happened that night? How had Claire seduced Dylan? Sierra was sure it was seduction. They might have been young, but Dylan had loved her with every fiber of his being. He wouldn't have knowingly betrayed her. She hadn't believed that at the time, but she did now.

She leaned her head back against her pillows and thought about those awful days. The fight they'd had, his date with Claire, his promises the next morning that everything was going to be fine between them. Then, less than a month later, the news that he was marrying Claire.

She folded the first letter and returned it to the envelope, then opened the second. The familiar handwriting made her eyes burn with unshed tears. She blinked them away, refusing to give into the weakness.

It was dated nearly a month after the first letter. In the beginning paragraphs, Dylan told her how much he loved her and missed her.

I heard that you've left to join the rodeo circuit. I still remember when you won the junior barrel racing championship. I was so proud of you. I know you'll do great. But I wish you were here. I'm scared, Sierra. Something's wrong and I don't know what to do about it. I'm more and more convinced Claire set me up because she wanted to marry me. But I still can't remember what happened that night.

I don't... I need to tell someone this, and you're my best friend, so you're the only person I trust. But I know you don't want to hear this. Damn.

I still can't remember being with her that night. She kissed me the other night and it was like kissing a stranger. Nothing was familiar. I had to walk away because all I could think of was you.

And there's more. I went to talk to her a couple of nights ago and she wasn't home. When I asked her about it, she said she'd had dinner with friends. But she'd told me she was tired and wanted to stay in that night. I can't help wondering if she's seeing another guy. I have this knot in my gut. What if she is? What if he's the father of her child and not me? What if I've destroyed all our lives for nothing?

Sierra closed her eyes. She couldn't bear to read anymore. If Claire had tricked Dylan... But she hadn't. Rory was his son. He had custody and was raising him. He wouldn't do that if the boy wasn't his.

She read the rest of the letter. Dylan still swore he loved her and couldn't stop thinking about her. He begged her to write him back. The silence was killing him. Couldn't they at least be friends?

That made her smile bitterly. No, they couldn't have been friends, not after all they'd meant to each other. She could have loved him, or hated him, or tried to forget him, but she couldn't have survived having contact with him.

The third and fourth letters were more of the same. His confusion about his lack of memory with Claire. His growing belief that there was another man in Claire's life. His distressing conviction that the child she carried wasn't his. He begged her to write him back, to tell him what was going on. He couldn't believe she'd forgotten him so easily.

Sierra picked up the last letter and tried to read the postmark. The small numbers blurred and she realized she was crying. She wiped her face impatiently and cleared her throat.

"I'm not going to lose it," she said aloud. "Not after all this time."

But it was so hard. All those old feelings overwhelmed her. She'd never loved anyone but Dylan and it was painful to read about his life with Claire. Maybe Kirk had been wrong to keep the letters from her, but right now she was grateful to have ten years between these words and herself. Back then, she would have written Dylan back. If he'd asked her to meet him, she would have gone. They were too much in love to have denied each other, and they would have found themselves in a very ugly situation.

She opened the fifth letter.

My darling Sierra,
This is the last time I'm going to write you. It's been nearly six months and you haven't been in touch. I can only assume you're truly over me. I respect you for that and wish I could say the same.

But I can't. I still love you with every breath I take. I still want you and need you in my life. There isn't an hour in which I don't think of you. Last night I dreamed of you, of being with you, talking to you, touching you, loving you.

And now I have to let you go. I went to the doctor's office with Claire yesterday while she

had an ultrasound. For the first time, I understand there is a life depending on me. The child
is a boy. I don't know if he's mine or not. I still
haven't slept with Claire. I'm not sure I ever
can. But I've taken on the responsibility of this
infant and I won't turn my back on that. On him.
To be a good father, I must let the past be the
past.

I will love you forever. You are the best part
of my world and without you every victory is
hollow. In my first letter to you, I said I wanted
you to keep on hating me so you wouldn't forget me. I take that back. I want you to be happy.
If that means putting me aside and loving someone else, then I hope you do that. I hope all
your dreams come true. If you ever need anything, anytime, just contact me. I will always be
available to you. No matter what.

Dylan

A sob caught at her throat and tears spilled from
her eyes. Sierra clutched the letter to her chest and
cried for all they'd lost. For a love that had been
tested, and never died. For either of them.

She waited until dawn before driving to Dylan's
ranch. About three-thirty, she'd given up trying to
sleep and had sat on the porch awaiting the sunrise.

She tried to close her door quietly, but the sound
was still loud in the still morning. She leaned against
the hood, not sure what time he woke up, or if she

should even be here at all. What was she going to say to him? That knowing the truth made a difference? Did it? The past couldn't be changed, but what about their future? Did they have one? Could she risk that?

A light clicked on in the kitchen. Sierra walked toward the back door. Through the half-open curtains, she could see Dylan moving around, filling the coffeepot and flipping the switch. He wore jeans and nothing else. His body was still beautiful—broad and strong with honed muscles.

She wasn't sure how long she stood there, watching, wondering what she was going to say to him. At last she gathered her courage and knocked on the back door.

He opened it and stared at her. A welcoming smile pulled at his lips. "I didn't expect you this early."

"But you did expect me?"

He stepped back, inviting her in. "I hoped you would want to talk to me after you read the letters."

She moved into the kitchen. "How long have you known Kirk kept them from me?"

The coffeepot sputtered. He pulled down two mugs from a cupboard and poured them each a cup. When he handed her one, he motioned to the kitchen table. She sank into one of the chairs and cradled the mug in her hands.

He took the seat across from her. "I always wondered why you didn't answer. After a couple of years I got to thinking that maybe you hadn't received the letters. You might have been home to receive the first one, but you were on the rodeo circuit for the rest so it would have been easy for someone to intercept them. Kirk was a logical suspect.'' He took a sip of coffee.

''When I first showed up last month, he confronted me,'' he continued. ''Said something about you not being interested in me. That if you had been, you would have answered my letters. When I asked him how he knew about them, the look on his face confirmed what I'd been thinking.''

She'd come here because she hadn't had a choice, but now that she was here, she wasn't sure what to say. She studied his familiar face. Stubble darkened his cheeks, emphasizing the stubborn strength of his jaw and the tempting curves of his mouth.

''Is Rory yours?'' she asked.

Dylan ran his fingers through his hair and sighed. ''No,'' he said at last. ''When he was born, I had the doctors do a blood test. There's no way he's mine.'' He shrugged and looked at her. ''I was going to walk out on her. I figured I'd give her a couple of weeks to get on her feet, then I'd leave and come find you.''

''What happened to change your mind?''

His lips turned up at the corner. ''I made one mistake. I held him. Claire didn't want to breast-feed, so while she and Rory were still in the hospital, I had one of the nurses show me how to bottle-feed him. It just took one time.'' His gaze shifted to the window and he stared at memories she could only imagine. ''He fell asleep in my arms and I realized

I couldn't walk away from him. Once Claire figured that out, she used Rory to keep me. It worked.''

Sierra searched her heart, but couldn't find any anger. "I wouldn't have expected less of you," she said. "You're wrong, Dylan. Rory might not be your biological son, but you are his father.''

"I know. I couldn't let him go. I was prepared to use all kinds of threats to keep him when Claire wanted out, but in the end, she didn't fight me.''

He leaned forward and stretched his arm across the table. Palm up, long fingers pointing toward her, he invited her to touch him. She hesitated, not sure what was happening between them. But she'd never been able to resist him. She placed her hand on his. When he squeezed gently, she returned the pressure.

"I committed two sins in my marriage," he said. "The first was writing you as long as I did. I kept hoping you would write back and demand that I leave her. I would have...for you. Even though it was wrong. My second was always loving you. I was the best husband I could be to Claire, but I never loved her and in the end, that's what drove her away.''

Sierra drew in a deep breath. "After how she manipulated you, I can't say I'm sorry.''

"I am. About a lot of things. Mostly the time we've lost." His gaze was steady. "Sierra, I came back here for you. If you'd been married, I wouldn't have approached you or even bought this ranch. But when I found out you weren't, I let myself hope that we could give this another try. I meant what I said.

I still love you. There's never been anyone else in my heart. Was I wrong to come back?''

She didn't know how to answer him. There were still too many questions. Fear lurked in the shadows of her soul. Would Dylan betray her again? Did she dare trust him? Did she dare not?

In the end, she couldn't find the words, so she stopped looking for them. She rose to her feet and walked around the table. He rose to meet her and pulled her into his embrace. As his mouth claimed hers, she knew she'd made the right choice. Dylan's arms had always been home.

Chapter 9

She was all he remembered, all he'd dreamed about, and more. No fantasy from the past could compare with the perfect joy of holding Sierra in his arms, feeling her mouth against his as they kissed.

Dylan wrapped his arms around her and held on tightly. He was willing to admit that a part of him was afraid this was just a dream. That he would soon wake up and find himself alone in his bed. Yet even as he told himself this time it was safe to believe, she parted her lips. The silent invitation was more than he could resist. He reached forward and touched his tongue to hers.

Her sweet taste made him moan low in his throat. Electricity shot through him with all the subtlety of a lightning bolt. She leaned closer so they touched from shoulder to thigh. He could feel the soft pressure of her breasts against his chest and the firm hold of her fingers as she clung to him. He was too hard, too ready, for this to be a dream.

He angled his head and continued to rediscover her mouth. The familiar shapes and textures, the heat, the need that drove him. He moved his hands up and down her back, feeling her strength. Her job required her to be physically strong and she had lean muscles under soft skin. Just like he remembered. Just like it should be. She was different from Claire's sharp angles and nearly visible bones. Flesh moved in response to his touch. She had shape and substance.

"Just like I remember," he murmured, pulling back long enough to trail kisses along her jaw to her neck. She arched into the caress. He stopped at the sensitive skin right below her ear and licked the sweet spot. She groaned low in response.

"Dylan."

His name was a prayer. He heard the reverence, felt it himself. "I was afraid," he confessed, pulling her tightly against him and burying his face in her hair. "So damned afraid the past would always stand between us. If you knew how much I've wanted you, loved you. You are everything to me, Sierra."

She pushed back a little and studied his face. He wasn't sure what she was looking for but he knew he was completely exposed to her. Everything he was thinking and feeling would show. He had no defenses left—he wanted her too much to pretend.

He wasn't sure what she saw, but after a minute, she nodded, then cupped his jaw and brought him closer. She brushed her mouth against his, her lips moist and warm. They clung to him, then she swept her tongue across the seam and he parted for her.

This time she was the aggressor. She invaded and discovered. He met her touch for touch, savoring the flickering fire raging between them. His blood swirled hot. The scent of her intoxicated him. He dropped his hands to her waist, then lower to her rear and hauled her hips against him. Her belly pressed against his arousal. He rocked her back and forth, creating a decadent friction that tempted his self-control.

She broke the kiss and gasped for air. "I want you," she said.

Her words were fuel for the need that raged between them. "Yes," he growled. "I want you, too. In my bed, naked, under me. I want to be inside of you."

Her lids half lowered over smoky, hazel eyes. A smile tugged at the corner of her mouth. "Gee, Dylan, stop hinting and come out and tell me what you really want."

He took her hand and tugged her toward the hallway. "I really want you."

They had to stop halfway up the stairs so he could hold her. He paused with her a step behind him, and gathered her close. She pressed her face into his chest and he felt the heat of her breath and the dampness of her mouth against his bare skin. His body tensed in response.

"I can't believe what you're doing to me," he murmured.

She laughed softly. "I know what you mean. I'm half expecting to find out this isn't really happening."

He touched a finger to her chin, urging her to look up at him. She was so beautiful. "It's real," he said. "We're finally together." Silently they continued up the stairs.

His bedroom was at the far end of the hallway. It had originally been two rooms, but the previous owners had torn down the dividing walls to create a huge master suite. Dylan hadn't had time to do much in the way of decorating. A large king-size four-poster brass bed stood against the wall. There were several windows and an open door leading into the master bath. The sheets and blankets were a tangle at the foot of the bed.

"I wasn't expecting company," he said.

"Good. Then we shouldn't be interrupted."

He stopped by the foot of the bed and turned toward her. She flowed into his embrace, her body leaning into his, her hands tracing a path from his elbows up his arms to his shoulders and back. They kissed, softly at first, barely touching, then deeper, with mouths open and tongues entwined.

He reached for the first button of her shirt and unfastened it. She took a half step back to give him room. Her hands dropped to her sides and she gazed at him, her eyes filled with trust and desire. It was a heady combination.

He unfastened the second button, then struggled for a moment with the third. "I feel like I'm seventeen again," he said. "My hands are trembling."

"I'm glad." She tossed her head and her long, loose hair flew over her shoulder. "I want you to tremble like you did back then. I want everything to be the same."

He pulled her shirt free of her jeans and pushed it over her shoulders. The garment fluttered to the floor. She wore a plain white cotton bra. Full curves spilled over the top. He bent down and kissed the swell of her right breast.

"It can't be the same," he told her, inhaling the arousing sweet fragrance of her skin. "But it can be better."

"Oh, Dylan." She clutched his head and buried her fingers in his hair. "If you knew how many times I've longed for this, for you. I wanted to forget, to hate you, but I never could. Not for long. You're a part of me. I just wish..." Her voice trailed off.

He looked at her. Unshed tears made her eyes glitter. "What, lover?" he asked and touched his mouth to her cheek, then her eyelids. "What's wrong?"

"I'm so afraid," she whispered. "I want this to be real and I'm afraid that it isn't. I don't want to care about you again. I don't want you to hurt me and leave me. I don't think I would survive that."

"I won't do either," he promised. "I just want the chance to love you."

She nodded once, briefly, but he wasn't sure she believed him. Perhaps there were no words with which to convince her. Perhaps he would have to show her how he felt.

He wrapped one arm around her and pulled her close. While his other hand reached for the fastener of her jeans, he brushed her mouth with his. She yielded to him instantly, parting, drawing him in, sucking gently in a way designed to drive him wild. It worked, too.

After he unzipped her jeans, he released her and bent to help her remove her boots and socks. Next, he tugged off her jeans. Her panties were as sensible and plain as her bra. He loved her for that. Sierra wouldn't think to buy satin and lace unless he asked her. Then she would blush and protest the expense, but ultimately, she would agree. His arousal flexed as he thought about seeing her in black lace and nothing else, then he shuddered at the even more erotic thought of seeing her naked.

He urged her up on the bed. She stretched out on the rumpled sheets and he sat next to her. Her hair fanned over the pillows. He stroked her cheek. "You're so beautiful."

She wrinkled her nose. "Yeah, right."

"I mean it. I could drown in your eyes."

"And leave me unsatisfied?"

Her teasing made him smile. He lowered himself next to her and gathered her close. Fierce emotion filled him. He wanted to get lost inside of her and never find his way back. "I've missed you," he told her. "Every day. With every breath."

Her answer was a kiss. He teased her lips with his

tongue while his hands made quick work of her bra. When her full breasts were free and bare to him, he moved his fingers around the generous curves, rediscovering magical country. Her nipples were already taut. He brushed his thumbs against the tight peaks. Her hips surged against him, bringing her feminine heat in contact with his desire. He arched into the caress, wishing away the layers of clothing.

Moving slowly, beginning the ritual of their ancient dance, he slipped between her thighs. He lowered his mouth from her lips to her neck, then lower still until he had trailed a damp path to the valley between her breasts.

Sierra kept having to remind herself to breathe. Dylan's touch was more exciting and intoxicating than she remembered. Her skin was hyperaware of every brush of his fingers or tongue. As he drew closer to her aching nipples, she raised her shoulder slightly off the bed, urging him on, silently begging him to take her in his mouth.

At last he did, closing his lips over her, tasting, sucking gently. Each tiny pull coiled down inside her, rippling through her belly and exploding in her sweet spot. She curled her fingers into the mattress, clutching the sheets. Her hips rose and she found herself pressing against the bulge in his trousers.

The temptation was too great. She moved up and down, rubbing herself against him. They both groaned low. It had been like this ten years ago. Undeniable passion that rapidly burned out of control. Trace memories combined with current reality to give their lovemaking a sense of inevitability. Even if she wanted to, she could deny Dylan nothing.

He cupped her breasts, pushing them close together and dividing his attention between them. As the pressure built, she moved her hips faster.

"I want you," he said, raising his head and looking at her face. "I want you."

The words had too much power. She began to tremble uncontrollably. He seemed to understand because instead of returning his attention to her breasts, he moved his hands all over her body. He stroked her belly, her thighs, her hands, her arms. His fingers stilled as he felt the still-healing scar from her run-in with the steer when she'd rescued Rory.

He stretched to the side and traced the red line. "You're still bruised," he said.

"For a couple more weeks. It was a hard kick."

"I know. I'm sorry."

"It's not your fault."

"I'm sorry because you got hurt. But I'm grateful you were there." He touched his mouth to the tender spot and his sweetness healed her battered soul.

"Thank you," she whispered.

He straightened. With one long, easy movement, he stripped her of her panties, then settled back in place. Once again he kissed her breasts, finding the sensitive tips and teasing them with gentle nips. Then he moved lower. Down her chest to her belly, then lower still, to the apex of her thighs.

He urged her to part for him. He cupped her rear with his hands and bent his head to taste her.

Sierra had enough warning to remind herself it was going to be like an explosion. Even so she gasped as the bolts of pleasure shot through her. She arched into him, instantly breathless and close. So very close.

He was perfection itself. A slow, steady, relentless assault on her senses. His tongue found and teased her sweet spot, circling it, stroking it, moving a little faster as her breathing increased. It was as if he could feel what she was feeling. As if he were somehow linked to her body.

When her release came, it was unexpected and life changing. Suddenly she was on the edge of the cliff and, with no warning, she began to fall. A thousand pleasure-points convulsed in satisfaction. Her body trembled, she called out his name. And in the end, he caught her in his arms and held her close.

It took several minutes for her body to return to normal. Dylan stroked her hair and murmured softly. Words of comfort and love. She finally opened her eyes and looked at him. "You're right," she said at last. "It is better than I remember."

He grinned. "I'm glad."

She thought about how quickly she'd climaxed. "And quicker."

He raised his eyebrows. "I hadn't noticed."

"Liar."

"Okay, I noticed. I chose to think it's because we're so good together."

She touched his cheek. "I know that's it." They'd

always been able to please each other. "I'm glad we didn't lose that."

"Me, too."

Something hard flexed against her hip. She reached down and ran her hand along the impressive length of his desire. "I wasn't aware we were dressing for the occasion."

"I could change that if you'd like."

"I would like. Very much."

He sat up and unfastened his jeans, then tossed them aside. As he reached toward the nightstand drawer, she shifted so he knelt between her legs, and drank in the sight of him. Time had been kind, honing a young man's body into mature strength. She ran her hands along his rock-hard thighs, then up his chest. He quickly opened and used the protection.

Her throat tightened. He hadn't even bothered to ask or try to talk her out of it. "Always the gentleman," she said, again fighting tears.

"You are precious to me," he told her. "I want to protect you."

"Thank you."

She felt him press against her feminine place. Suddenly the ache inside returned and she desperately needed to feel him there, filling her, joining with her. She pushed toward him, enveloping him in her heat. He groaned once, low and deep, then set his teeth.

"This isn't going to take long."

"Then we'll be even."

His dark gaze met hers. Passion dilated his pupils and pulled his face taut. "I love you," he said.

The words combined with his maleness filling her were more than she could stand. "I love you, too," she said, at last confessing the truth she'd kept hidden all these years.

He thrust into her, going deeper, taking them back to the edge of the cliff, then forcing her off with him. It was a moment of perfect joining and for the first time since Dylan had left her, Sierra truly felt that she belonged.

Later, when they'd recovered, made love again and dozed for a couple of hours, Sierra glanced out the window. "It must be close to noon," she told him. "When is Rory due back from his sleepover?"

"Not until dinnertime," Dylan said. "You up for another round?"

She laughed. "You're not that impressive, cowboy. I doubt you could—" Something hard nudged her leg. She felt under the covers and laughed. "Okay, so maybe you could. Obviously I was wrong."

"Damn right you were. I have a lot of time to make up for." He grinned. "I've been thinking about this for years, Sierra. I think you're going to enjoy some of the things I've been planning."

Her arousal was as quick as his. "I can't wait."

He pulled her on top of him. "What would you like to start with?"

"Well, how about a conversation?"

"Sure. What do you want to talk about?"

She bit her lower lip, then figured she didn't have

a whole lot to lose. After all, Dylan had finally convinced her that he cared about her. She wanted to be with him. Although their lives were heading in different directions and something permanent wasn't possible, they could still work out a compromise. Assuming he wanted one.

"Is the foreman job still open?" she asked.

"Of course. Are you willing to consider it?"

She nodded. "I'd like that. I can make this ranch successful for you. I'll be close enough so that we can be lovers when you're around and no one has to know. It's the perfect solution. We both get what we want without worrying about a permanent commitment."

Chapter 10

Dylan sat up and stared at her. "What are you talking about?" he asked. "I want people to know that we're together. And what's all this about being with me when I'm around? Do you think I expect you to be my mistress, at my beck and call whenever the urge strikes?"

Sierra pushed her hair out of her face and smiled. "You're overreacting. I'm not going to be your mistress, in the traditional sense of the word. I would like a shot at running the ranch and I think we can be happy together."

"But not on a permanent basis?"

"Well, not really. No."

He couldn't believe it. He'd finally gotten her to admit she cared about him; she was willing to work for him but she didn't want anything permanent. What the hell was going on? How had he failed?

He glared at her. "Damn it, Sierra, I want to marry you."

She didn't even blink. "Don't be ridiculous. It would never work."

He'd spent a lot of time in the past few weeks thinking about proposing to Sierra. He'd imagined her saying a lot of things—everything from throwing herself into his arms to telling him she would never forgive him for the past and slapping him across the face. But he hadn't imagined she would say he was ridiculous.

"I just asked you to marry me."

"I know. It's very sweet, but completely impractical." She slid out of bed and reached for her underwear. "I'm not a politician's wife, Dylan, and we both know it. This is my world." She motioned toward the window. "I understand ranching. I'm good at it. I fit in. Where you want to go—" She shook her head. "I'd be a joke."

"You'd be wonderful." He forced himself to focus on her words and not the sight of her beautiful bare breasts. Then she slipped on her bra and the distraction was covered, although he could still see the shape and imagine what they felt and tasted like.

He shook his head to clear away the erotic images. "We belong together."

"No, you have plans that don't include me." She pulled on her shirt and jeans, then began to fasten the buttons. "You've already started. I didn't realize you were running a practice that specialized in helping those in need. I really admire and respect that."

"So what's the problem?"

"You're going into politics. You're going to move to Washington. I don't think I could do that."

"Of course you could. You're just afraid."

She bristled slightly. "Fear has nothing to do with it. I don't want to get in your way." She tucked in her shirt then sat on the edge of the bed and took his hand. "I'm not stupid. I sat in your dining room and listened to those men talk. They have plans for you. Important plans that don't include some hick from Montana."

He didn't like the way this conversation was going. "You're not a hick. You're a smart, funny, wonderful woman and I want you at my side."

She touched his cheek. "It's very sweet of you to say so, and I'm sure you believe it right now, but in time you'll see that I'm right. You need someone who understands where you're going. Besides, you have to think of Rory."

"I *am* thinking of Rory. You'll be a great mother to him. He already adores you."

"I don't know anything about raising children."

"You've done terrific so far."

"I've given him a couple of riding lessons and helped with a birthday party. That does not qualify me for mother of the year."

The growing ache in his heart made it difficult to do anything but gasp for his next breath. He couldn't have come all this way only to lose her now. He had to make her see. "Sierra, I—"

She cut him off with a quick smile. "Don't try to

convince me otherwise. I know what I'm saying. For now, for as long as it's convenient, I'll run your ranch and be your lover. When you get to the point where it's important for you to marry, I'll step aside.''

"How can you say that?"

"Because it's the right thing to do."

"No." He stood up and glared down at her. "You're taking the coward's way out. You don't love me. If you did, you couldn't stand for me to be married to someone else."

Her eyes darkened with sadness. "It's because I love you I want you to be with the right person. Someone like Claire."

He swore. "I've been married to someone *exactly* like Claire and it was hell. I don't want an arm-piece or a decoration. I don't even want a politically correct wife. I want a partner, someone I can love and respect and want to wake up next to for the rest of my life. I want you, Sierra. I want to tell the world that we love each other. I want everyone to know that we belong together. I love you and I want to marry you."

She turned away, her loose hair shielding her face from his gaze. "Don't," she murmured. "You're making this difficult."

"Good. I want it to be damned difficult for you to leave me."

"I'm not leaving."

"It looks that way from here."

"I'm offering you everything but marriage. What else do you want from me?"

He grabbed her arm and turned her to face him. Tears swam in her eyes. "I want it all," he said quietly.

She jerked free. "You don't get it all. It's my way or forget it."

He felt as if she'd slapped him. "Just like that?"

"Exactly like that." She turned to leave.

Dylan watched her go because he couldn't think of any words to keep her at his side. But he would. He hadn't gotten where he was by accepting defeat. One way or the other he was going to convince Sierra that they'd been given the miracle of a second chance and neither their past, nor her fears were going to interfere with that. There was a reason he was the best in the business and Sierra was about to have that fact proven to her.

Sierra shoveled the smelly straw into the wheelbarrow. She didn't normally spend her day cleaning the stables, but a couple of the cowboys were down with the flu and there was extra work for everyone. Actually she'd volunteered for this detail. If nothing else, it gave her time to think.

Her body still ached pleasurably from Dylan's lovemaking the day before. If she moved a certain way, or stiffened her legs, she felt the muscles protest and that was a wonderful and tangible reminder of what they'd done together. Who would have thought they could find each other after all this time? It was, in its own way, a miracle.

Maybe it was a mistake to love and trust him again. This time, when he left her, she wasn't sure she was going to survive. But it would be worth it, she reminded herself. After all, she hadn't been alive all this time without him. Even though it was only temporary, she would enjoy their weeks or even months. She would have a chance at making his ranch one of the most successful in the country and she would get to feel that she belonged.

She pitched fresh straw into the stall and then smoothed it. Last night, before she'd fallen asleep, she'd allowed herself to pretend. For a few minutes, she daydreamed about what her life would be like if she'd chosen to believe Dylan's proposal and had accepted it. Idle dreams that had made her smile.

But reality was very different. She wouldn't fit in where he was going. He needed someone who understood the workings of that world. She would just be a liability to him. It was love that made her refuse his proposal. Love, not fear.

A voice in the back of her mind whispered a single word. "Liar."

She straightened. "I'm not lying," she said aloud. "This is better for Dylan. I don't belong there."

But even she couldn't bring herself to believe that...not completely. If she let herself trust him enough to marry him, then she would have no control over the future. She would have to take a step of faith, with nothing but his promise standing between her and certain emotional destruction. A promise that he'd broken once, so many years ago. If she refused him and forced him into a relationship on her terms, then she was still going to get hurt, but she got to say when and how much. She could control her emotional involvement and therefore her pain. The whole concept didn't make her feel very good about herself, but it offered sure survival. The other way— She shook her head. She couldn't even think about what might happen that way.

She wiped the sweat off her brow and knew it was going to take more than one shower to wash away the smell of horse manure. She moved to the next stall and reached for the shovel.

"You're looking mighty fierce about something," a man said.

Sierra jumped and turned toward the doorway. Ben Radisson stood silhouetted in the morning sun.

"This is high concentration work," she said and smiled. "What are you doing here?"

"I came to see you." He took a couple of steps closer and nodded toward the stall. "This is how I paid for my car when I was in high school," he said. "I was hell on wheels."

"I'll bet you were. And I'll bet you still are."

He winked. "Could be." He shoved his hands into his trouser pockets and rocked back on his heels. "Little lady, we've got ourselves a problem."

Her heart sank. Had Dylan told them about her going to work for him? Was a single woman living on his ranch going to be trouble for the campaign? "What's that?"

"Dylan told me about the arrangement you two had come to. I don't think the voters will object to a man hiring a woman as his foreman, what with this being the nineties and all, but the cohabitation is another matter."

She swallowed. "I see." She managed to get out the words without stumbling over them, but it was hard. She'd hoped that she would have a little time with him before she had to give him up again. "You want me to step aside."

"No, I want you to think about marrying the boy."

Her mouth dropped open but she couldn't speak.

"I know what you're thinking. He's a sorry excuse for a fellow, what with him being such a bleeding heart about some things."

"He's not," she said quickly. "He's wonderful and idealistic. He's damn good at what he does, and you know it. If he wasn't, you wouldn't be interested. You people are lucky a man like Dylan is interested in running for office at all. You don't deserve him."

"But you do?"

That knowing gaze warned her she'd fallen neatly into a trap. Sierra leaned the shovel against the stall wall and pulled off her gloves. "I don't know what I deserve. Everything is a little confusing right now."

Ben touched her arm. "I know what you're thinking, Sierra. You think Dylan needs some senator's daughter to smooth his way. For most candidates, I'd

agree with you, but not Dylan. He'll do things however he wants to because that's how he's always
done them. Did you know I met Claire once?''

Great. She glanced down at her stained shirt and
grimaced. So much for impressing anyone. ''No, I
didn't.''

''She's an attractive woman. On the outside. But
on the inside, she's cold and self-centered. Marrying
Dylan means wading in some horse manure a lot
deeper than this.'' He motioned to the stall. ''He
needs someone who isn't afraid of hard work. You're
smart and you learn fast. You're exactly what he
needs. So why are you so afraid to be a part of the
one thing you've always wanted?''

She looked into those wise brown eyes and knew
she couldn't answer the question. She was just afraid.
Of being hurt, of not surviving it this time, of losing
the dream. But was keeping the dream alive better
than taking a chance on making it real? It shouldn't
be, and yet she was acting as if it was.

''I'll think about what you said,'' she told him.
''That's the best I can offer right now.''

''I can't ask for more than that.'' He winked.
''Okay, I can ask for it, but I know to quit while I'm
ahead.''

He walked out of the barn and Sierra was left
alone to try to figure out if she had the courage to
take another chance on love.

Kirk stalked into her bedroom without knocking
and planted his hands on his hips. ''You're not living

with him. You got that?''

Sierra looked up from the book she'd been pretending to read. "I'm sure I have no idea what you're talking about," she said, even though she knew exactly what Kirk meant.

"I just spoke with Dylan. He told me about your plan. I think you'd be a great foreman, but no sister of mine is going to shack up with some guy. Not unless you marry him."

She rose to her feet and stood toe-to-toe with her brother. Unfortunately he topped her by several inches and didn't seem the least bit impressed by her angry stance.

"You want me to marry Dylan? I don't think so."

Kirk had the grace to look uncomfortable. "I'm willing to admit I might have misjudged the guy."

"How did that happen? You get a message in a dream?"

"We talked." He said the words grudgingly.

She raised her eyebrows. "You mean he talked and you listened."

"Yeah, something like that. Look, Sierra, it's been a long time and things have changed. At first I wasn't sure he was right for you, but maybe he is, you know? The guy is a mess. I think he really needs you in his life."

She turned away and crossed to the small window. "I feel as if I'm being maneuvered into making a decision before I'm ready," she said. "I don't think I like that."

"I thought you'd already decided that you weren't going to marry Dylan."

"I have."

"So he's just trying to change your mind. Is that so bad?"

Was it? Did she mind that Dylan wanted to be with her so much he would mount a calculated campaign to win her? Did that mean he really cared about her? Was that so horrible?

"I don't know," she admitted. "I don't know what to think."

Kirk came up behind her and hugged her close. "It can be scary, but it's worth it. I know. When love finally caught me, I didn't know what hit me. You deserve this, Sierra. Don't let him get away again."

Sierra was afraid to get out of her truck, but she had a riding lesson with Rory in less than five minutes and she refused to let her concerns about Dylan's next step make her late for that lesson. Rory was depending on her and she wasn't about to let him down.

Dylan had planned his strategy well. After bombarding her with visitors bearing messages, he'd left her alone for a couple of days. Just long enough for her to realize what life would be like without him, to start missing him. Last night she hadn't been able to sleep because her body had ached with longing. She'd come to the conclusion that she could lose herself in the fear and never experience real love, or she could take another chance. What other choice did she have? In the past ten years she'd never been able to love anyone as much as she'd loved him. It was unlikely she ever would. So why not risk complete, perfect happiness? They both deserved it.

She walked to the corral, half expecting to be ambushed. But there was only silence. Had he changed his mind or given up? Had she waited too long? She wished he would find her and ask her to marry him again so this time she could say yes.

A noise caught her attention. Her heart thundered in her chest, but it was only Rory leading his horse out of the stable.

"Hi, Sierra," he called when he saw her and grinned. "I've got your saddle on. Doesn't it look great?"

"Totally cool," she said.

The boy's grin got bigger. "I think you'd be a great mom," he told her.

She froze in her tracks. "What did you say?"

He wrinkled his nose. "Dad said it's gotta be your last objection." He fumbled over the unfamiliar word. "About being my mom. I told him I thought you'd be great, so he said I should explain it to you."

He moved closer until he was standing directly in front of her. "Dad says he wants to marry you and make you part of the family. I'd like that. I'd like you to live here always." Earnest blue eyes widened slightly. "We love you, Sierra."

A lump filled her throat. She dropped to her knees and pulled Rory close. He wrapped his arms around her in a fierce hug. She felt as if she'd finally come home. "I love you, too," she whispered. "Both of you."

"So you gonna marry us?"

"If your father asks me again I will."

"Sierra?"

She heard Dylan's voice. Slowly she rose to her feet and turned to face him. He stood just outside the barn, a tall, handsome man in jeans and long-sleeve shirt. His hair needed cutting and there were shadows under his eyes, but he'd never looked more wonderful.

"Do you mean it?" he asked. "You'll marry me?"

"Yes," she said and flung herself at him. He hauled her hard against him and kissed her. "Yes," she repeated, between kisses. "Always yes."

He moved his mouth over hers in a bone-melting caress and she felt her knees go weak. He'd always had that effect on her.

"I'm glad you came to your senses," he said at last. "I was running out of messengers."

"I can't risk losing you again," she said. "I was afraid of being hurt, but I'm more afraid of being without you. I love you, Dylan. I never stopped loving you."

"I'd like to get married soon."

She laughed. "That's fine with me."

He brushed his mouth against her cheek. "What's so funny."

"I was remembering how annoyed I was when I

caught the bouquet at my brother's wedding. I didn't realize it was a sign that everything in my life was about to turn out exactly right.''

Epilogue

A warm hand settled possessively against the small of her back. Sierra smiled without turning around. She didn't have to look to know the man standing so close behind her was her husband of less than two hours. Every part of her recognized Dylan; he was, and always had been, her destiny.

"You're a beautiful bride," the minister's wife said. "And the ranch is so lovely."

"Everything did come out perfectly, didn't it?" Sierra glanced around at the large tent Chayce had erected on the front lawn. Debate had raged for days about where to hold the wedding, because Dylan's house was in the middle of renovations and neither he nor Sierra had wanted to put off their wedding much longer. It was already fall and they had lots of time to make up for.

As the Derringer ranch had already been the site of two weddings, Chayce and Abby had offered it as the perfect solution.

When Dylan tugged on her hand, Sierra excused herself from the other woman and turned to her husband. As always, Dylan's handsome face took her breath away. Or maybe it wasn't his appearance at all, but the love she saw shining in his eyes. Love that had lasted through time and heartache for both of them.

"Are you happy?" he asked.

"Yes. Perfectly. I never thought it would be like this." She leaned close and kissed him.

"I see they're still at it," a familiar voice grumbled.

Sierra looked up and saw her brother standing next to them, his arm around his wife. Felicity nudged him playfully. "You're hardly in a position to judge anyone. You're certainly always ready to kiss me."

"That's different. Sierra's my baby sister."

"Not anymore," Chayce said, coming up to join the group. His wife, Abby, was with him and as they paused by the newlyweds, he slipped his arm around her. "Now Sierra is Dylan's wife."

A ripple of pleasure started at Sierra's toes and worked its way up. "I like the sound of that," she said.

Dylan squeezed her close. "Me, too."

In the background the small musical combo finished one song, then started another. Abby cocked her head. "It's time, Sierra." She pointed to the lovely bouquet of white roses. "Are you ready to throw your flowers?"

Sierra nodded. "I still remember how shocked I was when I caught them at Felicity's wedding. I was pretty annoyed by the whole tradition, but now..." She grinned.

"So they're lucky flowers," said Dylan.

"I guess so."

"I can't wait to see who catches them this time."

She thought about how far she had come in such a short period of time. Of the woman she'd been when she'd caught the bouquet and the woman she was now. "I can't wait to see, either," she told her husband, and walked to the front of the tent.

All the single women attending the reception gathered around her. Sierra turned her back, sent up a quick prayer that whoever caught her bouquet would be as blessed with happiness as she and Dylan had been, then she raised her arm and let the flowers sail through the air.

MONTANA MAVERICKS:
RETURN TO WHITEHORN

continues with

A FATHER'S VOW

by Myrna Temte

Available in May

...only from Silhouette Special Edition

Turn the page for an exciting sneak
preview....

Chapter One

Julia Stedman hesitated outside the Hip Hop Café, collecting herself after the long hot drive from Sheridan, Wyoming, to Whitehorn, Montana. The Hip Hop looked like one of those busy cafés found in almost any small western town—the kind that included a juicy serving of gossip with every cup of strong coffee and piece of homemade pie.

Julia stepped inside. A cute blond waitress with a perky ponytail zipped toward a booth filled with teenage boys, her hands and arms laden with plates of burgers and fries. "Be right with you," she called. "Have a seat if you can find one."

"Thanks." Julia glanced around the room, but every table had at least one customer.

An older woman, whose blond hair undoubtedly

had benefited from a hairdresser's magic, flashed a smile and nodded toward the chair opposite hers. "I always enjoy company."

Julia wasted no time accepting the invitation. Every café she'd ever worked in had had at least one customer like this woman—an unrepentant gossip who sincerely loved her work. If she didn't personally know the information Julia had come here for, she would know how to get it.

The woman offered her hand across the small table, three inches' worth of silver bracelets jangling with the movement. "I'm Lily Mae Wheeler. I don't believe we've ever met."

Shaking Lily Mae's hand, Julia smiled. "Julia Stedman. And I'm sure we've never met, because I've only been in Whitehorn for about five minutes."

"Are you here on vacation?" Lily Mae asked.

"Partially," Julia replied. "My father grew up and lived in this area. He's passed away now, but I'm hoping to find some of his relatives or at least some people who knew him."

"How fascinating," Lily Mae said.

The waitress arrived at their table, order pad in hand. "Watch out for Lily Mae," she said with a teasing grin. "She'll have your secrets out of you in ten seconds flat if you're not careful."

"Oh, hush, Janie," Lily Mae said with a laugh. "You make me sound like a terrible busybody."

"Well, that's what you are." Janie laughed and nudged Lily Mae's arm with her elbow. "You only get away with it because you're so sweet."

Lily Mae rolled her eyes in mock disgust. "You little stinkpot. Why don't you go find that poor J. D. Cade fellow you've got such a crush on and flirt with him for a while?"

Janie wrinkled her nose at Lily Mae, then turned to Julia and wrote down her order. When Janie hurried away to the kitchen with Julia's ticket, Lily Mae sipped from her coffee cup.

"I'll admit I do enjoy gossip, but I'm not malicious," she said. "People are just my…hobby."

Julia had to laugh. "No problem. I don't have any deep, dark secrets to hide."

Lily Mae leaned forward, resting her forearms on the table. A bell over the door jangled and five big, swarthy men wearing jeans, work boots and yellow hard hats entered the restaurant. Lily Mae automatically checked them out before turning back to Julia. "Well, then, tell me all about your father, and I'll see what I can do to help you find his family."

"I'm afraid I don't know much about him. He and my mother separated before I was born, and she wouldn't talk about him."

"Oh, hon, that's so sad," Lily Mae said. "I've been around here a long time. I wonder if I knew him."

Julia swallowed. Well, here it was. Time to find out the truth about Lily Mae's character. "He was Northern Cheyenne. He lived at the Laughing Horse Reservation."

Lily Mae's eyes widened slightly and she tipped her head to one side, intently studying Julia for a moment. Then she smiled again. "Well, now, I guess that explains that gorgeous tan of yours so early in the summer. And I've seen Indians with blue eyes before, but is your hair naturally that auburn?"

Julia chuckled. "What can I say? I can't do much about how straight it is, but I like to see something besides black once in a while."

"I hear you, hon." Lily Mae patted her own perfectly coiffed curls, and glanced upward as if she could see through her fluffy bangs to the top of her head. "I get real sick of seeing gray hair, myself. I always figured why put up with it if you don't have to?"

"Exactly," Julia agreed.

Janie delivered her club sandwich and iced tea. Julia waited until the waitress left before bringing up the subject she wanted to discuss again.

"Is there a chance you would have known my father, Lily Mae?"

Lily Mae's expression turned serious. "I know a few folks from the reservation, but not nearly as many as I know here in town, of course. A lot of the Cheyenne tend to keep to themselves."

Janie hustled back to the entrance, counted out a stack of plastic-coated menus and escorted the burly men toward the middle of the restaurant. When they approached her chair, Lily Mae's expression brightened. "Well, Sam Brightwater, you're just the fella we want to talk to."

The tall, powerfully built man at the end of the line paused and waved the others on, then turned toward Lily Mae. Julia's breath lodged in the center of her chest when she caught her first clear view of his face. Holy smokes, but he was…arresting.

His black, piercing eyes, his bold, uncompromising nose, those sculptured cheekbones and the long, thick braid trailing down his back from the rear of his hard hat, left no question about his ancestry. A century or two ago, he would have been a proud, strong warrior, perhaps even a chief. His dark skin and the brooding ridge of his eyebrows made his quick, polite smile seem that much brighter by comparison.

He shifted his weight to his left foot, removed his hat and held it against the side of his sleeveless blue work shirt with his elbow. Julia's mouth went dry. Lord, she'd never seen a physique quite like his outside of a movie theater.

His voice was pleasantly low with a raspy quality to it. "Good to see you again, Ms. Wheeler. Need some work done on your road?"

"Not right now." Lily Mae gestured toward another empty chair at the table. "Sit down and have some lunch with us."

Sam Brightwater stiffened, shot a glance toward the table his crew had gathered around and took a step back from Lily Mae's. He'd been at the job site all morning, supervising while the guys staked out streets for a new subdivision on the south side of Whitehorn. He was hot, hungry and tired.

Lily Mae flashed him a coaxing smile. "My new

friend here needs some information and I think maybe you can help her. Her name's Julia Stedman.''

Sam looked at Lily Mae's companion, and felt a chill roll over him that had nothing to do with the Hip Hop's new air-conditioning system. Julia Stedman was striking with long, dark hair, big blue eyes and a wide, sweet smile that faltered when his gaze fully met hers for the first time. There was a jolt of...what? Recognition?

No, it couldn't be recognition. The idea was ridiculous, of course. If he had seen this woman's face before, he knew he would've remembered it. And yet, the startled expression in her eyes told him she had felt the jolt, too. Whatever it had been....

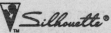

BEVERLY BARTON

Continues the twelve-book series— 36 Hours—in April 1998 with Book Ten

NINE MONTHS

Paige Summers couldn't have been more shocked when she learned that the man with whom she had spent one passionate, stormy night was none other than her arrogant new boss! And just because he was the father of her unborn baby didn't give him the right to claim her as his wife. Especially when he wasn't offering the one thing she wanted: his heart.

For Jared and Paige and *all* the residents of Grand Springs, Colorado, the storm-induced blackout was just the beginning of 36 Hours that changed *everything!* You won't want to miss a single book.

Available at your favorite retail outlet.

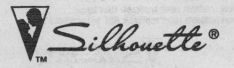

MONTANA Mavericks™

RETURN TO WHITEHORN

If you missed these great new titles in the Montana Mavericks series, don't miss this opportunity to order them from Silhouette Special Edition®:

#24154-2 LETTER TO A LONESOME COWBOY $4.25 U.S. ☐
by Jackie Merritt February 1998 $4.75 CAN.☐

#24160-7 WIFE MOST WANTED $4.25 U.S. ☐
by Joan Elliott Pickart March 1998 $4.75 CAN.☐

(quantities may be limited on some titles)

TOTAL AMOUNT	$
POSTAGE & HANDLING	$
($1.00 for one book, 50¢ for each additional)	
APPLICABLE TAXES*	$ _____
TOTAL PAYABLE	$ _____
(check or money order—please do not send cash)	

To order, complete this form and send it, along with a check or money order for the total above, payable to Silhouette Books, to: **In the U.S.:** 3010 Walden Avenue, P.O. Box 9077, Buffalo, NY 14269-9077; **In Canada:** P.O. Box 636, Fort Erie, Ontario, L2A 5X3.

Name: _____

Address: _____ City: _____

State/Prov.: _____ Zip/Postal Code: _____

Account #: _____ (If applicable) 075 SEN CSAS

*New York residents remit applicable sales taxes.
Canadian residents remit applicable GST and provincial taxes.

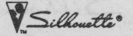

Look us up on-line at: http://www.romance.net PSMMWBPA